Manor for sale, BARON INCLUDED

A Romance of Rank Book One

ESTHER HATCH

For my fellow authors. You all have terrible jobs.
But it is also the best job, so here we are, still going...

CHAPTER 1

JONATHAN'S SOLICITOR was a horrible human being.

He was also one of his best friends, so he couldn't exactly tell him that. "I thought I made myself clear, I don't want to sell Greenwood Manor. What do you mean you have a buyer?"

Oliver pushed his spectacles lower on his nose so he could look above them. He didn't need the blasted things. He wore them so clients would take him seriously. When they were practically hanging off his nose it didn't make him look serious. It made him look ridiculous. Oliver sniffed—another annoying habit he had formed since becoming a solicitor. "It is your only property that isn't entailed."

Jonathan leaned across the desk and ripped the spectacles off of Oliver's nose, exposing his friend's fresh-faced good looks. Oliver didn't need to pretend with him. "That's because it was my mother's."

The office grew quiet. Outside a carriage rolled past. Of all the people in London, Oliver knew better than any of them the hole that had been torn in Jonathan's heart when his mother had passed away. The manor was the one place he had ever felt at home and now his friend wanted to rip it from him. Oliver blinked a few times, shuffled a stack of paper on his desk, and then returned the spectacles to his face. "I know. I know. But after our last conversation, I had an idea. It was highly improbable, but I let my colleagues know that I had a client looking to sell a manor house, and a manor house only. No land. The estate is one of the few you have that is still profitable and no one has used the house for years. I didn't think I would find anyone interested, for the house is expensive to maintain without the land to support it..."

Jonathan didn't need Oliver telling him how expensive his homes were to maintain. His barony had come with three of them in addition to Greenwood Manor. The past year had been filled with sheets of numbers cataloguing every expense and every penny coming in. The numbers had never added up in his favor. Britain's estates were still reeling from the repeal of the Corn Laws and the subsequent lowered price on grain, and his were no exception. While Jonathan hadn't opposed the change in theory or in vote, in action it had nearly bankrupted him. But his tenants at Greenwood Manor had sheep, not farmland. Unlike the rest of his estates, the lower price of grain had actually been a benefit to them.

"But Greenwood Manor? Oliver, how can I?"

Oliver slammed his fist on the desk and Jonathan jumped. "Some people don't have the luxury of holding on to items worth tens of thousands of pounds. And I'm sorry to be the bearer of bad news, but Jonathan, you are now one of them."

He didn't seem very sorry. His face was red and his breathing quick. In all of their years at Eton and then Oxford, Jonathan had never heard Oliver voice frustration about his situation. This outburst was the closest his friend had ever come to admitting he not only noticed, but resented his lower station. Oliver must not relish being the bearer of bad news, but Jonathan must look like a fool, every day getting closer to ruin, and not being willing to sell the one thing that would change his fortune for the better.

Jonathan took a deep breath. He should at least listen to what Oliver had to say. "So you found someone."

Oliver lifted his hand from the desk and his forehead smoothed. He put his glasses back on the end of his nose. He was back to being a solicitor, not a friend. "I did. And the offer is quite good. It should allow you to maintain your property for at least your lifetime. And the price of grain will have to come up at some point. You will be able to raise the rents back to what they were before. This could turn things around, even for your children."

His children? Jonathan sat back down on the chair in front of Oliver's desk. Greenwood Manor was supposed to be where he raised his children. They were to wander the grounds, learn about the flowers that grew there, and feel at peace just as he had. How exactly was he supposed to raise children without Greenwood Manor? The lines between Oliver's eyebrows were returning. It was almost as if he could hear Oliver's thoughts: Jonathan needed to grow up. For all his fairy-tale like attributions to Greenwood Manor, he hadn't even set foot on the grounds since his mother died. At first it was because his father hadn't let him, and then after his father had passed…well… what if it didn't live up to his memory? And how could it? It was empty.

But despite never going there, he couldn't bear to part with it. Not even to save his other estates.

He was a rubbish baron.

There was a knock at the office's exterior door. Oliver had left the door to his private office open to the foyer that connected it to the street. Oliver slid his chair out from behind him and stood. "That is probably her."

"Her?" Jonathan eyed the door. Who was Oliver meeting with?

"The buyer. I told her to meet us here today to discuss the possibility of a sale. She is the soul of discretion, so if you decide you really can't part with it, you can count on her not to say anything. But, Farnsworth…" Oliver lowered his glasses again, his piercing, icy blue eyes boring into Jonathan's own. "I don't think you have a better option than this."

A woman? Jonathan sat back, blinking hard. A woman was the client Oliver had drummed up to buy the manor? What kind of woman would buy a manor house on her own? A widow was really the only possibility—most likely one with too much money for her own good. Whoever she was, her husband must have left her a fortune. "You are trying to convince me to sell to a woman?"

"She was the only person to show interest. It shouldn't matter that she is a woman."

It shouldn't, but it did. A woman with money meant a lone woman. Greenwood Manor should belong to a family.

Oliver strode to the door, but Jonathan leaped toward him and turned him around by his elbow. "I'm not selling and I don't want to be introduced to her."

"You should stay and at least hear what she has to say. She could perhaps change your mind."

"If she does, I will eat my hat."

Oliver rubbed his forehead between his eyes. "What do you expect me to do? I can't not introduce you, not if you are in the room, and I do think you should stay and hear her out."

"Turn her away."

"I am not going to stand in the doorway and turn away a respectable woman while she stands in the street. The least I can do is invite her in and speak with her respectably. If you cannot handle that, then even though I highly discourage it, as this may be your only opportunity to get yourself out of this mess you are in, I suggest *you* leave."

Jonathan groaned. Hiring a friend for a solicitor had been a terrible mistake. Jonathan should be the one telling Oliver what to do. "If you insist I stay, I will. But tell her I'm your scribe or something."

"My scribe?"

"Yes," Jonathan hissed.

Oliver shook his head. "Have you seen your handwriting?"

Jonathan slapped a hand to his forehead. "I'm not actually going to be your scribe."

Oliver's eyes widened as if the thought of Jonathan working for him was abhorrent. "Of course you're not. You are brilliantly under-qualified."

Through gritted teeth Jonathan managed a smile. He cocked his head to one side. "Your clerk, then."

One side of Oliver's face scrunched together. If he wanted to disguise his youth and looks, he should make that face more often. "Your organization skills aren't exactly stellar either."

Jonathan let out an exasperated puff of air. "For heaven's sake, Oliver, just make up something. I will not be introduced to this land-grubbing woman. I will never have another reason to spend another second in her company and I don't even want to be here now. Just pick whatever skill you think I am worthy of pretending to have and tell her I do that."

Oliver frowned, examining him like he was some sort of experiment gone wrong. Jonathan raised his gaze to the ceiling. This was ridiculous. The man couldn't think of one thing he was good at? They had spent years together at Eton as well as Oxford. And it wasn't as if he actually had to be good at any of those things—they were only pretending, for heaven's sake.

Oliver went through the doorway, crossed the foyer and reached for the handle of the outside door. Jonathan strode over to the large window, as far away from the entrance of the office as he could get. He put a hand at his waistcoat and did his best to look as though he were a working man. What did a working man look like?

Tired? He rubbed his eyes and raked a hand through his meticulously styled hair. Although he couldn't see the result, it would be unruly in an instant. His hair much preferred a natural state of dishevelment. He didn't have time to change the lavish knot in his cravat, but a matronly widow surely would not inspect his clothing closely. She wouldn't be in the room long; it didn't really matter.

Oliver opened the door and a young woman walked in. Her hair was dark and piled up on the top of her head with perfect curls. She held herself straight and looked Oliver unabashedly in the eye. Jonathan's jaw dropped. *This* was the woman who was to buy Greenwood Manor? He leaned forward on his toes. What the devil was going on?

He fell back on his heels a moment later when an older woman strode in just behind the dark-haired surprise. *She* was exactly the type of woman he had expected: impeccable clothing, hair already mostly gray, and an upturned chin exuding wealth. This had to be the widow interested in Greenwood Manor, and the young lady a daughter or a companion.

The young lady put out her hand and Oliver shook it. Women were never so forward with Jonathan, at least not in this friendly manner, with no fluttering eyelashes or heads lowered in false modesty. Did she and Oliver already know each other from somewhere? Jonathan typically only spoke of business with his solicitor. Yet it seemed as though Oliver should have mentioned such an intriguing acquaintance to him. Was he hiding this relationship?

"Mrs. Merryweather," the young lady said, turning to the older woman, "allow me to introduce you to Mr. Oliver Beechcroft."

"A pleasure." Oliver gave her a short bow. Mrs. Merryweather didn't extend her hand. Oliver motioned for the two women to enter his office and sit at the chairs in front of his desk.

Jonathan waited for his introduction, but Oliver must have taken his wishes seriously, for it never came. He didn't mind escaping an introduction with the elderly woman, but he would have liked to have known her companion's name. There was something about the tilt of her head and the comfortable way she shook hands with Oliver that was...different.

He had determined to stay by the window, hopefully ignored, but something about the spark in the young lady's eye drew him like the warmth of a fire. He strode over to the desk and stood behind Oliver's chair, ignoring the feeling that he was like a young pup hoping for some attention. He was a baron, he reminded himself. He might not feel like one, but it didn't change the fact that he was. He should be able to take or leave this young woman's introduction.

But he would prefer to take it.

Mrs. Merryweather and her companion cast a quick glance over his person from their seats. The young lady paused at his waistcoat, her eyes focusing on his chest. For some reason he felt the need to take in a deep breath to expand it, but he controlled himself. He only half-expanded it. He didn't have a tall, dashing figure like Oliver, but he did have an impressive chest.

The young lady turned questioningly to Oliver.

"Ah, yes." Oliver turned to him. "Miss Duncan, Mrs. Merryweather, I'm sorry, an introduction is in order."

Miss Duncan. He finally had a name to go with the face. It suited her.

"This is Jonathan..." He paused before mumbling an incoherent last name that could have been anything. "He is my..." Oliver paused again, hesitation in his eyes. If the blasted man was calculating any skills or talents Jonathan could possibly have, it was taking him much too long. Oliver was excellent at math, history, and governing wealth, but his skills at deception were sadly lacking. Whatever he said now would hardly be believed by the two astute women sitting before him. With a final squint and a wave of his hand in Jonathan's direction, Oliver spoke. "He is my pugilist."

The women blinked.

His pugilist? True, Jonathan *had* gotten into trouble in his youth for rows that had turned to fisticuffs, and his knowledge and expertise in the sport had come in handy. But, really? That was really the only skill Oliver could think of?

And who employed a pugilist?

Jonathan ignored the urge to slap his hand to his forehead and start the whole introduction over. He would have to wrangle Oliver's words into making some sort of sense.

"You are a pugilist?" Mrs. Merryweather asked. Her eyes went to his hands, which were thankfully still clothed in his gloves. He had a few scars from his lessons with Mr. Ashton in the garden of Greenwood Manor, as well as his escapades in university, but nothing like what a real pugilist would boast.

"Why do you employ a pugilist?" Miss Duncan asked. Her wide-open, honest eyes were positively curious.

"Yes, Oliver." Jonathan couldn't help it. His friend was the one who had come up with the ridiculous idea. Somehow *this* was more believable than him being a scribe? "Why *did* you hire a pugilist?"

Oliver pushed his spectacles up on his nose—a movement that would only make the two women less distinguishable to him.

7

Perhaps he lied better when he couldn't make out people's faces. If that were the case, he should have pushed his spectacles up five minutes ago.

"In this business, you never know when a pugilist could come in handy. He isn't here every day. But he does provide some protection when I bring in clients I am worried about."

Miss Duncan flashed her dark eyes toward Oliver. There was just enough gold smattered in with the brown to make them spark. "And you believe you need protection from me? Or is it Mrs. Merryweather you are worried about?" She raised an eyebrow in a fashion much too forward and familiar for mere acquaintances. How closely were those two connected? But when she turned her eyes on Jonathan, they contained just as much fire. Perhaps she looked at everyone in such an open manner. "Would you strike a woman if Mr. Beechcroft asked you to?"

Jonathan reared back. "No, of course not." What did the woman take him for?

She turned to Oliver. "It seems to me you haven't chosen your pugilist wisely. He just admitted he wouldn't do his job."

"No, no...indeed, he is a fine pugilist. And, no, I am not worried about either of you. He was meeting with me before this."

"Well, I would rather not discuss my offer on the Greenwood property with an uninvolved man in the room."

Her offer? Jonathan snapped his jaw closed and forced his gaze onto the longcase clock across the room. It wouldn't do for Miss Duncan to see his surprise. *Miss Duncan* was the woman who had offered to buy Greenwood Manor? She was so young. Where had she come up with the capital for a home like that? No wonder she was so forthcoming with Oliver. She was the one here on business, and if she had the type of wealth that would afford her a large home in the country that brought in no income, she was most likely used to dealing with businessmen.

Oliver pulled down his spectacles, looked Jonathan in the eye and nodded toward the door. Jonathan gave Oliver a subtle nod. If Miss Duncan didn't want him there, he wouldn't stay. Oliver pushed his spectacles back up. "Thank you, Mr. ..." He mumbled another or perhaps the same unintelligible family name.

Jonathan crossed the room, all the time aware that Miss Duncan watched him. He left Oliver's office and paced about in the small foyer. What were they saying? He pressed his ear to the door. He couldn't make out much more than the low rumblings of Oliver's voice. There were pauses where he assumed Miss Duncan must have been talking, but perhaps because she was facing away from him, he couldn't even make out the timbre of her voice.

He pressed his ear tighter to the hard grain of the wood. There it was...a soft but firm vibration rolling out from behind the door. What were they discussing? How would Miss Duncan take his refusal to sell? Coming here had been a complete waste of her time, and she didn't seem like the type of woman who would appreciate that.

The sound of wood scraping on wood caught his ear. He jumped away from the door and ran to the opposite end of the foyer on his toes. He crossed both arms across his torso and tried to stand like a pugilist would.

Pugilists definitely threw back their shoulders and expanded their chests. It was part of their persona, certainly.

The door opened and, without meaning to, he caught Miss Duncan's eye. She was the first through the door, so it was only natural that he would.

She held his gaze for a moment and then her eyes slid down to the top of his waistcoat again. His pugilist pose had been a good idea. He may not have the scars of a pugilist, but his thickness could pass muster.

"That is a very fine waistcoat for a pugilist. It makes me wonder if perhaps I have heard of you."

Jonathan pushed his shoulders back further. "I'm still quite new to London. Most likely you haven't, but hopefully someday you will."

"Well." She stepped forward. The foyer was miniscule and there were now four people in it. In a movement that was as unexpected as an uppercut to the jaw, she lifted her hand and seized the top edge of his waistcoat just above his heart. She rubbed the fabric between her thumb and forefinger—not fast enough to create a spark, but a shock still ran through him when the tips of her fingers grazed his chest.

She leaned forward, the top of her head just below his eyes. "This is a very fine silk. And what is more—based on this brocade pattern, it was not produced in Great Britain."

Her hand was still on his chest. All he could do was nod. The air in his lungs was quickly running low, but he didn't dare release it. It might be time he was introduced to more wealthy trade families if their women were all like Miss Duncan.

"And the buttons..." Her fingertips dotted their way down his waistcoat until the fabric disappeared under his jacket. "Those are also imported." Miss Duncan's voice was not loud, but it was firm, as if touching the buttons on his chest was simply a business transaction, not unlike buying his mother's home. "But not from the same country. The silk is most definitely from East Asia, but the shape of the button underneath is most likely Persian. This isn't simply a fine article of clothing for a pugilist, it is a fine article of clothing for any man. It must have cost a fortune."

Jonathan swallowed. She removed her hand from his person. She had barely touched him, and yet the inappropriateness of it all had him feeling like a confused Eton boy all over again. All three other occupants in the foyer looked at him as if waiting for an explanation. The truth was, this was one of his favorite waistcoats, for all the reasons Miss Duncan had just mentioned, as well as the superior fit. He had bought it the year before his father had passed away, yet somehow it had remained timeless.

It *had* cost him a fortune. But that was back before he understood the position his family and his tenants were in. Honestly, two years ago his situation had not been so dire. He hadn't thought it an extravagance.

Jonathan eyed Oliver. It shouldn't bother him that his friend knew he had expensive clothing, but since he was the one man in London who knew Jonathan's financial situation, it irked him to think Oliver would judge him as frivolous. "I bought it years ago. And the milliner who sold me the fabric had assured me it was well-priced," he said to the room.

"I wasn't disparaging you." Miss Duncan's mouth formed an open, inclusive grin, which made him wish the two of them could be friends. "Whatever you paid for that fabric, it was worth it. The colors accentuate the blues and grays of your eyes, and it will hold its shape well for years." She gave him a wink. "It is striking on you."

Jonathan blinked. How had he never heard of this Miss Duncan? What part of the country did she hail from? Wherever it was, he would like to visit, if for no other reason than to meet more women like her.

Miss Duncan turned to Oliver. Would she compliment his eyes as well? "It is a pity we couldn't come to an agreement with Lord Farnsworth." Her eyes flashed to Jonathan's once again. And though she was speaking to Oliver, she didn't stop looking at Jonathan. "If he changes his mind, I hope you will let me know."

The air left his lungs in a rush. It was never his chest she had been looking at. It was his waistcoat. No amount of disheveled hair and tired eyes could hide the fact that his clothing did not belong to a working man. She knew exactly who he was. And what was more, she still wanted Greenwood Manor, only now she was asking him directly.

Oliver mumbled a quick "for certain" even though Miss Duncan hadn't been addressing him. Then he opened the door for the two ladies. Miss Duncan gave Jonathan one more nod before turning to leave. She also must have known how to pick just the right fabric to compliment her eyes, for suddenly they weren't simply dark—they were a painter's palette of browns and golds and greens.

Once the women were safely away from the office front, Jonathan turned to Oliver. "What is your relationship with Miss Duncan?"

"I have no relationship with her except this one. Her solicitor sent her to me when he heard about Greenwood Manor."

"You have no other interest in her?"

"Interest? Whatever do you mean?"

Jonathan raised an eyebrow.

"Oh, heavens no. That woman was the sole owner of British Vermillion Textile. It would be impertinent for me to even think…"

British Vermillion Textile. He had heard of it. It was an older company and well established. How had Miss Duncan become the owner? Jonathan gazed out the window of the office door. "She was quite beautiful. I don't believe I've ever met a woman quite so…" What was the word for it?

"Interesting?"

"Yes." Emphatically, yes.

Oliver removed his spectacles. "Jonathan?"

"Call her back."

"But I already told her you wouldn't be selling."

"I know you did. I've changed my mind. Call her back."

"How will I explain…"

"For Pete's sake, Oliver. She knows who I am. Did you not hear all that silk brocade nonsense? She is no fool, and you are no deceiver of men. Remind me to never enlist your help in deception of any kind."

"Even still I must have a reason."

"Then tell her the truth. I didn't understand how well the situation fit my problems. Tell her all the things you said before about my other lands not operating at a profit, and how this is the only way to save them. Now that I have thought it over, I see the brilliance of this particular business transaction."

Oliver placed one of the ear pieces of his spectacles to the side of his mouth and chewed on it. "Are you certain you want to sell?"

"I've never been more certain of anything in my life. Tell me, Oliver—have you been to Greenwood Manor in the past few years?"

"I visited before making inquiries."

"And only the manor is to be sold? Not the hunting lodge near the home?"

"Why are you so interested in the hunting lodge? You can't even properly load a gun."

"Thank you for reminding me of one more thing I cannot do well. Honestly, Oliver…a pugilist?

"It is the only thing you do well. You certainly can't hunt."

"We were pretending." It was a concept Oliver apparently had no capacity for. Jonathan shook his head. "I don't want the lodge for hunting. Just tell me if it is to be included in the sale or not."

Oliver sighed, a deep, soul-searching sigh that seemed to question the way his life was being run. "The lodge was to be retained by you. The only property listed with the sale is the ground directly surrounding the manor and the land adjacent to the roadway leading to it."

"And Miss Duncan? She is unattached to anyone romantically?"

Oliver narrowed his eyes. "I didn't think to look into it. That isn't part of my job."

There is no possible way Oliver would have lined up this sale without investigating Miss Duncan. "Oliver..."

"As far as I know, she is romantically unattached."

That was good enough for Jonathan. He had never entertained the idea of marriage before. He had always thought to wait until he was at least twenty-five. He was two years ahead, but nothing was wrong with that. This would be a business transaction. He would spend enough time with Miss Duncan to be certain they enjoyed each other's company, and then he would propose they marry. As a tradeswoman, she would see the value to both of them in such a transaction. His parent's marriage had only been complicated by the fact that his mother had loved his father. Happiness shouldn't depend on other people loving you. But life would be more entertaining if he was at least intrigued by his wife. "I'll sell Greenwood Manor, but only to Miss Duncan."

"You are acting as if you are doing me a favor. I am the one trying to help you."

Jonathan smiled. One of the best things he had ever done was pummel the boys who had picked on Oliver for coming to Eton with the help of a sponsor. "And I am trying to let you."

Oliver's shoulders drooped and he sighed heavily. "Farnsworth, this is a bad idea."

"No," Jonathan said, a spark of excitement rising in his chest. It wasn't a bad idea. "It is a challenge." He loved a challenge, and Miss

Duncan would be an amusing one. "And when I best this challenge? Miss Duncan will be my prize."

"I'm not certain Miss Duncan would like to be considered a prize."

Jonathan put his eyes heavenward. Oliver and his semantics. "You haven't been to a ballroom with me. Trust me, there aren't many women in the world who would snub their noses at becoming a baroness."

Oliver rubbed his forehead. "But she doesn't strike me as similar to the women you have been meeting in ballrooms."

"Precisely." She was much more interesting. But she was still a woman, and thus far, he had never met a woman whose face did not light up when they learned he was a baron. "This is one of the best ideas I have had since I became baron. Don't you see?" His head whipped toward the door and his heart beat escalated. "She is the answer to everything. I don't want to lose Greenwood Manor; she will own Greenwood Manor. I need capital to keep the barony running despite a net loss; she has an astounding amount of capital." Jonathan slapped his friend on the shoulder. "Oliver, do you realize what you have done? You have solved all of my problems, and done so in a bewitching package."

Those fiery eyes; her strong chin. That smile. He had always known he would need to marry one day. It might as well be to someone who interested him. "How quickly can she take possession of the manor?"

"As long as negotiations go well, within a month." Oliver sighed.

Within a month. Wooing her would take a month or two at the most after that. Within three months all of his financial burdens would be gone. Those butterfly-soft fingertips would gently land on his chest daily—not a bad prospect. He could get used to the idea of having a wife if she had fingertips like that.

His solicitor was an absolute genius.

CHAPTER 2

DID those two men think she was a complete simpleton? Sally Duncan took her footman's arm and swept up the step into her carriage. She had thought better of Oliver Beechcroft. Mrs. Merryweather might have been fooled by the whole pugilist idea, but even *she* had most likely caught on that something was amiss. Sally had managed to run a textile company for three years on her own. She was perfectly capable of spotting a very rich privileged man from across the room. This Jonathan with the imperceptible last name was no more a pugilist than she was a horse.

But even that deception she could have forgiven if they had allowed her to buy the manor. The moment she had first seen it, she had known it was perfect—secluded with extensive gardens and, most importantly, far from London.

Mama might not have loved the idea of her two daughters living so far from home, but she would have acquiesced eventually. Victoria would have loved the home and the adventure of being away and out on her own. The past three years, Sally had been so focused on British Vermillion Textiles that she hadn't even noticed how much Victoria had wasted away.

Now it had all come to naught thanks to a chest-padded lord.

Or at least she assumed the man must have been Lord Farnsworth. What other rich young man would be interested in her meeting with Mr. Beechcroft?

Mrs. Merryweather fidgeted in the seat next to her. "I'm sorry you weren't able to purchase the estate." Her features didn't seem overly disappointed. "However, I can't help but think it might be for the best. You should be in London meeting with suitors and enjoying the end of the Season."

Besides wanting to give Victoria a true home, suitors were the reason she *wanted* to leave London. Her broken engagement from Mr. Harrison had been kept a secret, but the last thing she wanted to do was fend off more men like him. Sally had thought Mr. Harrison had understood her, loved her, and even loved Victoria. She had thought Mr. Harrison was a man like her grandfather. He had seen her potential and—society be hanged—had given her the company he had started on his own as a young man. Her grandfather knew what she had been capable of, and she had lived the last three years going above and beyond his expectations to prove him right.

In the end, Mr. Harrison had been more like her father than her grandfather. She winced. Her father had been a good man. She had loved him deeply. But he had always wanted a son; someone who would take over the company. He had only ever seen Sally for what she was not, and not for what she could be—not even for what she was.

The longer she lived, the more she realized her grandfather was a strange man, to look at his granddaughter and see an heir. It was a rare thing even her father hadn't been able to do.

"Where are we going?" Mrs. Merryweather asked.

A fair question. Sally no longer had an office, so home was the only choice. She opened her mouth to say as much when there was a rap on the carriage door. Sally bent her head out only to find Mr. Beechcroft, his spectacles practically falling off his nose, standing below her.

"Mr. Beechcroft?"

"I beg your pardon, Miss Duncan, but would you consider coming back inside? Something has changed and Lord Farnsworth is now willing to entertain your offer."

Sally's eyes narrowed. Mr. Beechcroft was slightly out of breath, but the way his eyebrows furrowed made it obvious he knew exactly how unprofessionally he was behaving.

Lord Farnsworth apparently didn't. The so-called pugilist was still standing outside Mr. Beechcroft's office, and when her eyes caught his, he threw a hand up in salute.

A salute? Was the man mad? Had the padding on his chest gone to his head?

She shouldn't have touched his buttons. But he had been so smug, and he had put his solicitor in a very awkward position. She hadn't wanted to leave without making known she was no dunderhead incapable of knowing a gentleman when she saw one. And if she could manage to make him uncomfortable in the meantime? Even better.

"Will you come back in?" Mr. Beechcroft awaited her answer.

Her spine stiffened. Of course not. Who offered a home and then rescinded the offer, only to offer it again? She took a deep breath and reminded herself this was no different from her trade deal with China for unprocessed cocoons. Their price had seemed unreasonable, but with British sericulture crushed by disease, she had swallowed her pride and accepted their terms. Being the first of the British textile companies to do so had proved extremely profitable.

"Will your pugilist be present?" she asked.

"He doesn't need to be."

"And the terms will be the same? He hasn't raised his price?"

"He has not."

"Very well, then."

Mr. Beechcroft opened the carriage door and helped her down. He motioned for her to go ahead of him as they walked across the street. She turned to look for Mrs. Merryweather only to find Mr. Beechcroft making frantic waving motions to his *pugilist.*

Lord Farnworth pointed to his chest and frowned, but eventually must have understood his solicitor, for he turned on his heel and walked away.

With the strange lord out of the way, the tightness that had started at the back of her neck began to loosen. She was about to become the owner of Greenwood Manor.

She hadn't been this nervous and excited since Grandfather had told her she was going to be running British Vermillion Textiles. It was a good sign, since she had sold the company in order to buy it.

~

"YOU'VE DONE WHAT?" Mama's eyebrows always rested high upon her forehead, but at the moment they lifted to the point of ridiculousness.

Sally reached for a biscuit and set it on her plate beside her tea. Victoria was in her room, reading. She usually joined them for tea at least, but she had found a book on Egypt that fascinated her enough to keep her in her room even longer than usual. Ever since Mr. Harrison had commented on Sally's neglect, she had made a point of getting Victoria outside in the garden every chance she had. But for this tea, it was best to speak with her mother alone. "I've bought an estate in Dorset. I didn't want to tell you until it was all settled, but now that it is, I wanted to let you know that I will be leaving London this week."

"First you sold Vermillion and now this?"

It had torn a piece out of Sally's soul to part ways with her grandfather's business. But these next few years with Victoria she would never get back. The manor hadn't taken all of her money. There was enough left that once Victoria was older and secure in the knowledge that she mattered, Sally could start up a business again. She would honor her grandfather by doing what he did—starting from scratch and leaving something beautiful behind. But for a minimum of two years, she would focus on Victoria. No one should feel unimportant and overlooked, and Sally should have seen that long before Mr. Harrison pointed it out.

"You never wanted me to run Vermillion. You told me I should sell it as soon as I inherited it."

"Yes, but not so you could buy an estate in Dorset, of all places. It is so far away."

"You are welcome to visit any time you like."

"But what of the Season? I wanted you to sell Vermillion so you could focus more on your social life and marry, not run off to the far corners of the world. How are you to marry when you live in Dorset? Do you expect Mr. Harrison to visit you there?"

Sally stilled. "I do not."

Mama's eyes narrowed. "What do you mean?"

"Mr. Harrison and I are no longer courting."

"Why?"

"We didn't suit each other."

"He is to inherit a barony. I find that very suitable."

"I know you do, mama." Sally reached forward and placed a hand on mama's wrist. "And I'm sorry to disappoint you, but it is for the best."

The muscles in mama's forearm tightened. "I cannot understand how it could be for the best. Frankly, I'm having a hard time understanding you at all."

It was a sentiment Sally was used to, but coming from her mother, it stung. "He wanted heirs, Mama."

"You don't want children?" Mama pulled her arm away, her eyes wide and her mouth clenched, making the muscles in her neck more pronounced. Sally was doing this all wrong. Surely she could have come up with a better way to break this news.

"I do want children. That is my point. He never spoke of children, Mama. He only spoke of *heirs*." For a baron, that meant sons. What if she didn't have any? Surely, her mother should understand that. She had lived with a husband wounded by this very fact his whole life. With a barony, that pressure would be double-fold. Sally would feel it, and until she did have a son, her daughters would feel it.

"He spoke of having children with you?"

Oh, no.

Mama leaned forward. "Your relationship had progressed so far that children had come up? Sally, that is enough to force an engagement. You should be taking advantage of that."

"I just told you he is no longer courting me."

Mama's head went into her hands. Sally waited, giving her a chance to come to terms with all the news Sally had sprung on her.

Thank the heavens Mr. Harrison had wanted to keep their engagement a secret.

"I think you could win his affections back. He was so taken with you." Mama stood in a frantic moment and paced behind her chair. "It wouldn't take much. The way he looked at you at the Reacher's ball, I was certain a proposal would come any day."

The proposal had come that day. He had been fascinated with her, and she had loved being truly seen by someone. And, yes, even the fact that he would be a baron had been enticing. It had been easy to say yes to him. But that had started the quiet conversations about the future. It was a future that, the more they talked about, the less certain Sally felt. Every time they spoke of children he spoke only of sons and heirs. She tried to forgive him. She tried to trust that if all they had were daughters, he would love them once he saw them. But a barony wasn't a business. It could only be passed on to sons, and there was no way around that. Still, she might have gone through with it if it weren't for their conversation about Victoria.

Sally had assumed Victoria would live with them and together they could launch her into society.

Mr. Harrison had been shocked at the idea. *You spend all your time working on Vermillion. How was I to know you wanted to live with her?*

And the worst part about it was he had been right.

That had been the end of her engagement and the beginning of a shift in her focus. Vermillion was sold, and Victoria's happiness was now her goal. Sally needed a few years to return Victoria to her happy, smiling self, and then she would make certain her sister married a man who could take over from Sally and continue to make her happy. Besides purchasing the manor, Sally had set up a very generous dowry for Victoria. When it came time for her to make her entrance into society, the problem would be keeping insincere suitors away, not finding suitors for her. Grandfather would be happy about both of her decisions.

"Mr. Harrison and I didn't suit one another. I've sold the company and I've bought this manor so Victoria and I can spend the next few years together there, making it a home."

Mama's mad pacing stopped. Perhaps she finally had come to terms with the fact that her daughter would not be a baroness. "Victoria has a home."

"She has a room full of books that she rarely leaves."

"She *likes* to read."

"But I think she may like other things as well, and in Dorset, we are going to discover what those things are."

With a deep sigh, her mother returned to her chair. "How will she even get to Dorset? A carriage ride like that could kill her."

"We will take the train most of the way. And she is made of much sterner stuff than you know. A carriage ride would not kill her—not even remotely." If Mama was so concerned about Victoria being killed because she had to sit in a carriage for hours a day, she should make certain she got out and about more often.

"You never know, though; the train and the carriage could make her worse. I didn't know..."

Mama paused, that haunted look returning to her eyes. It had been there ever since Victoria's unsuccessful surgery. The surgery should have helped her. Instead, removing part of her bone on each of her feet had made her condition infinitely worse. Her feet had been deformed before—something the doctor had promised he could fix—but now they were stiffened and unmovable in an even worse position, permanently turned in on themselves in a way that caused terrible pain if she stood on them for more than a few moments.

"You didn't know. You did what any mother would do."

"Not some mothers. Some mothers chose better. Their daughters aren't invalids. I just wanted her to be able to wear a beautiful pair of slippers."

Sally threw her hands in the air. Everyone in the house needed to move forward and not dwell on the decision made two years ago.

Victoria wasn't going to get better, but it wasn't as though she was getting worse, at least not physically. After Sally got Victoria settled in their new life she would send for their mother. Some time at Greenwood Manor might settle her nerves. But she wouldn't bring her until Victoria was comfortable in her new life. She couldn't risk Mama treating Victoria as if she could do nothing.

Victoria should have been taken out of this townhome months ago. Sally had simply been too frantic about growing Vermillion fabrics to notice. Mr. Harrison had been right about that.

"Mama, you have been sadly neglected these past few years. Victoria and I will remove ourselves to Dorset, and you will be completely free again to attend all the social functions and parties that you would like."

Her mother's face softened as she contemplated Sally's offer. "When will you be sending for Victoria?"

"In perhaps a week or two, so have the servants prepare her a new wardrobe—one suitable for being outside."

"Outside?"

"Yes, Mama. Outside. It will be full summer soon, and we shall be spending much of our time out of doors." Sally turned and left. The conversation hadn't gone well, but she had made her points clear, and her mother had finally accepted them. Now it was time to gather the renovation supplies she would need to bring with her to Greenwood Manor. By the time she was done with it, much of it would be unrecognizable.

CHAPTER 3

ONE MAN'S ruin was another's chance at redemption.

Sally ran her fingers along the stone banister leading up the stairway to the entrance of Greenwood Manor. The stairway was over fifteen feet wide but it narrowed as it reached the front balcony. On the opposite side of the balcony, a twin staircase made its way down and widened at the base. Each step was made from the finest marble she had ever seen. Despite its age and exposure to the unpredictable Dorset weather, it still shined in the sunlight.

Sadly, one of these stairways would have to be the first thing to go.

Sally held her sketch pad and fabric swatches. There would be a lot to do in the next few days before Victoria arrived, and she looked forward to every minute of it.

The staff had assembled in a neat line just outside the front door. "Welcome, Miss Duncan." Mrs. Hiddleson, her new housekeeper, gave her a curtsy. "Your trunks have been unpacked and your room in the west wing is ready."

"Thank you, Mrs. Hiddleson." Sally knew which room she was speaking of. It was a large chamber with plenty of room for wardrobes and bookshelves, both pieces of furniture she couldn't help but fill with treasures she found. She could get used to the life of a leisurely lady. Mrs. Hiddleson introduced her to the three maids.

Sally visited her room, which was still as grandiose as it had been during her tour with Lord Farnsworth's solicitor. She walked a large portion of her wing of the house which, despite having been left empty for roughly ten years, was still in good condition.

No surprise there. A baron should keep up a home like this, even if he was too busy spending his inheritance to visit.

The east wing needed a bit more work, which was the reason she had decided to give it to Victoria. She would have a whole wing of a house for her very own, after years of being stuck almost solely in one room. Sally couldn't wait to see her face. She hoped it would, at least in part, make up for her neglect.

Victoria had ghastly taste. She fell in love with every culture she read about and cared not a whit about current understandings of what was tasteful. Sally planned to indulge her every whim...at least in the east wing. They could always redecorate together in a few years when Victoria was an adult. Certainly by then her sensibilities would finally begin to show. But for now, Egyptian Sphinxes and Rococo vases would be mixed with Turkish rugs and English garden papers.

Victoria would not be neglected here.

After walking the inside of the home with Mrs. Hiddleson, Sally excused herself to go back to her room and change. She slid her fingers down the wall of the corridor as she strode back to her room, passing a grand drawing room situated at the back of the home. This was a room she would entertain in. The opposite side of the room was filled with windows and a door that led to a balcony overlooking the back garden. She crossed the room. What exactly did the back garden look like? She remembered a meticulously manicured rose garden, as well as hedges and a lawn. But other than that, she couldn't quite recall all there was for them to enjoy.

She unbarred the door and strode out into the crisp air, inhaling deeply. Even though they were miles from the sea, it was almost as if she could still taste it in the wind: the salty-sweet tang of water and sand without a hint of smog. The stone balcony was in sturdy condition and looked out over the lawn, then behind the lawn to the rose garden, which was only a fourth of the manicured part of the garden.

Leading off the balcony was also a long double stairway with a slow slope. One of the stairways would also need to be removed so that Victoria could visit the garden whenever she wanted to be out. Now that Sally was looking out over the grounds, she remembered the layout better. Four sections of gardens were separated equally by paths. In the center of the paths stood a circular fountain with stone seating all around it. The other parts of the garden were winter gardens, a statuary and a hedge maze. How had she forgotten that she now owned a statuary and a hedge maze? And beyond the maze and winter garden was another feature she only just recalled: a pond.

The sun glistened off the water, making her squint. Then squint again. She rubbed her eyes and leaned forward over the balustrade.

Merciful heavens, there was a man in her pond.

Blinking, she ran back into the house. "Mrs. Hiddleson!" she called. She poked her head back outside. No, she hadn't been seeing things. He was still there. "Mrs. Hiddleson, come quickly."

Mrs. Hiddleson had better be within hearing distance. Sally was certain that if she left the balcony, the apparition in the pond would be gone when she got back. She squinted at the sunlight reflecting off the water.

A man was swimming in her pond.

Was he even clothed?

She leaned forward and shifted to the right, removing the glare of the sun from where he was swimming. Not many men knew how to swim nor felt the need to. Who would be swimming in her pond? She employed a groom, a gardener and a footman. She still needed to hire a butler. The footman had arrived with her. He would not have made his way straight to the water to go for a dip.

Mrs. Hiddleson must not have heard her cry. And Sally didn't dare run into the manor and find her. If it was an employee of hers, she needed to inform him of her expectations, one of which would be that he didn't swim in her pond. How foolish would it be to inspect exactly what was going on by herself?

Foolish.

And yet, Sally didn't like the idea of a servant feeling free to bathe in the pond at a time of day where she could stumble upon him. What about when Victoria was here? Would she come upon a similar scene?

No, she would not. Problems must be met head-on without hesitation or wavering, and the sooner, the better. She was the mistress of this estate, and even though the servants had run the place for years without the interference of the owners, some things would have to change now that she was here.

She swept down the stairs on the right side of the balcony and stomped through the gravel pathway of the garden, past the fountain, until she reached the pond. The swimmer was on the far side and there wasn't a good path around it.

No matter. She hiked up her skirts and forged a path along the grassy banks.

When she was about twenty feet away, she stepped on a fallen branch. The man spun around with just his head above water.

His eyes met hers for a split second and then he spun back around.

She knew that face. But from where? She raised her skirts higher and quickened her pace. Which of the servants had she met? Only the footman, and this was definitely not the footman. Still, she knew the light brown hair and square jawline from somewhere.

"Pardon me," she called out. "Who gave you permission to swim in this pond?"

He didn't turn around to face her; instead, he ducked under the water and swam farther away.

The impudence.

She would not be treated thus. Especially not by someone in her employ. "Stop this instant."

He didn't.

The pond was not so large that he would be able to swim out of her sight. What in the world was he expecting to gain by swimming away? Unless he wanted to stay there all day and into the night, she would discover his identity and what would have been a small infraction would now be cause for dismissal.

The gall.

She followed along the shoreline, and although he did increase the distance between them, there was no way he could actually escape. He must have realized that fact, for at last he stopped.

She put her hands on her hips. "Turn around so I know which of my servants has ignored me so purposefully."

"I would rather not."

Oh, he would rather not, would he? Sally marched forward again. She passed a tree to her left and saw a pair of boots, a jacket, and a waistcoat neatly folded, resting against the trunk.

She knew that waistcoat: Asian silk and Persian buttons.

It belonged to the pugilist—the pugilist who was most definitely not a pugilist.

"Lord Farnsworth?"

His head dropped forward and a dripping arm rose out of the water. He placed his forehead in his palm, shook his head, then straightened and turned around.

"Miss Duncan." A drop of pond water fell from a lock of hair. He wiped it and pushed his hair back, then gave her a bow...or at least the closest thing a man could approximate to a bow whilst five feet underwater. It was a bob of his head, really.

"What are you doing in my pond? The sale of this property went through last week. You can no longer be here."

His head tipped to one side and the barest sliver of a shoulder emerged from the water. He was shrugging. "I thought you were to arrive tomorrow."

She *had* arrived a day early, but how did he know that? And more importantly—why did it matter? She thought her one visit with him would be her last. The man who had been so ridiculous as to try and pass himself off as a pugilist when he was quite obviously a man of fortune was now here, swimming about on her property.

"My day of arrival is irrelevant. I now own this pond and you should not bathe in it."

His chin lifted. "I'm not bathing in it." She raised her eyebrows. It

27

was a hard point to argue when she was watching him do just that. "I'm swimming in it."

She scoffed. "I don't see the difference."

His head bobbed closer to her, his arms pushing him forward. "Oh, there is a very large difference. If I were bathing you would also find my breeches and shirt in that pile of clothes next to you."

Sally cringed. Glancing once again at the pile of clothes, she was grateful to see that he was right. Her cheeks heated, but she refused to be embarrassed. *He* was the one swimming in *her pond.* She pulled her lips together, but she still let out the smallest of laughs. The whole blasted situation was ridiculous. And the baron hadn't needed to throw being naked into the mix to make it more so.

She shook her head and relaxed her shoulders. Lord Farnsworth was no employee she needed to disparage; he was a baron and a... guest? Where was he staying? He wouldn't think she would play hostess to him, would he? Simply because he used to own the manor? She hadn't sold Vermillion so she could entertain a man she barely knew.

"Please, just remove yourself from my pond. We can discuss this later when you are decent."

"Our pond," he called out across the water. "And are you certain you would like me to come out?"

"Of course I am certain. I cannot have you swimming here in the middle of the day."

What exactly did he mean by *our* pond? Did the man not understand how the sale of a property worked? Did he think he still had some rights to Greenwood Manor? Swimming in the pond was one thing, but if he tried to come into her home uninvited...

He shrugged, his shoulder lifting from underneath the water. "All right, then." He kept his eyes on hers as he stepped closer. Each tread exposed more of Lord Farnsworth. First his shoulders...had they been so broad in the solicitor's office? They had, but she had assumed that was thanks to careful padding. The linen of his shirt clung to the rounded curves of his upper arms. Then his chest.

The weave of his shirt was not equal to the task of remaining opaque. Nothing about the baron's physique had been falsified. Every bit of his upper body was real. How did a gentleman have such arms? Most of the men she was acquainted with only exerted themselves by riding, dancing, and perhaps some fencing. None of those activities led to the thickness Lord Farnsworth displayed. Her face, which at the mention of Lord Farnsworth being naked had remained mostly unaffected, now heated with the prospect of a certainly not naked and yet a not truly covered Lord Farnsworth removing himself from the pond and speaking with her in his saturated clothing on dry ground.

She threw a hand out in front of her. "Stop." He stopped, looked down at his chest, now half-exposed, and had the audacity to smile. *Insufferable.* "You may remain in my pond."

"Our pond," he said again. She wouldn't look at his shirt. She stared directly into his eyes, and when she couldn't handle that, she inspected the clouds in the distant sky behind him. It seemed there was a distinct chance of rain later in the day.

She cleared her throat. "I understand you are most likely not in the habit of selling property, but when one does, it generally belongs to the new owner. That is me. This is my pond. And after I leave, I trust you will remove yourself from it."

He put both hands on his waist, the motion drawing her eyes. She jerked them back to his face. His grin was even broader than his shoulders. "It is true I don't often sell property, but I am not wrong in calling this our pond. I still own this half of it, so in fact you are currently on my property. I, however, will not ask you to leave. You are welcome to visit my part of the land at any time. I would be happy to have you."

Sally gritted her teeth. The man couldn't keep a smile off his face. And why didn't he just take a step or two back in the water? She was certain she owned the pond. It was used to water the lawn and gardens if there was ever a dry spell.

"I'm quite certain the property line is the pond."

"You are correct."

"Then I own the pond."

"A good portion of it, yes. When I stay at the hunting lodge, I use the pond for fishing and to water the horses. We both need the water from the pond, so the property line is the pond for each of our parcels of land. Meaning, the property line runs directly down the middle of the pond. I was swimming in my half of the pond, which, as Mrs. Hiddleson will tell you, I am prone to do, and which is completely within my rights."

At least that solved the riddle of where he was staying. Her shoulders relaxed slightly. "Are you telling me I cannot stop you from parading about in your shirtsleeves in full view of my balcony? How would you feel if I did the same on my half of the pond?"

Lord Farnsworth's eyes slid down her figure and then back up to her face. "I would say, don't limit yourself to your side of the pond. You would be welcome in mine as well."

Oh, this was ridiculous! She hadn't bargained on the baron staying on what was left of his property at all, let alone having him swim on his property in clear view of hers. She couldn't handle this. Not now; not directly after taking possession of her new home. When she had investigated the property before agreeing to buy it, she had discovered that neither the lodge nor the manor had been in use for the past several years. If he hadn't bothered to come in the past several years, why was he here now?

Whatever his reasons, she would not put up with the way he looked at her. Not only was this baron bad enough with money that he had to sell off property that had been in his mother's family for generations, but he was obviously also some sort of a rake.

If they were to be neighbors at times, they would be neighbors. But she didn't need to actually converse or spend time with such a man as this. She would simply warn him away, and then hopefully he would return to London and never be in her sight again.

CHAPTER 4

JONATHAN'S LIPS curled into a smile. He hadn't bargained on seeing Miss Duncan until tomorrow, but watching her blush had been a pleasure he was grateful he hadn't had to wait another day for.

His future wife. She was at least as beautiful as he had remembered her. And it seemed she wasn't completely unaware of his charms. His plan was already well underway. As neighbors, she would have to invite him to dinner or, at a minimum, tea.

He stood waist-deep in the pond, waiting expectantly for her invitation, but the offer didn't come.

"Lord Farnsworth, I cannot command you to leave your own property. As I'm still not certain if what you say about the pond is true, I will look over the documents I was given. But I will say this." She reached down and grabbed his waistcoat and jacket from the ground. She held them out in front of her as if accusing him of some sort of crime. "When you are in full view of my home you need to keep your waistcoat and jacket on. In a few days, my sister will be coming to live here. It is one thing for me to find you swimming in the pond; it would be quite another for my younger sister to—"

"I will give up swimming in the pond."

"—discover..." She paused, her head slipped to one side, and her hand that had been shaking his clothes in demonstration dropped. "You will?"

Happily. That blasted Mrs. Hiddleson had surprised him two afternoons ago just after he had arrived. He had slipped into the pond trying to get a better look at the back of the manor. Mrs. Hiddleson had always chided him as a boy for the messes he made of himself, so he hadn't wanted to admit to not having grown up in the past ten years. Instead he had made up the ridiculous excuse that he enjoyed swimming and planned to often swim in the pond.

Once Jonathan committed to something, he didn't turn away from it. If Mrs. Hiddleson expected him to swim in the pond, then swim in the pond he would...at least until given a reasonable excuse to stop. Miss Duncan asking him not to swim in it was perfectly reasonable.

The whole mess could have been avoided if he had simply made a point of visiting the manor before it was sold. Now when he had finally returned to the place of his fondest childhood memories, he could no longer enter it. He couldn't regret the time he spent investigating Miss Duncan, though. She was a fascinating woman. Every business owner he visited had touted her fine taste and acumen at finding the best producers of silks and cottons. The younger businessmen seemed to be half in love with her and the older ones very protective. Every interaction had made him more certain he had made the right choice.

Fate was a funny thing indeed. Of all the ways he had thought about finding a wife, this had never been one. But if all went according to plan, he would have to suggest to others the same process.

He still wished he had a way to explore Greenwood Manor. It was so close, and yet so unattainable.

Unless, of course, he was invited to tea. Now that Miss Duncan was here, he most certainly would be.

She seemed to be waiting for an explanation as to why he was so accommodating of her wish to no longer swim in the pond. "I assure you I plan to be the best of neighbors. If you do not want me to swim here, then I won't."

The hand that wasn't holding his clothing went to her waist. "Well, we can hardly call each other neighbors when you are rarely here."

"In the past ten years I haven't had the opportunity to visit Greenwood Manor."

Miss Duncan nodded as if that statement satisfied her.

"So, I obviously plan to spend a bit more time here from now on... to make up for that."

Miss Duncan blinked. Her eyes flashed to the waterline and everything above it before jerking back to his face. "You will spend more time here now? When you don't even own the manor?"

"I suppose I didn't realize how much I would miss it until it was gone."

Miss Duncan muttered something under her breath but he was too far away to catch it. It was summer and a sunny day, but the water was starting to chill him, especially with the upper half of his chest exposed to the air. He could step back into the water, but he rather enjoyed the rose color of Miss Duncan's cheeks. Besides, if she were to be his wife in only a few short months, she may as well grow accustomed to his form.

In London he had been the soul of propriety with women. He had considered himself too young to marry and had been careful with every interaction, as the last thing he had wanted was to raise the hopes of a young lady—or even worse, her mother—when he had no intention to wed as of yet.

But knowing the woman that stood before him was to be his wife? His need to make every interaction completely benign was lifted and the freedom of speaking his mind brought a lightness to every word he said to her. Familiarity, comfort, and ease; other than Oliver and his other Eton friends, he hadn't had the pleasure of enjoying an openness of mind with someone since his mother had died.

Jonathan hadn't really seen the point in a wife before. Even now he probably wouldn't be considering the prospect if he hadn't had to sell Greenwood Manor. But the idea of spending his evenings with Miss Duncan was surprisingly intriguing. What would they talk about? Would she open up to him about what it had been like for her taking over her grandfather's business and making it flourish? Did she like to read? A vision of his head in her lap while she read to him in the library flashed through his mind. Once again the library could be a library of belonging and peace. But in the family he created with Miss Duncan, they would always stay together. There would be no need to weave fairy tales about happy families. They would be their own happy family. Would she be playful when they were reading in the library and none of the servants were around to watch them? He glanced at her face. Or would she always be as serious as she was now, with that line of disapproval forming between her eyebrows and her plump lips curved into a frown?

Either way...intriguing. He was going to quite enjoy getting to know his wife.

"I shall bid you farewell, Lord Farnsworth. Thank you for agreeing not to swim in the pond. I assume you are correct and we will make good neighbors."

"I'm sure of it," he answered back. And then throwing caution to the wind, he pushed his legs forward through the water. Before he could get more than his waist out of the water, she gave him a quick businesslike nod, her eyes only slipping downward for the briefest of seconds before she turned on her heel to leave.

"Miss Duncan," he called. She paused, but then must have changed her mind, for after only a moment she strode forward again, this time at a faster pace. He was nearly out of the water now, only his calves and feet still slowing him down. He lifted his legs higher and splashed his way out of the pond. "Miss Duncan, you have my waistcoat and jacket."

Miss Duncan once again murmured something under her breath, and even though he could not hear what she had said, he was quite certain from her tone it wasn't language he was used to hearing from a young lady's mouth.

He smiled. The mouth of a tradeswoman—he could get used to that as well.

Water dripped from his shirt and trousers in steady streams as he made his way to where Miss Duncan stood. She remained facing the manor with her shoulders back and her head held high. He smothered a chuckle. Something told him the future Lady Farnsworth would not like to be laughed at. "Don't be alarmed. There is no need to turn around. I'm directly behind you." He leaned forward and reached out to pluck the clothes from her grasp.

"I am *not* alarmed," she said, and although he couldn't see her face he could practically hear her teeth grinding. "I simply do not want to embarrass you." Her arm bent backward, awkwardly holding his clothes away from her. He took them, and made certain their hands only touched for the briefest of seconds—just a brush of his thumb against the outside edge of her smallest finger. Compared to his pond-chilled hands, hers were warm, dry, and soft in a way his hands would never be.

"I shall take my leave. You won't find me in the pond again."

"Thank you."

"If you change your mind, though, simply say the word and I will return to my previous habits. I could even teach you to swim if you like. We could each stay on our own side of the pond, making it completely proper."

She shook her head, making the few curls not tightly bound up on her head sway back and forth. "Nothing about that would be proper."

Jonathan curled his lip. The knowledge that the woman who stood before him would one day be his wife brought down all his barriers of propriety. One day they would know everything about one another. "Well, then, I bid you good day. Welcome to Greenwood Manor." That didn't seem enough. The manor and the gardens spread out in front of Miss Duncan; her well-groomed figure still in her well-tailored traveling clothes blocked only the view of the east side of the house. Miss Duncan now belonged here, a fact that seemed to make his future settle into place. "Welcome home."

He turned on his heel, content with their first interaction here in Dorset. If he stayed any longer, he might say something much too forward. The inevitability of what Miss Duncan would become to him was clear to Jonathan, but she would need at least a few more days of interactions before the subject could be breached. No matter how logical the relationship, women wanted to be wooed, after all. Or at least so he had heard.

It wasn't until he was halfway back to the hunting lodge that he stopped and looked back at Greenwood Manor. Only the roof was visible above the trees that separated the pond from his lodge.

Miss Duncan had forgotten to invite him to tea. He had no idea how to see her again.

CHAPTER 5

WHAT KIND of neighbor didn't invite a visiting baron over for tea? It had been three days and he hadn't heard a word or even received a note from Miss Duncan. Jonathan paced outside the lodge. When he reached the front right edge of open space in front of the lodge there was a hill and he could just see the roofline of Greenwood Manor. He stopped and surveyed it. How could she be so close and not even think to invite him? His groom was a terrible cook and it seemed like she should at least guess at his less-than-fortunate cuisine choices.

True, she was a single young woman, but she had a companion and a house full of servants. He was stuck in the small hunting lodge with only his valet and a groom. It wasn't as though he could invite her.

Something had to be done.

A neighbor didn't need an invitation to visit. After all, Miss Duncan was new to the area; it would be customary for him to walk over and bring a gift of some sort. He had actually brought a gift for her from London, something he had picked up from one of the merchants when he had investigated her. But he wanted to save that for when he proposed. It would be much too intimate a gift to be considered only neighborly.

He looked around the lodge. There were a few books in the library, but most of them were either on hunting or some of his mother's favorites—ones he had requested to be brought over from the manor before the sale, and he wasn't ready to part with those. He needed all the pots and pans in the kitchen, and he doubted those would be an appropriate gift for a lady anyway.

"Howard," Jonathan called.

A door shut upstairs and his valet's footsteps plodded down the stairs. "Yes, sir?"

"Do you hunt?"

The corners of Howard's lips turned down. "I've never had that opportunity."

Blast. If his valet didn't hunt, he was going to have to go shoot a pheasant himself. His father had always loved hunting, but that was one of many ways Jonathan didn't resemble him. He had no dog to drive the pheasants out. He could try for a hare. Somehow a pheasant seemed a better gift. A deer would make for a larger target. He might be able to hit a deer. But it would be practically impossible for him to deliver it to her.

"Do you know how to load a gun?"

"I do not, but I do know how to clean them, and since the guns have been here for over ten years without being used, I feel that should be the first step."

"Yes, of course it should be." Good thing he had Howard. Jonathan might have remembered to clean the guns once he had them in front of him, but he also was in a rush to visit Greenwood Manor. It had been torture being so close to the home and not having a chance to see the inside. "Do we have powder and shot?" It wasn't as though he had never gone hunting. If Howard could clean the guns, he would be able to remember how to load them.

Howard nodded.

"Great, then we are all set. Let's see if we can't drum up some game."

It took over an hour to get the guns ready, and two hours into hunting Jonathan was starting to question his plan. Perhaps a book on hunting would have been a better idea. She might not have much use for it, but at least it would be something, and by now he could have been enjoying her company for quite some time.

"By all rights, this land should be encompassed by game." Jonathan ran a hand through his hair. "No one has hunted it for years."

Howard cleared his throat and mumbled something under his breath. Howard wasn't one to typically mumble. A tree branch whacked Jonathan in the face and he brushed off the dampness it left there. They were following what he hoped was a game trail, but he had no idea if he was correct. "What was that?"

Howard cleared his throat again. "To be fair…it isn't as though we haven't seen any game."

Jonathan sniffed and brushed aside another branch before it hit his face. "I couldn't have brought Miss Duncan one of those deer we saw." Not that he hadn't tried to shoot one; he had.

"Quite right. It would have been too great a burden for certain."

"And the hare? There is barely even any meat on a hare." It had been frightened by his shot as well.

"That is true."

"It is. I suppose I didn't mean that there wasn't *any* game here, just that there hasn't been the right kind of game."

"And what kind of game would that be, sir?"

"The kind that allows me to shoot it."

Howard cleared his throat a third time. Jonathan might need a new valet.

"Miss Duncan." Mrs. Hiddleson knocked softly on her bedroom door. "You've a visitor."

Sally set down the plans for the front of the home and frowned. Who would come calling? She didn't know anyone in the area and the nearest neighbors were miles away. A wet shirt and water dripping down from a lock of hair flashed in her memory. Lord Farnsworth? Surely not. What possible reason could he have for coming to her home? "Who is it?"

"Lord Farnsworth."

She closed her eyes tightly. How much longer was the man going to remain near her property? By all accounts, he hadn't ever felt the need to spend time here before she purchased it.

She stood and opened the door. "Where did you put him?"

"In the east parlor."

"The east parlor?" Sally had just put her book of papers and a few mock-ups of Victoria's rooms in there. It would be the first room she renovated after the stairs were done. "That is where I have all my work."

Mrs. Hiddleson frowned. "I'm sorry, miss. I didn't realize. Would you like me to move him?"

"No, I'll go there now. The sooner the better." Even now he could be looking at the drawings and plans for the east wing. Her book of wallpapers was there, complete with larger samples of the papers she knew Victoria would love.

Mrs. Hiddleson nodded and waited for her to take the lead. They strode through the corridor, and each second Sally was more and more certain Lord Farnsworth would be thumbing through her things. The man had no sense of propriety or boundaries. Were all titled men so completely unaware of a woman's feelings? The two she knew certainly seemed to be. Mr. Harrison wasn't technically titled yet, but he would be, and that had been reason enough for him to assume he could make all the decisions in their relationship.

"He brought you a housewarming gift. I sent it to Cook." The words tumbled out of Mrs. Hiddleson's mouth in a rush.

"A gift?"

"Yes."

Sally furrowed her eyebrows. "What was it?"

Mrs. Hiddleson cleared her throat as if she would rather not answer. She sighed. "A squirrel."

"A squirrel? Why on earth did he bring me a squirrel?"

"You will have to ask him. There wasn't much left of it, but I suppose Cook will find something she can do with it."

Sally's stomach turned. The last thing she wanted to eat was squirrel. How did one even cook squirrel? Lord Farnsworth must mean something by the gift, but she couldn't imagine what. A warning to stay away from the better game on his lands? She was no hunter. He hadn't needed to worry about that. Perhaps a reminder that she was small game compared to him?

Mrs. Hiddleson opened the parlor door and, just as Sally had feared, Lord Farnsworth was rifling through her book of wallpapers. He stood when she entered, but he kept the book in his hands. She stomped over to him and pulled it from his grasp.

"What are these?"

"Papers."

He raised his eyebrows. "For the walls?"

"Where else would I put them?"

"For Greenwood Manor?"

"Yes, for Greenwood Manor. Unlike yourself, I have but one home."

"But have you seen them?" He pointed to the one still on top: a gaudy, deep red accented by gold flowers. And that one was the least of her concerns. The one with rotating angles of fish would certainly be too much for him to handle.

"Of course I have seen them. I am the one who brought them."

"Even the one with the fish?"

Blast. "Have a seat, Lord Farnsworth." Most of the furniture had stayed with the home, so none of the rooms were empty, even if they were outdated. "I am certain you aren't here to concentrate on my papers for the walls."

"I wasn't, but now that I see them…" He paused. "No matter. As you said, it is your home to decorate as you see fit. This room hasn't changed since I was last in it. Even the furniture."

"Yes, well, it was included in the sale."

He nodded and then eyed the book of papers in her hands. "Do you have plans for the library?"

She didn't really have plans for the library, but something about the way he leaned forward in cautious interest made her want to pretend she did. "You saw the fish paper, didn't you?"

41

His face went white. "You are going to paper the library in fish?"

She smiled. Perhaps Lord Farnsworth seeing her papers was not the worst thing in the world. What would a completely inept designer say? "We aren't far from the sea. It seems fitting."

"Not far from—" He sputtered, then stopped and swallowed. "When exactly do you plan to do the papers?"

She smiled. "We will do them one room at a time." Lord Farnsworth relaxed slightly, his shoulders dropping and the line between his eyes softening to a wrinkle. "Starting with the library, of course."

He coughed and then a muscle in his jaw clenched. After blinking a few times, he leaned forward in his chair as if to protest, but then stopped himself. He must have remembered this was her home, and if she wanted to paper the library in hippopotami, it was her prerogative. A perverse sense of pleasure at the sight of Lord Farnsworth so agitated overtook her. He had made her uncomfortable many times, not the least of which was their meeting at the pond, and it seemed as though papering the library was the perfect topic of conversation.

"I'm not certain we need a library, really. I have been debating removing the bookcases and repurposing the room as…" What type of environment would a strangely unfettered baron dislike? If he was used to swimming in ponds and pretending to be a pugilist, it would take no small thing to disquiet him. "I was thinking perhaps a menagerie."

Lord Farnsworth stilled. He blinked several times and his hand tightened on the arm of the chair he was sitting in. "A menagerie...in place of the library."

"Of course." The veins in his neck became more prominent as he clenched his jaw. His perfectly squared chin was even more conspicuous when frustration was on his face. She held in a smile. What was it about this man that made her want to disquiet him? "Why else would I paper the walls with fish?"

"And you would have live animals in this menagerie? Inside the home?"

There was something about watching this man, a peer of the

realm, and one who had been given everything he wanted in life, nearly having a convulsion at the thought of her running amok with just one of his many homes that made her insides swell with jittery excitement. It was the same excitement she would feel whenever she signed a large contract for fabric. Men always thought they had the upper hand in these situations, and she loved proving them wrong.

"Of course we would have live animals; a few reptiles, some fish of course, and a moose."

"A moose? Where would you find a moose? And have you seen one? They are hulking. One would never fit in the library."

"You mean the menagerie."

He ran a hand through his hair—it had been combed so nicely before—and then kept his hand at the back of his neck. "You know what I mean."

"I've been thinking about having one shipped from the Americas. It is exciting, is it not? I never could have had a menagerie in my home in London."

He removed his hand from his neck and ran it down his face. When he looked up at her, his eyebrows were furrowed, his expression pleading. "Perhaps you should wait a few months. Tearing out a library seems like it would be a lot of work. Don't you want to enjoy the property a little first?"

"I do, but I can't help but think I will enjoy it even more once it has a menagerie."

"I could help you build an outdoor menagerie in the garden. It seems like that would be a better place for it. Can you imagine a moose being stuck indoors all the time?"

"Well, of course my plan would include part of the garden. That is why the library is perfect for it. The doors that lead outside could be used as a passageway for some of the larger animals, like the moose and the snow leopard."

He sat back in his chair, defeated. "You cannot be serious."

Of course she wasn't serious. What type of woman did he take her for that he would think she was at all serious? His offer of help proved he thought her completely incapable of managing a home by herself.

Why else would he have shown up at the exact time she was taking possession? "Lord Farnsworth, why exactly are you here?"

"I brought you a housewarming gift. We are neighbors now, after all."

Sally clenched her teeth together. She had not bargained on Lord Farnsworth being her neighbor. "But why a squirrel of all things?"

"Truthfully?"

"Please."

"I'm not much of a hunter. I would have loved to bring you something much better, but it was all my valet and I could drum up."

"You don't hunt?" What the devil was he doing here? He was staying in the hunting lodge, for heaven's sake. Had he come only to torment her? What had she ever done to him?

"Not usually. Obviously, I'm here hunting now, but it was my father who was a great hunter. To his utter disappointment, I never had a passion for it. But I did use my few skills to bag you a squirrel today." A crooked smile spread on his face, making him look more like a neighborhood boy sharing a jest than a condescending baron. "I'm not sure what you will do with it."

She would not be distracted by his neighborly charm. Something was very wrong, and the squirrel proved it. "So, you came to the hunting lodge and yet you do not like to hunt?"

Lord Farnsworth cleared his throat and shuffled around in his seat again. "Yes."

"Why in the world would you do that?"

He opened his mouth, then shut it so quickly his teeth clacked together. He leaned forward, as if he changed his mind and would talk, but then stood from his chair and paced in front of it. There really was only one explanation as to why he would be here. He must be trying to keep an eye on her. He never cared for the manor while it was his own, but now that it was hers, he suddenly needed to be certain she didn't do anything upsetting to it.

If he thought she was the sort of woman to buy a home and then completely run it to ruin, who was she to disappoint him? From now on, she would make certain the baron was privy to all the worst of her plans. Somehow he would see the Sphinxes and the vases that Victoria had fallen in love with. She had every right to do whatever she wanted to with the manor. If he wanted to control what happened to it, he shouldn't have squandered his money on things less important than this home.

Lord Farnsworth stopped his pacing and turned toward her. His arms raised as if he were about to place them on her shoulders, but then he dropped them. "I do have a reason for being here—a good one, I think, and I hope you will come to agree with me. I am hunting something, but I cannot tell you of it yet."

What a strange thing to say. If he indeed were here to make certain she didn't wreck the house, did he expect her thanks for his interference? Her lips curled. She supposed she would thank him for stopping her from doing something so ridiculous as putting in a menagerie. But he didn't know that.

"And when do you think you will be able to tell me of it?"

His eyes scanned her face, pausing on her mouth, which still had her silly, vindictive grin on it. She quickly sucked her lips inside her mouth, but it was too late. He had already caught her smirk and had moved on to studying her eyes. His toe, which had been tapping a steady nervous beat, stilled, and his face relaxed into a hesitant half-smile. "Two weeks," he said.

"Two more weeks?" A day or two of tormenting him with her plans would be more than enough, but two weeks? Victoria would be here by then and he would only get in the way.

His smile from earlier faltered slightly. "Perhaps three. Yes, three should be plenty."

Three weeks? She *never* should have assumed the baron would stay away simply because he hadn't been to the property in years. She should have specified in the bill of sale what times of year he could come, and she could have made certain she and Victoria were in London while he was here. The last thing Victoria needed was another gentleman muttering incomplete sentences to her like Mr. Harrison had done. The edges of Sally's vision darkened. The sooner she got rid of Lord Farnsworth, the better.

Lord Farnsworth shuffled his feet, his head cocked to one side as he watched her distress. "At the very most four."

"And what are you hoping for? Two weeks or four?"

"Me? I would rather make it two." He leaned slightly forward. His eyes searched her face, and whatever he saw there made one corner of his mouth twitch upward. "I would much rather make it two."

His declaration should have made her breathe easier, but he was near enough for her nose to catch the faintest scent of gunpowder. Could the two of them not have even one customary interaction? First he pretended to be something he was not, and then she caught him in a pond, and now he was bringing her a squirrel and conversing with her much too intimately. Still, she could handle his interfering for two weeks. "Well, then, I hope you get your wish."

His eyes brightened. The man was full of all kinds of moods she could not follow. "As do I."

Sally stood. "Thank you for your kind gift, Lord Farnsworth. I'm certain it will be…" What? Will be what? What exactly did one do with a squirrel? She couldn't tell him it would be put to good use, for she in all honestly wasn't even sure what that would mean. "Remembered. I hope you enjoy the rest of your stay in the lodge."

He rose, his eyebrows furrowed. "Are you dismissing me?"

"Dismissing seems like a strong term. You came to deliver a gift and I have received it. What else were you expecting?"

"I don't know...a chance to get to know one another better?" His eyes shifted to the door as if he was worried she was about to throw him out of it. How long did he expect her to wait on him? His gift was...kind...she supposed, but there was work to be done. As entertaining as it was to ruffle a few of the resident lord's feathers, she needed to get back to planning. And with Mrs. Merryweather on her way back to London to fetch Victoria, Sally wasn't about to spend much time with Lord Farnsworth on her own. He could get the wrong idea and think she was trying to pursue him.

"Didn't you say you were going to be here for two more weeks? I am certain we will have plenty of opportunities to see one another again."

"You are certain?" He tipped his head to one side as if he wasn't.

"Of course. We are neighbors, after all." It was hard to think of a time when they might actually run into one another, but it was completely possible. She walked toward the door and he followed.

When they reached the foyer, Mrs. Hiddleson was waiting to see him out. Sally needed to see about employing a butler. She hadn't expected guests yet and had been slow to go about looking for one.

Lord Farnsworth gave his farewell with a bow and a look in his eye that she couldn't place. Disappointment? Boredom? He seemed distressed to be parting ways with her, but why? Hunting must not be keeping him entertained well enough. If that were the case, he should return to London, where there would be more than just one neighbor to interact with.

As the door shut behind him and Mrs. Hiddleson shuffled away, Sally shook her head and returned to the east parlor. She picked up the paper with the fish and squinted. Would she be mad to hang it in the library? She clicked her tongue and threw the paper back down on the side table. Victoria was starting to wear off on her. The library was a beautiful room as it was.

Still, if she could do it in two weeks before Lord Farnsworth left and show it to him, the look on his face might be worth the expense.

CHAPTER 6

JONATHAN DRUMMED his fingers on the small writing desk in the library of the hunting lodge. He was on his third day of waiting for Miss Duncan to return his call, but to no avail. It seemed three days was the absolute maximum number of days he could handle sitting alone in the lodge without going mad. She was probably busy planning her indoor-outdoor menagerie that would completely ruin the library.

She couldn't have been serious. She couldn't.

But why have samples of fish wallpaper if she wasn't going to use fish wallpaper? He had heard so much about her excellent taste, and yet she was considering papering something in the manor with fish. Were all the textile merchants he talked to mad, or was Jonathan completely mistaken about what was stylish in decor?

He had certainly never seen any room papered with fish before.

Jonathan stood and eyed the door. He couldn't just sit in the lodge and wait for Miss Duncan to come to him. By the time she finally did, who knew what she might do to the manor? Whether it was stylish or not, the last thing he wanted was for the manor to be papered in any of those gaudy papers. The sooner he asked her to marry him, the better. The parlor seemed relatively unscathed, but he had no solid memories of it—that had been a room for guests. And Jonathan was never a guest. The manor had always been home.

And he *still* hadn't been offered any tea. He had brought her a perfectly good squirrel; the least she could do was offer him some tea.

A knock at the door interrupted his thoughts. Jonathan straightened in his chair. Had Miss Duncan come at last? He smoothed down his hair and checked his cravat. "Yes."

Howard cracked open the door. "Sorry to disturb you..."

"No need to be sorry. What is it?"

"I was wondering if you wanted me to send Robert into town to ask about getting a few more servants—specifically, a scullery maid and a cook."

Jonathan sunk back into his chair. He still had no visit from Miss Duncan, then. He pursed his lips together. The squirrel had been a mistake. Never bring a young woman a squirrel. Young ladies liked flowers and sweetmeats, not wild game.

Howard was right, though. He had been so distracted by Miss Duncan that he had neglected some of his duties. They desperately needed a cook. Robert was no skilled craftsman in the kitchen, and the three of them had suffered enough from his cooking. Not only that, but this could also be an excuse to go to Greenwood Manor.

Jonathan spun on his heel. "Of course. But first, I will go to Greenwood Manor and ask Mrs. Hiddleson if she has any recommendations."

"I would be happy to—"

"No." Jonathan didn't allow Howard to finish his sentence. "I will do it."

Jonathan bounded out of the corridor and into the front hall. He threw open the door and leaped out of the dim cottage into the bright afternoon sun. He finally had an excuse to visit Greenwood Manor, and he wasn't going to waste it.

It only took a few minutes to reach the pond. He smiled as he passed the spot where Miss Duncan had mistaken him for one of the servants. She knew how to make her mind known. He would always know where he stood with his wife; there would be no unspoken pain in a marriage with her. Perhaps his parents could have had an easier time of it with that sort of honesty. Jonathan and his mother had always missed his father when he was away from them, yet she had never spoken of it.

How much more she must have missed both of them when Jonathan was also away.

From the outskirts of the back garden he could just make out the different sections: the winter garden, where he spent most of his time, was mostly green without much color, but the rose garden was vibrant in a multitude of shades. He had never seen it quite so adorned, even though he had often dreamed of it as a boy. He had made it past most of the back garden when he heard Mrs. Hiddleson call his name.

He looked up from the path to see Mrs. Hiddleson coming down the back stairs of Greenwood Manor, waving a handkerchief in the air.

Well, that seemed as much an invitation to the grounds as anything. He stepped into the garden and met her at the bottom of the staircase.

"Not going for a swim today?"

Jonathan raised his chin. He was a grown man, and he would not be intimidated by his childhood housekeeper. He could simply tell her that he *had* been snooping around the grounds that day, and when she had startled him, he had fallen in. "Miss Duncan has asked me not to swim in the pond any longer, so unfortunately, I won't be getting my exercise in such a manner for the time being."

She tipped her head to one side.

Poppycock. The woman didn't believe him.

"I will miss it," he added lamely.

"I'm certain you will; how could you not? Nothing like getting wet on a fine summer's day like today."

There was quite a chill in the air for summer. There often was in Dorset. He never had been able to pull the wool over Mrs. Hiddleson's eyes.

He nodded his head in agreement. "Nothing like it. You should try it some time, Mrs. Hiddleson. It is very restorative."

"I shall not. And why would I need anything restorative? I am in just as good of health as I was when you lived here, Lord Farnsworth. Now, since you aren't swimming, what can I help you with?"

"I was hoping to speak with Miss Duncan about finding a few servants for the hunting lodge."

"What types of servants are you needing?"

"We are quite desperate for a scullery maid and a cook."

"I know all the girls in town. Miss Duncan isn't familiar with anyone yet."

Blast. The woman had a point.

"Even still, perhaps she might like to know that I am looking. If she needs anyone, I would make certain she finds her servants first. After all, I won't be hiring mine for a permanent position."

"We have already done all the hiring, but for the butler. Wait here and I will get you a list of ladies. You've been at the lodge a week now, and no cook." She clucked her tongue.

"We've managed."

Mrs. Hiddleson gave him the exact kind of look she had when he was a boy and had been caught trying to light fires in the hearth—like he didn't even know what he didn't know.

Mrs. Hiddleson was back up the stairs before he could stop her. He paced at the base of the stairs for several minutes waiting for her return.

Mrs. Hiddleson returned with a paper in her hand. She handed it to him and wished him luck. He turned to leave. Mrs. Hiddleson grabbed his elbow. The contact was not unpleasant. None of his servants at home touched him without permission. There was something about being around a woman who had known him as a boy that made Mrs. Hiddleson's touch feel like family. And it had been much too long since he'd had a family—in some ways he'd never had one. She squeezed her fingers. "Have you seen Mr. Ashton yet? He was asking about you."

Jonathan froze. He should have stopped and seen Mr. Ashton, just like he should have come to Greenwood Manor before it was sold. "No. Do you think he would want to see me?"

"Of course he will want to see you. We have all wanted to see you grown."

Once again he was a small boy being reprimanded. Other than his friends from Eton, Mrs. Hiddleson and Mr. Ashton were some of the very few people who cared about him. As a child, Father never allowed him to visit or write to them after Mother had passed away. He couldn't understand why Jonathan would want to. His father had never allowed him to form relationships with the help at his estates.

And when he reached adulthood? Well, what if they had forgotten him? It was better to keep them in memory.

That was a poor excuse when he was less than a mile away, though. He would have to go visit Mr. Ashton...as soon as he figured out one more reason to visit Miss Duncan.

"I'll make it a point to see him soon." Jonathan waved to Mrs. Hiddleson. She shook her head as he strode away.

That had been a waste of his time.

He stomped back to the hunting lodge and flung the list of names down on the kitchen table.

There had to be a reasonable excuse to visit with Miss Duncan. The new servants had been a bad idea. Of course Miss Duncan would have no real way to help him with that problem. He needed something specific to her—something only she could help him with.

Jonathan pulled the door open to the library and hauled out the bill of sale. Spreading the papers out on the desk, he scanned them for anything that could be of use. There had to be something here that he might need to discuss with Miss Duncan. He just needed to find it.

After reading through most of the papers with only a few less-than-stellar ideas, he slid one paper to the side, only to find exactly what he was looking for. He pressed his finger on the paragraph.

Animals.

All the animals of the estate still belonged to him. That obviously was meant to pertain to sheep, but over the years there had been other animals housed at Greenwood Manor, namely his grandfather's hunting dogs.

So any dogs at the manor should belong to him. After all, what good was a hunting lodge without dogs? He highly doubted there were still any dogs living on the estate, but it would be remiss of him if he didn't at least check. He strode out of the room, purposely leaving the papers behind. If he had to follow Miss Duncan into her library to get her bill of sale, even better. The library was the heart of Greenwood Manor, and he would do a lot more than drum up an excuse about dogs to see it.

He would look ridiculous returning only a few minutes after his last visit, but he didn't care. He was done waiting on Miss Duncan. How in the world were they supposed to get engaged if they never saw each other?

This time he skirted the pond and kept to the trees. He didn't want Mrs. Hiddleson or another one of the servants to see him coming. Clanging sounds reached his ears not long after he passed the pond and back garden. He broke through the trees after passing beyond the manor house and turned to see a group of men working on one of the stairways leading up to the house.

That was strange.

What could be wrong with the stairs?

He hadn't noticed a problem with them when he'd delivered the squirrel. He had been distracted by finally getting a chance to enter Greenwood Manor. He may not have noticed some loose stonework or deep marks from overuse. Perhaps they were aging, after all.

But as he drew closer, he could see that the opposite stairway hadn't been touched, and it not only looked in good condition, it was made from Purbeck Marble. That would have cost a fortune to put in. Why in the world was Miss Duncan removing it?

As if his thoughts could conjure her, Miss Duncan stepped through the door and onto the floor above him.

Some of the men stopped, but she waved them on, simply surveying their work.

He strode over to the men. Miss Duncan noticed him after only a few steps and she raised an eyebrow.

What? She was surprised her one and only neighbor would come to pay her a visit? Did she not know anything about country life?

"Miss Duncan," Jonathan said over the noise of the pickaxes. "I trust you have been well since I last saw you?"

"Yes."

"It seems you are already beginning your improvements."

"Yes."

There wasn't much he could say in response to that. Nor did he want to continue yelling over the noise of the workers, so he crossed over to the opposite stairway that hadn't been disturbed and climbed it. The grey and pink hues from the marble jumped out at him. What substance could she possibly feel was better suited than this? He reached the top and leaned against the balustrade. "You are starting your renovations with the Purbeck Marble stairs?"

"Yes."

At least it wasn't the menagerie, but still, their conversation was hardly going as he had expected. How was he supposed to get to know her better if she only answered every question with a "yes"? Perhaps he should simply ask her to marry him now and save himself the trouble of courting—if you could call living in a hunting lodge and sulking that he wasn't invited over more often courting.

What the devil was she doing to the manor? He had quite talked himself out of taking her menagerie idea seriously, but if she was removing marble from the stairs, he might need to rethink his assumptions. Had she bought it only to take it apart piece by piece and sell each item?

That would be a terrible investment, and so much work. It was ridiculous. The woman whom many merchants had touted as a pleasure to work with, having the keenest eye for fashion and design, seemed to be very different from the woman he was meeting with now that they were in Dorset.

"And what exactly are you planning to do with these stairs?"

"I'm getting rid of them." She said it like it was a perfectly normal thing to remove stairs from one's home.

"You mean the marble? You are getting rid of the marble."

"No, the stairs. They won't work with the plans I have."

Stairs wouldn't work? *Stairs?* "What exactly are your plans for the house? You aren't perhaps planning to scavenge it and sell off any valuables." He laughed to show that he was in jest, but even she must have noticed he wasn't entirely certain she wouldn't do such a thing.

"Of course not. Don't be ridiculous."

Ridiculous? He wasn't the one destroying a perfectly good set of stairs.

"Then what exactly is going on?"

"Need I remind you that I own this home now? Nothing I do should concern you."

"But I find tearing up perfectly good marble does. What are you planning to replace it with?" The house couldn't function without stairs; she must be planning to rebuild them with something grander. That was the only thing he could think of that would reconcile the woman standing before him and the one he had heard praised in London.

She tipped her head to one side as if considering whether or not he deserved an answer. The way she smiled before speaking didn't make him feel as though he had passed any tests. "For now, Portland cement."

The clanging hammers suddenly raised in pitch and caused a sharp pain in his head. "You are replacing marble with Portland cement? Why would stairs be improved upon by making them out of cement?"

"They wouldn't be, but I'm not making stairs. I'm taking them out, aren't I?" She made no sense. He had decided to marry a crazy woman. That smile that at first had seemed so open and friendly now seemed a bit too open and friendly, as if she had no concerns in the world; as if the fact that she would own a home with no steps to gain entry to it was nothing to worry about. "And marble does seem a bit posh, doesn't it, for what I have planned? Can you imagine a moose traipsing about on marble? It would be quite ridiculous."

Jonathan shook his head to try and clear the ringing in it. But as it was coming from the men working, there was not much he could do. He could turn around now, never see the manor again, and never see Miss Duncan again. Selling the manor had been a mistake, but it was a mistake of loss, not gain. What if he married Miss Duncan and she wanted stairs removed from all of his houses?

She propped one hand on her shapely hip and waited for his reply. He closed his eyes for a moment. Nothing had to be decided today. Everything he had discovered about Miss Duncan, apart from the stairs and the menagerie, seemed to point to the fact that she was not only sane, but a hard worker with excellent taste.

Her raised eyebrows seemed to be a challenge. Would he accept the fact that she was the one who owned the manor or not?

If he didn't, there was no way she would ever see him as anything other than a snobbish lord who thought nothing of her power and opinion—not a good way to start a courtship or a marriage. Her smile was friendly, not crazed. Her plans made some sort of sense, or at least they had to in her mind. And he would feel those delicate fingertips on his chest again. He simply needed to adhere to his plan.

He smiled at the workers below Miss Duncan and then turned and looked back at the stairs he had just climbed. Would they meet the same fate as the others? He didn't dare ask. The marble truly was beautiful. It was such a shame. But when he returned his gaze to Miss Duncan, her flashing hazel eyes made the marble seem suddenly dull and lifeless.

It was nothing compared to the life and activity hidden behind those orbs.

"I have come to get the dogs." He couldn't handle seeing or hearing the mess that was going on in front of his mother's house. "Perhaps we could speak inside?"

The door was just behind Miss Duncan. She would simply need to turn around and motion him in, and this time he wasn't leaving without either enjoying some tea with his future intended, or setting foot in the library.

CHAPTER 7

LORD FARNSWORTH WAS NOT SETTING another foot in her home. Mrs. Hiddleson had let him in once, and Sally saw no reason he would need to be allowed in a second time. And dogs? What dogs? No amount of talk about dogs or that strange way he pulled back his shoulders and puffed out his chest was going to change her mind.

"What dogs, Lord Farnsworth?"

"My hunting dogs. Their trot is on your property, but the dogs actually belong to me." He stepped closer to her. He was wearing another fine waistcoat—not one that would have cost as much as the first one she had seen him in, but one that would still have been out of reach for almost anyone but nobility. Men like Lord Farnsworth were the reason she had been able to expand her grandfather's business from a well-run company to an exclusive importer and creator of extremely fine fabrics. It didn't mean she had to like them.

"I do remember seeing a dog trot. I haven't been inside, but I haven't heard anything about these dogs."

"Would you like to look over the bill of sale? There is a section that mentions the inclusion of all animals. I can follow you inside—"

"No, I have no issue with you taking any dogs that may be here. I simply don't believe there are any. Follow me. We can inspect the dog trot, but I assure you, I haven't seen any dogs."

She went back down the stairs that Lord Farnsworth had just climbed. It was fortunate Greenwood Manor had a double staircase. Otherwise she would be reduced to having to use the back stairs until the ramp was put in.

After descending the stairs, she followed the path that led to her right. Lord Farnsworth must be behind her, but she didn't turn to look. Her eyes would probably be drawn to that fine chest of his again. She needed to stop inspecting his waistcoats, or perhaps hire him to model some of the newest designs being made from Vermillion textiles.

She shook her head. Lord Farnsworth no longer owned this manor, and she no longer owned Vermillion. They both needed to accustom themselves to those facts.

Sally felt, rather than saw, Lord Farnsworth come to her side. He wasn't particularly tall, but he was indeed built like a pugilist and contained so much pent-up power in his upper body it made the air feel different around him—very different from Mr. Harrison. Mr. Harrison's tall and slender frame had never made her nervous. She strode forward and slightly to her right to give Lord Farnsworth more space.

"And how are your hunting goals coming along? Are you still thinking two weeks will be enough to accomplish them?" Sally asked without trying to hide the hope in her voice.

Lord Farnsworth's steps slowed and she matched his pace. "It depends." His voice was drawn out as if he was thinking it over on the spot.

"It depends on what?" She snuck a glance at him, but only his face.

His eyebrows rose and one corner of his lips quirked up. "On my prey."

"What exactly are you hunting? I hope it isn't anything too elusive." Was that too rude? She was practically telling him she hoped he would be leaving soon.

Lord Farnsworth didn't look hurt. If anything, he looked

intrigued. He stepped closer and into the space that most of society would consider too intimate for two neighbors on a stroll. "I hope so as well."

Her mind went blank for a second and her eye roamed down to the point where his shirt disappeared beneath his waistcoat. "Oh." She shook her head and once again moved her trajectory slightly to increase the space between them. He must be hunting something quite interesting indeed for his eyes to light up like that. What game lived in the area? She made a note to herself to discover it.

"Here is the kennel and dog trot," she announced as if Lord Farnsworth didn't know that better than she.

"It is quiet, isn't it?"

"I told you, I'm fairly certain there are no dogs here. I've never heard any."

"Can I have a look?"

"Suit yourself."

Jonathan ducked his head and shuffled into the darkness of the kennel. It was tall enough inside that he didn't have to crawl, but he had to remain bent at the waist. When he was a boy there had been at times upwards of twenty dogs here. His mother had never hunted much, but his grandfather had. After his grandfather passed away, the dogs were sold rather than have them not put to use. However, the summer before his mother had died, she had taken in a litter of abandoned puppies. They weren't hunting dogs, but a type of cocker spaniel mutt that no one had wanted. But he and his mother had loved them as pets. He understood those dogs, and he felt they understood him. No one wanted to feel cast off and unwanted.

Of course they were gone. Even if the staff had continued to care for them, they would have been too old indeed to have survived until now.

One more thing he should have returned for.

How much had he missed because he had listened to his father?

Jonathan walked down the middle of the stalls, not ready yet to return to Miss Duncan. They were musty and showed no signs of use. Those dogs had most likely been gone for years.

He placed a hand on one of the rough wooden beams. He had begged his father to come to Greenwood Manor and bring even one of those dogs home to their estate in Bedfordshire. But after Jonathan was born, his father had never set foot in Greenwood Manor when mother was alive, and he wasn't about to after her death, either.

Nor would he send a servant.

Jonathan was left to mourn his mother alone, for his father certainly never did.

Jonathan shook his head. What was done was done. What he needed now was an excuse to charm Miss Duncan. Once again his plan had fallen short. Perhaps she would walk with him. He could give her a tour of the grounds.

He squinted his eyes at the sunlight as he emerged from the kennel. "No dogs."

"I had thought not."

"And there are no dogs in the house?"

Miss Duncan shrugged, her eyes wandering back to the manor as if she had much more pressing things to do. "I haven't seen any."

"Of course there wouldn't be anything as mundane as dogs in your home; you have far more exotic plans, like moose and fish and who knows what else."

The corner of Miss Duncan's mouth quirked as if she wanted to laugh, but was controlling herself. Jonathan had no idea what was happening with the stairs, but the menagerie had to be fictitious.

Didn't it?

What kind of woman wanted a menagerie in her home? Or for that matter, what kind of woman made up a menagerie?

That quirk of a smile made him think she was, if nothing else, an interesting one. He hoped he had the time to find out. How exactly did one go about courting a woman who lived less than a mile away? In theory it should have been easy. In practice, it would have been much easier to simply ask her to dance one too many times. "Would you like me to show you around the grounds? Since I am here, I fancy a walk."

She raised both of her eyebrows. "You would like to give me a tour of my grounds?"

Blast. That had come out very wrong. "You could give me a tour—that is, if you have time." Jonathan leaned forward and smiled. She glanced back at Greenwood Manor, that same longing to return gracing her face. "Or I could come back tomorrow. You could give me a tour then. If that doesn't work, the next day. I'm free most days."

Miss Duncan pulled her shoulders back and gave him a winsome smile, not quite as winsome as the one she had given Oliver in his office, but winsome nonetheless. "I'll take the time today. No need to keep returning. The manor can wait for a few minutes." And then she started on her way. He jumped ahead to catch up with her.

If a few minutes was all she could spare, he would have to make the most of them. What had she liked about him so far? He needed to find some way to accentuate it. His chest? He had to have something more to offer the woman than a broad chest. He was a baron. In the past that had been enough to tempt most women. He eyed Miss Duncan. She didn't walk like the women he was used to. They strolled, but Miss Duncan marched. His title would have to be saved for a last resort. His eye for fine fabrics? That might hold some sway. He had a lot of fine friends back in London—other than Oliver, most of his friends were titled—and they all came to him for advice on clothing. And if all else failed he would compliment her. Women loved compliments. He had seen more than one marriage happen because of a well-timed mention of a woman's sparkling eyes.

He may not have the handwriting of a scribe or a brain for numbers, but he could flatter women in his sleep.

CHAPTER 8

SALLY HAD plenty of experience dealing with needy and indulgent clients. When you sold fabric that only the highest crust of society could afford, it came with the territory. She broadened her smile and made Lord Farnsworth feel that he was in charge of the situation, but once she had the opportunity to slip away, she would be back inside the manor. Victoria was arriving in only a few days and there was still much to do.

"What part of the grounds would you like to see? I believe you have already had a tour of the pond." She couldn't help that quip. Lord Farnsworth seemed bent on wasting her time, but at least he had provided her with some entertainment.

Lord Farnsworth smiled, his face open and compelling. If she didn't know better, she would think he also had to deal with difficult clients. "Our pond," he said.

Those deuced property lines. Who put a line directly through a pond? And how had she missed that when looking over the details of the contract?

It was unfortunate they hadn't found a dog. It might have helped him catch whatever game he was looking for. And even if it didn't, perhaps it would keep him busy and off of her property. She glanced at him out of the corner of her eye. At least he could keep up. Mr. Harrison had always wanted to walk at a leisurely pace. It had unnerved her to no end. That should have been her first sign that the relationship was never going to work.

"It seems as though you are already well-acquainted with the back of the home; would you care to walk down the lane until we meet the main road?" That would give them a finite amount of walking time. In a garden, couples could meander about all day—not that they were in any way a couple. She pushed away from him slightly, keeping her skirt from brushing the bottom half of Lord Farnsworth's leg.

"I haven't actually seen much of the back garden other than to pass by it. I saw the rose garden yesterday. Is it in bloom?"

Her short, finite walk was evaporating. The lane would have been much quicker. And he had most definitely seen the rose garden. It was visible from the pond. "Yes, it is. Would you like to see it?"

He leaned toward her, eyes shining. "I would love to see it." The intense excitement in Lord Farnsworth's manner belied the simpleness of their plan. He must be quite bored, indeed. He held his arm out and with a sigh she took it. His arm was thick and sturdy. Everything about his physical appearance, other than his clothing, made him seem like he would be more at home on a dock than in a ballroom. He led the way further behind the house, his pace matching hers from earlier—if anything, it was even quicker. "I've never had a chance to see the roses in bloom...at least not in full bloom."

"You were never here in the summer?"

"No, I only came here while my father was in London for the parliamentary session."

Mrs. Hiddleson had spoken to her as if the family had always been there. She hadn't realized they hadn't lived here in the summer.

"I suppose that explains the winter garden," she said. The winter garden was more impressive than the rose garden in both scale and variety. It wasn't in bloom now, but Mrs. Hiddleson had boasted numerous times about the flowers that would bloom there.

"I would like to see the winter garden as well." Lord Farnsworth walked with his shoulders tilted forward. Sally found her feet following in his forthright, steady rhythm. The grounds were beautiful—she had made certain of that before buying—but she hadn't yet taken the time to walk and enjoy them. Trees dotted the pathway, some of them hulking enough that they might have been planted a century ago. No trees grew like that in the places she had lived in London. Victoria would love it here. After the stairs were done, Sally would send some workers to flatten out the pathway so Victoria could enjoy the garden when she came.

Lord Farnsworth cleared his throat. "Your dress is very beautiful. A fine muslin, perfect for the country."

Her dress was plain. She had planned on a full day of work, not on entertaining a gentleman. The fabric was of course fine, though; he wasn't wrong about that. Just because she sometimes needed to wear muslin didn't mean she needed to wear coarse muslin. "Thank you."

"Is it also from another country? Like my silk?"

He seemed genuinely curious, although why, she had no idea. "No this is good, old-fashioned English muslin. Nothing very special about it."

He stopped and pulled himself away from her but kept hold of her, sliding his hand down her arm lightly until he held her by the fingertips. He tipped his head to one side as if he was examining a bolt of fabric. "On you, any material would shine like a gaslamp."

She held in a laugh. She'd heard her fair share of flattery, but what? Who wants fabric that shines like a gaslamp? What if it were a nightgown? She would get no sleep. "I have seen many fabrics in my day. None of them were as bright as that."

"Then perhaps it is you that is so bright." Lord Farnsworth smiled, and then stood there, waiting, as if his asinine comment deserved a reply, or even worse, gratitude. If she were still the owner of British Vermillion Fabrics and he were a stuffy nobleman wishing to impress her, she would have smiled and indeed voiced a thank you. But she no longer had to live under the thumb of impressing those who might help her company.

She pulled her fingertips from his grip, and let out a laugh that was more of a scoff than anything. She didn't need to placate the strange

64

baron simply because he had a title, lands, and thick forearms. "I assure you, Lord Farnsworth, I bring no light to a darkened room."

Lord Farnsworth's eyes followed her hands and then went back to her face. He quirked his lips. "That is an experiment I wouldn't mind testing."

For a strange moment her breath caught. She was used to men paying her compliments, but most of them were because they were trying to gain her favor and get a better price on her fabrics. It had been too long since she had walked or talked with a gentleman in something other than a business-like manner. Even Mr. Harrison hadn't said anything as forward as Lord Farnsworth's comment, and they had been engaged.

She turned and started walking again. They would soon be in the back garden. Hopefully he would leave and head to his hunting lodge from there and she could return to overseeing the work her men were doing on the front stairs.

He hadn't liked those stairs being removed.

He wasn't going to like the rest of the changes she was making.

Her lips lifted into a smile. He may be able to unnerve her with wet shirts and overly forward remarks, but she owned his previous home and there was nothing he could do about that.

The back garden came in full view. Two stone paved paths cut the garden into four sections with a fountain surrounded by stone benches where they intersected in the middle. One of the fourths closest to the house was the rose garden. The other was the winter garden. Both of those options were better than the hedge maze or the statuary. At least in the flowering gardens they would be in full view of the manor. Lord Farnsworth's strange manner was a bit concerning out in the open, and she didn't want to end up somewhere out of sight with him. There was no telling what he would do.

She eyed him. He had said a few things that would make her think him a rake, but other than standing in a wet shirt in her pond, he hadn't ever done anything untoward. It was hard to know exactly what to expect from Lord Farnsworth. He was a study in contradictions. At times, like now, his face was full of light like a young boy discovering new things around every corner. But at other times, he was suggesting he teach her to swim or hinting at being with her in the dark.

They passed the winter garden first, but she didn't try to turn him deeper into the small paths found there. If they only spent time in the rose garden, she would be rid of him sooner. When they passed the last small pathway leading into it, she felt it would be safe to comment without running the risk of adding to their walk. "I have been very impressed with the winter garden. It has been immaculately kept over the years. I don't think I have ever seen a larger winter garden anywhere."

Lord Farnsworth followed her eye to the last corner of the winter garden. "I see the hellebore is still growing. You will have some lovely violet blooms early this winter. I will have to pick some for you." Sally furrowed her brows. He would not be here in winter. He would be in London for the Season. It wasn't as if he would come hunting twice in a year...would he? He didn't notice her concern; instead, he still spoke of the garden. "And the primroses will come out early in the spring, before you think flowers should be blooming at all. My mother and I always had a little competition to see who would spot one first. I always won."

She tried to picture the sturdy man beside her as a young boy. He would have been given everything, even flowers during a time when by all rights nothing should be blooming. "If you always won, it was most likely because your mother let you."

He stopped and turned back to look at the winter garden now behind them. He scrunched his face together. "You know, Miss Duncan, I hadn't ever thought of that, but I'm sure you are right."

"I don't tire of hearing that."

He laughed. "I'm certain you have plenty of opportunity."

"Just as I'm certain you had plenty of things given to you by your mother." She didn't mean it as a compliment, but he seemed to take it that way, his shoulders pulling back as he took one last look at the winter garden.

"I did," he said softly. "She wanted to give me everything she could."

The baroness certainly could have given him a shocking number of things. His statement solidified everything Sally thought of him, and yet the way he said it did not. He spoke of his mother with a reverence that defied her notion of a self-serving lord who cared for no one but himself.

She shook her head. It didn't matter who exactly the baron was. He would be leaving soon and then she could get on with her preparations for Victoria. "The rose garden is in front of us. Is there a particular variety you would like to see?"

"Rose du Roi," he said without hesitation.

Blast, she had no idea where that rose would be. They could be in the garden for hours looking for it. "That one is red, isn't it?" she asked, not certain he would know.

"Yes, mottled with violet, making it a deep shade. It has a yellow eye and the most heavenly scent."

"I thought you hadn't seen it in bloom."

"I haven't, but I learned all the names of the roses, nonetheless. I dreamed of someday seeing them in bloom and taking in their scents." He turned his head and surveyed the garden in front of them as if planning his pathway through it. With a smile like a boy in a candy shop, he took her hand and tugged her into the small path meandering through the roses. His excitement was contagious, and the touch of his hand seemed to send layers of curiosity into hers, like a rose opening to the sun. "I know where they are—or at least where they were." He navigated her garden with ease. His eyes shot here and there and he stopped to exclaim the name of a variety of a rose every other foot or so. Her eyes remained for the most part on their hands linked together. It was an impertinence, surely, but his demeanor wasn't ungentlemanly—it was innocent, as if he had been transported back in time, and the two of them were children on an adventure. Where would the impertinence be in that? His only disappointment was "the old cabbage rose," which he had thought would be much bigger. "That is what I get for having an avid imagination, I suppose. I truly thought it would be the size of a cabbage."

The energy coursing from his hand to hers was too much when they were simply standing still. She tugged her hand free without any resistance on his part. Had he even noticed what he had done? "It is beautiful, though," she said, touching one of the large round blooms. How did a flower manage to produce so much beauty?

He lifted a hand to pluck it, and then stopped. "I suppose I cannot give you this flower, since it is yours."

She shook her head. "No, you cannot." Flowers from Lord Farnsworth would be a problem. It was one thing to receive a squirrel from him. She could laugh that off, but taking flowers? It was too much like what she would have received from men in London. And they were not in London, they were in Dorset, the place she had come to leave London behind and start a life focused solely on Victoria. "But you may take it for yourself. I'm sure your mother would have wanted you to have it."

He grinned and then reached down and twisted the stem of the rose, breaking off the flower and holding it in his hand. Now that he was holding the rose, he wouldn't thoughtlessly grab her hand again. It had been a smart move to allow him to pick it. She flexed her left hand. It was much more proper to explore the garden without contact.

After they meandered through what must have been half the rose garden, they finally reached his Rose du Roi. He immediately bent low and inhaled its scent. Then he didn't move; he simply stayed there with his face in the deeply colored bloom. When he arose, his eyes were alight. He moved his blossom into his left hand and pulled her over to the Rose du Roi by her elbow. "Come, you must smell this." A small laugh escaped her lips as she was jostled forward. There was much to do in the manor behind them, but that all slipped away as she buried her face in the brilliant blooms. "This one lives up to all my hopes for it. Mr. Ashton hadn't exaggerated."

She stood upright. "You know my gardener?" As soon as the words left her mouth she wanted to call them back. The man had only just walked her through the whole rose garden from memory, for heaven's sake. Of course he knew the gardener.

"I do. Thank you for keeping him on. He has been tending to this garden as long as I can remember."

What did he take her for? The kind of person who would turn out a man who had lived and cared for Greenwood Manor for most of his adult life? "Of course." She had only spoken to Mr. Ashton once but the care he took in the gardens was evident. There weren't many manors whose grounds would be so immaculate when the proprietors hadn't lived there in over a decade.

Lord Farnsworth's head turned in the direction of the gardener's cottage. "I would like to speak to him sometime."

"I will let him know. I assume he is welcome to come to your lodge."

"Of course, but if it isn't an inconvenience I would also like to visit with him here in the garden—to see the work that he has done and have him show it to me."

Now he wanted to come to her home and dally about in the garden? When would she ever get her work done? "Why don't we find him now?" Sally had wasted too much time exploring the garden with Lord Farnsworth. If Mr. Ashton would take him through it, she could get back to the workers on the stairs.

Which admittedly didn't seem quite as pressing as it had a few minutes ago.

They were not far from the edge of the rose garden, and the path from there led to Mr. Ashton's cottage. Sally led the way, and for the first time since they had left the dog trot, Lord Farnsworth's pace did not keep up with hers, as if he was hesitant to meet the man. Was there something about Mr. Ashton that worried Lord Farnsworth? The one interaction she had had with him was pleasant, and his care of the garden alone was reason enough to respect the man.

Lord Farnsworth fell further behind as soon as the cottage came into view. Lilacs and peonies surrounded the area. Mr. Ashton knelt next to the flowers with a pail set beside him. After only just entering the clearing, Lord Farnsworth's footsteps on the gravel path stopped.

Sally turned to find him staring at Mr. Ashton with warring emotions in his face. Did he want to meet with him or not? Something must have alerted Mr. Ashton to their arrival, for he turned. When his eyes met hers, he quickly grabbed a hoe by his side, used it as leverage to rise to his feet, and gave her a short bow. Then he glanced behind her and took a step forward.

Lord Farnsworth must have found whatever bravery had left him earlier, for he stepped around her and in an action she wouldn't expect from a baron to a gardener, he bowed his head low and slow. "Mr. Ashton. It has been much too long."

Mr. Ashton's arm holding the hoe shook and he leaned forward. He scanned Lord Farnsworth's face. "John?"

Lord Farnsworth's shoulders drooped. He took two steps forward and then stopped, then rushed the rest of the way to the gardener and threw his arms around him. The hoe dropped to the ground as the old man reached around Lord Farnsworth's broad shoulders and enveloped him in an embrace. Mr. Ashton's head knocked the hat off of Lord Farnsworth, but rather than try to right it, Mr. Ashton stroked the back of Lord Farnsworth's hair. The shaking in Mr. Ashton's arms spread to his body, his chin quivering and tears filling his eyes. Lord Farnsworth held him tighter until the shaking subsided.

Lord Farnsworth, burly pugilist lord that he was, held the frail gardener in his arms as if he were his long-lost father.

Tight pinpricks of emotion clouded Sally's eyes and she turned to face the manor. It had been too long since she had embraced her grandfather. Her father had almost never held her, and Mama embraced her publicly, but almost never when they were alone. Even Mr. Harrison had not been so bold as to enfold her in his arms, although there were times she would have welcomed it.

Sally took a deep breath. Lord Farnsworth hadn't needed her to accompany him. He should have had this meeting on his own. She wouldn't begrudge him walking across her property to visit an old friend.

She had taken two steps back to the manor when a sound stopped her.

A bark.

She spun around to see a golden-haired dog walking gingerly around the two men. They were no longer embracing—now Lord Farnsworth was kneeling and scratching the dog's head. "I thought you said there were no dogs on the property," he called out to her.

Everything about him had changed in the few moments he had been near the cottage. He didn't look like a pugilist or a haughty lord. With his hat on the ground and his fine wool trousers in the dirt, he didn't look much older than a boy.

And his smile was as broad as the bow of a merchant ship.

Sally raised her hands. "I didn't know about this dog."

"Do you know what this means?"

She raised her eyebrows. No, she didn't seem to know what anything meant anymore.

"This means he is my dog. I have a dog."

Mr. Ashton placed a hand on his shoulder and squeezed it. "He has waited long enough for you to return. He and I both."

Lord Farnsworth stood and gripped Mr. Ashton by the shoulder as well. She fought the need to turn around again. For whatever reason, she had been invited to this reunion. She might as well join it. The work on the stairs would continue without her. She had come to Greenwood Manor to work less and connect more. She had thought to connect mostly with Victoria, the person who mattered the most to her, but perhaps she could commence that goal by establishing new connections with the people who would be a part of her life here. Mr. Ashton was a good person to start with.

CHAPTER 9

THE DOG'S name was Bernard. Jonathan had named him that when the dog was not much bigger than his open palm, and Jonathan had been only twelve years old. Mr. Ashton had happily told Jonathan to take Bernard back to the hunting lodge.

The last two days had been spent getting him accustomed to his new home. Jonathan bent down and stroked the gray head that lay in his lap as he finished his noon meal. Seeing Mr. Ashton had brought back more memories and more guilt that he had been prepared for.

Mr. Ashton had not blamed him for staying away. He must have understood. Miss Duncan hadn't stayed long and so his courting, if he could call it that, had been cut short, but now that he had Bernard, he would always have an excuse to return to the property. It wasn't as if he could keep Bernard away from his old home.

Bernard was the last of the litter that his mother had saved. Jonathan had helped her name all of them with names that had started with the letter "B." He couldn't remember Bernard specifically, but Mr. Ashton had told him Bernard must have remembered him. Based on the way the dog came and laid his head in his lap every time Jonathan sat down, he was inclined to believe him.

It was strange that a place he had left behind so long ago would still have so many traces of him.

Mr. Ashton. How many times had he taken Jonathan into the garden and explained to him the different types of flowers? And when flowers weren't enough, he led him into boxing. Flowers and boxing. Mr. Ashton would probably have liked him to make more use of his horticultural knowledge than his fists while at school, but life at Eton hadn't lent itself to much practical use of gardening skills.

Indeed, his first fight came after he had explained the difference of how to trim a rose bush versus a peony. He wasn't as tall as the other boys. Despite them knowing he was the son of a baron, the fact that he spoke like a gardener's son made him an easy target—at least the bigger boys had thought so, until he displayed his other skill set. Jonathan's penchant for flowers was forgotten quickly enough once his fists had been put to use. After his first scuffle, the other boys had learned to leave him alone. It wasn't until Oliver was being teased that Jonathan had needed to use his fists once again.

He stood from the chair and Bernard looked up at him expectantly. The distance from the lodge to the manor wouldn't have been long for Bernard when he was younger, but now...

Jonathan scooped Bernard up into his arms and strode out the door. He kicked the door closed behind him and marched toward Greenwood Manor. Before reaching the pond he set Bernard down and pushed him forward. He and Bernard had bonded, but not well enough for the dog to forget the home he had lived in for the past ten years.

Bernard hobbled for a bit and then, with his joints warmed up, he managed a shuffling jog. Jonathan chased after him, which excited Bernard to the point that he ran and stayed ahead of him. He wouldn't be able to keep this pace for long, but the exercise was good for Bernard, as long as he didn't get too much of it, which is why he had carried him most of the way.

Jonathan needed a way into Miss Duncan's heart, or if not her heart, at least her head. Thus far he had been woefully unsuccessful in capturing her interest. She seemed pleasant enough about spending some time with him, but never tried to seek him out. He had been distracted by the rose garden and Mr. Ashton yesterday and had only managed a few compliments before turning into the sad Eton boy that loved flowers and his gardener. Jonathan needed to be more deliberate. There would be plenty of time for Miss Duncan to discover his strange habits after they were married. Bernard had reached the back garden, and as expected, when he reached the fountain he turned left.

As much as Jonathan would have loved another chance to reminisce with Mr. Ashton, he needed Bernard to find his way to Miss Duncan, not Mr. Ashton. He could reminisce all he wanted with Mr. Ashton once his position with Miss Duncan was secured, and hopefully that could be done before Miss Duncan started tearing apart the library.

He quickened his pace. Bernard was not quite as feeble as he imagined; if anything, he had only sped up the closer they got to his old home. The path bent around a tree and Jonathan hurtled around it.

But he wasn't the only one on the path. Directly in front of him was a lanky girl standing behind a wheeled bath chair. Jonathan jumped to one side. He landed strangely on one foot and quickly shifted his balance to his other in an awkward leap that left him standing and also kept him from charging head-on into the girl in front of him.

The girl he had almost run over was staring at him open-mouthed. The last thing he had expected to see on his walk today was a young lady with plaited hair, pushing around a wheeled chair. Bernard, oblivious to the humans around him, continued on his path and Jonathan let him. The dog knew where he was going.

The apparition was at that hard age of being somewhere between childhood and womanhood: fourteen, perhaps. Too old for a nursery, but not yet an adult. "Who are you?" she demanded. "The gardener? No, he is old. The gardener's son, perhaps?"

Flashes of being teased at Eton made him stand up straight. What gardener dressed so well? Did a man ready himself for digging in the dirt by dressing in such well-tailored trousers? For a moment he didn't answer, though, for a dissenting answer indeed felt like a lie. He was not Mr. Ashton's son. The world would have been much simpler if he had been, for his father's barony had done him no good. He would have rather been a gardener's son.

Jonathan's eyes went back to the chair. What was she doing with it? "Is Mr. Ashton well?" He craned his neck to look as far down the path as he could. What if something had happened to him? An uneasiness settled deep in the pit of his stomach. "He hasn't been hurt?"

"I'm certain Mr. Ashton is well. This is my chair."

Her chair? He blinked, letting the world shift back into place. He took a deep breath. "What are you doing with it?"

She lifted her eyes heavenward. "At the moment, trying to turn it around. The gravel is too loose here and the wheels keep sinking in." She leaned forward and pushed the handles at the back of the wheeled chair a few inches to her right, and then, placing a good deal of her weight on the back of the chair, she gingerly took two steps to the side, each of which produced a wince.

It really was her chair.

He stepped back onto the path and to her side. "How may I help?"

She lifted her chin. "I can do it."

Instead of answering, he leaned forward. "We haven't been introduced. May I ask with whom I am speaking?"

"I don't think it would be appropriate for me to tell you until you answer my question; besides, you should know who I am."

He should know who she is? Was she someone from the village? She was too young to be someone who would remember him. There were no babies that he could think of associated with the property before he left. She was too well-dressed to be a part of the household staff. Perhaps she was someone from the village who often visited, but if that were the case she would have known he was not the gardener.

"I should know who you are?"

Her head lifted. "Definitely."

He looked her up and down. The lift of her chin reminded him of the way Queen Victoria lifted hers when she walked through a crowd; a person comfortable in her own importance and place in the world.

He snickered. "My best guess is that you must be Queen Victoria and you are here as some sort of a plot to take over Dorset."

Her eyebrows furrowed and a snort escaped her mouth. "If I were Queen Victoria, why would I need to take over Dorset? I already rule Dorset."

He snapped his fingers. "So you admit it."

She tipped her head to one side. One long plait dragged along the armrest of her wheeled chair. "I admit to nothing. However, I will say that you are not completely wrong. And now that you know something about me, I would like to know your name."

If she was Queen Victoria, he figured he could be whomever he wanted as well. "I am Jonathan Francis." True enough. He put both hands on his hips and pulled his shoulders back. "The world-renowned boxer." Not so true.

"You are a boxer?"

Oliver had gotten into his head, and now even he was telling people he was a pugilist. "Not simply a boxer." He raised his eyebrow. "A world-renowned boxer."

She raised an eyebrow. "And I am Queen Victoria?"

"Yes."

She shrugged. "Fair enough." She pulled on the wheel to her right, trying to move the chair to one side, but she was stuck in some of the gravel on the path.

"Were you trying to go somewhere?"

"I wanted to meet the gardener, Mr. Ashton. My sister told me I have to explore for at least two hours and I'm not allowed to read any books until I have. She said Mr. Ashton could teach me about flowers. I know his home is this way, but here, the path isn't smooth and packed down like in the garden."

So this was Miss Duncan's sister. Jonathan had studied Miss Duncan enough to know that her grandfather had passed away three years ago, and her father even earlier than that. The only family she had left was her mother and a sister who would be about this young nymph's age. He hadn't known she was in need of a wheelchair. The gravel was deep the rest of the way to Mr. Ashton's cottage, and it wouldn't be easy to push her through it, nor did he want Miss Duncan to find him removing her sister from the garden. "Would you like me to run and fetch Mr. Ashton? I believe he has my dog, anyway. I was headed in that direction."

"Yes, I would like that. Thank you..." She paused, obviously uncertain about what to call him. "Mr. Francis."

He didn't correct her; he had been Mr. Francis for most of his adult life. Lord Farnsworth still felt as if that were his father's name, and besides, he didn't want to intimidate this young queen. She seemed quite sure of her possession of the garden, and he didn't want that look of independence and pride to leave her face. Besides, Mr. Ashton was certain to let her know in one way or another.

He jogged down the path until it opened up to the front garden of Mr. Ashton's cottage. Mr. Ashton was standing just outside his front door, bent over and petting Bernard on the head. No doubt Bernard had made his presence known by scratching at the door.

Mr. Ashton had always seemed ancient. In a strange way it was almost as if he had stayed the same age these past years, but Jonathan and Bernard had felt the years. Jonathan waved. "Bernard wanted to pay you a visit."

"Only Bernard?"

"Of course only Bernard. If I visit you, you will put me to work. Miss Duncan doesn't want a baron trimming her rose bushes."

"Something tells me Miss Duncan wouldn't mind that at all."

Jonathan raised an eyebrow. Had Miss Duncan been speaking of him to Mr. Ashton? "What do you mean by that?"

Mr. Ashton laughed. "Only that she is a woman who isn't going to be intimidated by a title."

He didn't want her intimidated, but he had hoped perhaps Mr. Ashton had meant something more with his offhand comment. "Has she said anything about me? Asked anything about me?"

Mr. Ashton's hand rested on the top of Bernard's head. "She hasn't."

Oh.

Mr. Ashton stepped toward him, Bernard following. "Of course, other than the time we spent together, I have hardly had a word with the young lady, so that shouldn't be surprising."

"Speaking of Miss Duncan, I've a young queen in the garden waiting to meet you."

"A young queen?"

"Yes. Miss Duncan seems to have told her you would be willing to show her some of your skills in the garden."

"My skills in the garden, eh? Who exactly is this young lady?"

"Come and see." Jonathan didn't bother to tell him about the chair. Mr. Ashton wouldn't treat her any differently because of it.

They strode down the gravel path. Bernard trailed behind them, breathing heavily, but not willing to be left behind. Halfway to Victoria, Jonathan stopped and scooped up Bernard. It seemed as though he would have to get used to carrying the dog about.

"Well, well, well," Mr. Ashton said as soon as Victoria came into sight. "Who is this young lady we have here?"

Her chair was in the same position Jonathan had left her in, pointed toward them, only now she was sitting in it. "I'm Victoria Duncan."

"Queen Victoria Duncan," Jonathan added with an elaborate bow. "We are your humble servants."

She raised her chin. "Are you?"

"Of course," Mr. Ashton said, copying Jonathan's bow. "I am nothing if not loyal to the queen, and at least as loyal to the new owners of Greenwood Manor."

"Well, then." Her head raised and her chin jutted out. "I require you to turn this chair around so I can go back to the garden, and I would like to be taught about flowers."

Jonathan marched to her side and deposited Bernard into her lap. She squealed, but not with displeasure. "If you don't mind, Bernard is quite fatigued and isn't able to walk much farther. Would you mind carrying him?"

Her eyes flashed to his. Even though she was younger than Miss Duncan, her eyes seemed more guarded. Miss Victoria Duncan was less likely to admit people into her inner circle of friends, whereas

Miss Duncan seemed perfectly willing to smile and encourage anyone. What kind of life had this girl had up until this point? She could stand, but it caused her pain. Had that always been the case?

He and Mr. Ashton both took hold of an armrest and lifted Victoria, chair and all, off the gravel. They spun her around and started marching toward the garden.

"Tell me what you know about flowers already," Mr. Ashton said. "Then I will know where to start."

"I've read lots about flowers. My favorites are the foxgloves, but I didn't see any on my way here."

"No, we don't have any foxgloves. But that is something that could be remedied soon enough. I can add some in the statuary."

"I saw a part of the garden with no flowers. It is only greens. Why don't we plant them there?"

Mr. Ashton shook his head. "That is the winter garden. It blooms in the winter."

"You have a garden that blooms in winter?"

Mr. Ashton winked at her. "No, *you* have a garden that blooms in winter. This is your garden. I'm only the caretaker."

A smile transformed her face. "I think I shall like having a winter garden. What grows there?"

They had reached the edge of the garden where the path was paved in stone rather than gravel. Mr. Ashton and Jonathan stopped and set down the chair. Without waiting, Mr. Ashton took hold of the handles at the back and pushed Victoria toward the winter garden. It wasn't in bloom, of course, but Mr. Ashton would be able to describe the snow drops, daphnes, and Christmas roses in such detail that Victoria would practically be able to smell them by the time they left that section of the garden.

Jonathan trailed behind them. He hadn't entered the winter garden yet. That was his mother's garden. Mr. Ashton had helped her decide what to plant and where, but she was the one who had always wanted a winter garden. Jonathan had spent hours outside with her when he had lived here.

"Do you know this winter garden was planted with a child in

mind?" Mr. Ashton said to Victoria. Jonathan's ears perked up. He hadn't ever heard that. "There was a young boy that would live here, but only in the winter, and his mother wanted him to see how beautiful Dorset was, even when most of the land was no longer green."

Jonathan stopped, his breath catching. Of course that was why she had planted the garden. How could he not have seen that?

"Where did the boy live in the summer?"

"In the summer he lived in a few other places. He had a home in Bedfordshire and Lincolnshire, and one other shire."

Cambridgeshire, but Mr. Ashton was exaggerating by calling them homes. They were estates. Greenwood Manor had been his only home. No one had planted him a garden in any of those other houses.

"That is a lot of houses. I'm happy to have this one."

"And where did you live before?" Mr. Ashton asked.

Jonathan was several paces behind them, so he couldn't see Victoria's reaction, but she didn't answer right away. Her elbow poked out to the side of the chair and then returned a few times. She was petting Bernard. When she finally spoke, she only said one word: "London."

"And did you have a garden in London?"

"I suppose we did."

"You suppose you did?"

"We did. I just never had the chance to see it. At least not for the past few years."

Now it was Jonathan and Mr. Ashton's turn to be silent. Why in the world would that precocious young lady not be out in a garden? At least during the summer when the weather was better, one would think she would have spent hours outside, she seemed to love it so much. Had Miss Duncan kept her inside? Something deep inside his stomach twisted. Exactly what type of woman was he planning on marrying? First she threw out crazy ideas like menageries and tore out perfectly good stairs...

He stopped and hit his forehead with his hand. The stairs. She was taking out the stairs for Victoria. He watched the two of them move forward into the garden. The menagerie still made no sense, but the stairs were for Miss Duncan's sister. Greenwood Manor was undergoing some changes to make it more of a home for Victoria, just as it had undergone changes when he had lived here. Had his mother torn out something in order to plant a winter garden when she realized it would be the only time he was here? She must have.

Most likely whatever had been planted there instead had been as beautiful as those marble stairs.

Jonathan strode forward again, increasing his stride until he came up beside Victoria. "Well, now you will have a garden anytime you like."

"I think I shall come every day."

"And what will you do here every day?"

"What did the boy do? The one with the winter garden?"

"Well," Mr. Ashton said, "he helped his mother with the garden, and…" Mr. Ashton's weathered face crinkled into a smile. Heavens, what was he about to tell Victoria now? There was only one other activity he had spent time on in the garden, and it wasn't really the type of thing to interest a young girl. "He learned how to box."

Victoria spun her head around to eye Mr. Ashton. "Who taught him how to box? His mother?"

Jonathan snickered. His mother was a lady of the first order. She hadn't even known about *him* learning to box, at least not until that first letter home from Eton.

"No, not his mother. I taught him."

"You are a boxer?"

Jonathan placed a hand on Mr. Ashton's shoulder. "Mr. Ashton is one of England's finest boxers. The boy couldn't have asked for a better or a more qualified teacher."

"After we see the winter garden, could you show me?"

"I suppose if John here is up for it, we could spar for a bit."

Victoria tipped her head to one side. "I would like to see that, too, but what I meant was, would you show me how to box?"

Mr. Ashton skipped a step and the chair bounced to a stop. He smoothed it over quickly, but Jonathan knew what he was thinking. His first few lessons had been all about footwork. How in the world would they teach this young queen to box?

"It would be an honor to teach you how to box. I have missed having lessons with the boy. And you will have one solid advantage if you ever find yourself in a match," Mr. Ashton said, his voice merry. "You won't topple easily." Mr. Ashton spun her around in her chair so that she was facing him. "The flowers will wait a bit longer. Now, John, tell her how to position her body."

He took in Victoria, his mind adjusting to the advantages and disadvantages to fighting someone while sitting in a chair. He nodded at Mr. Ashton and then pulled his hands up in a defensive position. "When you are boxing you always want to get low. Your positioning toward your opponent could work to your advantage as long as you can learn to protect your head. Now, scoot forward in your seat and bend at your waist." She did. He winked at her. "Now, plant a good one into Mr. Ashton's middle."

Victoria's eyes widened and her mouth hung open. "Now?" Jonathan nodded at her. "But you haven't even taught me anything yet."

Jonathan chuckled. "Well, we are going to start by assessing your natural talent. There is much to learn in the sport of boxing, but you must not discount one's natural instinct to fight."

Mr. Ashton planted both feet firmly on the ground and braced for impact. Victoria's eyes fluttered closed and her chin lowered. "I don't think I have that instinct."

Mr. Ashton lifted her chin with a forefinger. "Of course you do. Everyone does. You simply need to find it." Her eyes opened and she stared at Mr. Ashton's age-lined face. Jonathan knew very well the confidence Mr. Ashton could provide. He had provided a bit too much in Jonathan, at least if you asked any of his teachers at Eton. Oliver hadn't minded, though. When he was teased for coming into the school thanks to a benefactor and not his own family, Jonathan's fists were able to put a stop to it.

At Oxford Jonathan was called on to repeat his trouncing of a few choice classmates. By then he no longer had access to Mr. Ashton's lessons, so he had taken up with a few less-mannered pugilists to train with.

Victoria pushed a fist into Mr. Ashton, but it lacked strength. Mr. Ashton shook his head. "You can do better than that."

"I don't want to hurt you."

"Because I am old?"

"Because you are kind."

Mr. Ashton stepped back. "Well, that is easily remedied. John, come over here and let Miss Victoria slug you."

Jonathan laughed. Victoria's eyes went back and forth between the two of them and then narrowed at a point in Jonathan's waist. Jonathan pushed Mr. Ashton aside in a friendly shove, stood in front of Victoria, and tightened his stomach.

"I will be sorely disappointed if you don't hit me with all your strength. I've had grown men, some nearly twice my size, go many rounds with me, so I promise I can handle what you give me. Think of something that makes you angry, something you wish you could change but you can't..." Victoria's hands tightened on the handles of her chair as she leaned forward. "Focus all of that energy on the second button of my waistcoat and—"

Victoria's arm flashed out, connecting with his middle. Jonathan doubled over and pushed the breath out of his lungs. It was a fair hit, with more force than he would have imagined Victoria could muster. He exaggerated his reaction, but he was impressed none-theless.

Mr. Ashton clapped and laughed and Victoria's hand went to her mouth. "I'm sorry!"

Jonathan blinked his eyes as if he were in pain. "You have the natural talent for it, I'll give you that," he wheezed. And she really did. Jonathan had spent enough time with men who had no idea how to hit, and Victoria at least knew enough to channel her energy and punch through her target.

With the chair taking up most of her reach and mobility, entering an actual boxing fight would be a terrible mistake, but women who boxed did so only for the exercise anyway; they would never be allowed in a ring. Victoria bent at the waist well, and he had seen her legs move as counterweights to her swing. Her problems must lie in her feet. What kind of injury did she have that confined her to the chair for mobility?

"Tell me, my Queen. What exactly are you capable of? I saw you standing earlier, so you are not in that chair because of a complete inability to move."

Victoria scrunched her nose together. "No, I can move everything, but to stand on my feet for more than a few minutes...it is painful." Her feet were well covered by her dress.

"So you can pivot forward and turn about at the waist," Mr. Ashton said.

"Yes."

"Well, then, that makes our job easier. And the fact that you can stand, even for a second, could provide an element of surprise if you ever need it."

"Do you think I will need it?"

"In a fight?" Jonathan bent low and brought his mouth to the level of her ear. "You need everything you have."

Victoria nodded in such a way as if to express the seriousness of the task she was about to undertake. "I will keep that in mind."

"Good." Jonathan straightened.

"Today let's start on hand positions." Mr. Ashton put his hands up, his dominant hand closer to his chest. Victoria followed suit. Jonathan stepped back and let them work.

So Miss Duncan's plans had to do with this precocious young lady. One piece of the puzzle finally clicked into place.

Now if he could only discover why she had that horrendous fish wallpaper.

CHAPTER 10

"You don't like that one?" Sally held up what was *supposed* to be a vase for Victoria to look at more closely. Victoria sat on the divan in what was to be her parlor. Sally had helped her take the two painful steps between her wheeled chair and the seat. They had spent the morning going over designs and plans for this room. Selling Vermillion had been like tearing out a piece of Sally's soul, but seeing Victoria blossom here was restoring the missing pieces of her heart. Every time Victoria picked a fabric for chairs or decided on which carpet to put in a room, she opened up more. She had only been here for four days, and already had more color in her face. Some of that had to be attributed to her afternoons in the garden, where she spent time while Sally dealt with the more mundane parts of running a new household. But renovating a home suited Victoria, even if her tastes didn't match the typical standards of the day. This vase, however, was even too much for Sally.

She had shipped it from a remote island in the Indies, and the thing looked as though it could steal a person's soul completely. It was all claws and feet. The legs of some hairy animal took up the bottom half of the vase, which was made of white stone. But there were too many appendages, legs on top of legs in a half circle. She set the vase down on the table in front of them. One of the legs acted as the base, while the others hovered in the air around it. The upper half were the creature's arms, made of copper. Thus far, she had found no head. Had Sally actually bought a vase so disastrous that even Victoria found it distasteful?

Victoria's face scrunched in disgust, not unlike the face she made when she had to put weight on her feet. "I don't like it at all. I hope it wasn't expensive."

It was expensive. It seemed the more distasteful the vase, the more expensive it was. This one had been very expensive indeed. "Don't worry, I'm sure we will find a use for it somewhere."

"The attic?" Victoria suggested.

Sally nodded. "Or the cellar."

"And frighten the poor servants when they go there looking for wine?"

"A good point. I suppose we could put it in the dog trot. Or..." Sally paused. She knew exactly where this work of art belonged.

"Or where?" Victoria asked.

Sally lifted the copper and stone vase up into the light. The sunlight shone off the polished claws that formed the rim. Lord Farnsworth had given her a squirrel, after all. It would be wrong of her to not return...something...to him.

This vase was something.

Sally flashed Victoria a grin. "I have the perfect place for it."

"I gathered that from the devilish look on your face. Where?"

"There is a man staying at a hunting cottage nearby. I think it is just the type of artwork he would enjoy."

Victoria cocked her head to one side and took in the full nature of the vase once again. "Is he all right in the head?"

Was he? Sally had seen a few instances—swimming in the pond and shooting squirrels—which might hint at something not being quite right with the man. But for the most part, yes, he did seem to have all of his faculties. "He is perfectly stable, if a little strange. In truth, he won't like the vase, but *I* like the idea of giving it to him." A smile kept teasing her lips no matter how hard she tried to push it down. First the fish wallpaper, then the stairs, now this...art? He would think her mad.

Victoria tipped her head to one side. "How old is this man in the hunting cottage?"

"Why do you ask?"

"Is he quite old?"

"No."

"Is he handsome?"

Sally pulled her head back. Lord Farnsworth was too rugged and indestructible-looking to be called handsome in any classical fashion. "No."

"So you want to give a young but unattractive man living nearby a gift."

Victoria had become much more inquisitive in the past four days. "I'll be giving it to him as a neighbor. It isn't as though we have many of those." Sally started wrapping the vase back in its papers. "Besides, he gave me one."

"He gave you a gift?"

"Yes, to welcome us into the area."

"Was it expensive? Like the vase?"

Sally did her best to keep her lips pulled in a straight line. "It was a squirrel." Lord Farnsworth had seemed so pleased with himself.

Victoria blinked. "He gave you a squirrel?" Then she closed her eyes and rubbed one of them. "Was it alive?"

"No, it was quite dead."

"Like in a basket? Or wrapped up in a cloth? How does one go about gifting a squirrel?"

"I don't know, actually. Mrs. Hiddleson gave it to Cook before I even got a chance to see it."

Victoria's eye widened to the size of saucers. "You *ate* it?"

"I...I don't think so." She had never dared ask what cook had done with the poor thing. But she didn't think it had ended up on her plate. Or her soup bowl.

"How are you going to get it to him?"

"I suppose I will have to deliver it."

"Yourself?" Victoria's eyes grew suspicious. "Are you certain he isn't handsome?"

"Quite certain." Perhaps not completely certain, but Victoria didn't need to know that. "Besides, he is titled, and you know how uninterested I am in any man who has a line to preserve."

"I know how uninterested you are now. There was a time when you were quite interested in one."

"Mr. Harrison isn't titled."

"He isn't titled yet. But he is in line to be. You could have been a baroness."

Sally rubbed her temples. How many times had she tried to get that man's voice out of her head? *Daughters are not a problem. If we have them first I would never be upset with you. Soon enough you would produce an heir.* So benevolent. To a woman who had inherited and successfully grown her family's business. So much like her father. So much like any man except her grandfather. "Trust me, I have no desire to be a baroness. At the moment, I am perfectly happy to remain only your sister."

"Then perhaps I will become a baroness. Just how unattractive is this neighbor? And what is he doing here?"

If Sally only knew. "Heavens if I know. I don't think he will be here long."

"Not long enough for me to catch his eye?"

"Victoria, you are much too young to be thinking such things, and he is much too old." Any man of marriageable age would be too old for Victoria. She didn't need to know Lord Farnsworth was young enough that in the few short years it would take for Victoria to become a woman, a match between them wouldn't actually be out of the question. She shook her head, banishing the thought from her mind. "I wouldn't want either of us to end up with a peer. They are so haughty and all they care about is money and appearances." And male heirs.

"And I have neither."

The amount of dowry Sally had set aside for Victoria was a small fortune. "You have both, which is why I will protect you from them."

"What do you mean I have both?"

"If you haven't looked in a mirror lately, that is your own fault. I don't need to give you a reason to suffer from vanity."

"No, I mean the money part. What did you mean about the money part? Sally, what have you done?"

"Grandfather wanted us both to have Vermillion; you were simply too young." Victoria was going to find out about her dowry at some point, and it might as well be now.

"How much?" Victoria had gone pale. Perhaps this wasn't the time to tell her.

"I have always considered Vermillion to be ours. Half."

"My dowry is half the value of Vermillion?" Victoria leaned back in the sofa, eyes blinking.

"Yes."

"Sally, what have you done?"

"It is what grandfather would have wanted."

"Men are going to be positively accosting me in London when I come out in society."

"Would you rather they weren't? You have always been the romantic one between the two of us."

"I would rather the insincere ones wouldn't. How are we going to weed out all the bad ones?"

"I'll be there. You won't be the only heiress each Season; there are always quite a few. I cannot believe having money makes it impossible to marry well."

Victoria took a deep breath. "I suppose I will have to trust you on that one. I hadn't thought..." She ran a hand along the top of her thigh. "This changes a lot of things for me."

"I can always take it back if you want, or we can donate it somewhere. If it ever becomes a burden, talk to me and we will figure something out. But no door will be closed to you in London. We have a few more years to prepare for that."

"But you won't let me come with you to deliver this monstrosity to the hunting lodge?"

"I will not."

"Why don't you simply send a servant to deliver it?"

Sally stopped trying to hide her smile. "Because that would be much less entertaining." Victoria's eyes narrowed, but it didn't matter. Her sister could think what she wanted. Sally was simply returning the favor by bringing a neighborly gift.

A horrid and perplexing but thoughtful gift.

CHAPTER 11

OLIVER'S SUMMARY of what Jonathan's stewards had been able to accomplish at his other estates since the sale of Greenwood Manor was precise and detailed. Many of the tenants' homes had been reroofed, a problem that had been weighing on Jonathan for months, and several roads had been improved, making it safer for the farmers to take their crops to the market. He folded the letter and placed it inside the writing desk's drawer.

He tipped his chair back on its hind legs in a manner his mother would have disapproved of and surveyed the dim room surrounding him. Usually the library afforded more light, but the skies were dark today with threatening rain. Compared to his libraries in his other homes, this one was small, but some of his favorite books sat on the shelves and they were easier to find with fewer shelves. People put far too much weight on the grandness of things.

A knock at the door interrupted his thoughts.

Howard stepped through the doorway. "There is a woman coming up the path."

Jonathan leaned forward and the two front legs of his chair slammed down onto the wooden floor. "The path that leads to Green-wood Manor?"

"Yes."

"And is she walking?"

Howard's eyes squinted. "Yes. She is walking, not in a carriage."

"And is it a young woman?" So help him, if he got his hopes up and it was Mrs. Hiddleson coming this way…

"Her step seemed spry to me."

Jonathan shot up from his chair. "How is my cravat? Is it straight? My hair—" Had he been running his hands through his hair? He did that sometimes when he worked. Howard stepped forward and tugged on one side of his cravat. He only nodded at Jonathan's hair.

"I shall put her in the front parlor."

"We only have one parlor here."

Howard smiled. "It sounds better though, doesn't it?"

"You don't need to pretend graces with Miss Duncan. I don't think she would appreciate it. But, yes, put her in the parlor. I'll await your knock."

Howard slipped back out the door and Jonathan paced in front of it. Miss Duncan was coming to see him. What could it be about? Was she going to invite him to join her for tea tomorrow? Or had she discovered his boxing lessons with Victoria? What would she think of that?

Perhaps he should have asked her permission before starting the lessons.

He closed his eyes and tried to picture Miss Duncan being upset over Victoria learning jabs and blocks. There were plenty of women in London who wouldn't want their younger sisters engaging in such a low sport.

Miss Duncan was nothing like any of them, though. She may be upset with him for not telling her, but if anything, she would be proud of her sister for learning something new. Miss Duncan was beautiful in ways the women of his previous acquaintance could never compare, and her ability to take on huge endeavors with a gleam in her eye for the challenge was one of them. She wouldn't deny her sister the same type of pleasure.

Miss Duncan must have knocked softly, for a murmur of voices near the front of the house announced that he had a guest in his home. He pulled on his lapels, making certain they were straight.

Miss Duncan was finally in his home.

And she had come here on her own.

If all went well during this meeting, he could be proposing within a week.

Despite waiting for it, Howard's knock made him jump.

Jonathan pulled the door open and rushed past his valet, then turned around and skipped backwards. "She is in the parlor?"

"The front parlor, yes."

Jonathan threw his eyes to the ceiling. Of the two of them, shouldn't Jonathan be the more snobbish?

Despite practically running to the room, he stopped in his tracks when he reached it. Behind this door was the woman who had been occupying his thoughts ever since he met her in London. It was time to be his most charming self.

He took a deep breath and opened the door.

Miss Duncan was still standing. In her hand was a wooden crate twice as tall as it was wide and tied up with cording. He gave her a slow and low bow. That was charming, wasn't it? "Miss Duncan, it is a pleasure to have you in my home."

A hint of a smile. "It is a pleasure to be here."

She said nothing about what had brought her, nor what was in the box. She simply stood there, with that strange half-smile on her face.

And so he smiled back, because smiling without talking was charming as well, wasn't it? Or was he making himself look like a fool? He blinked and returned his gaze to the box instead of her dark, mischievous eyes. He couldn't help but feel they were hiding some-thing, and whatever it was they were hiding, Miss Duncan found exciting. He swallowed. It wouldn't do to get ahead of himself. "Would you like to set that down?"

Her half-smile blossomed and she stepped forward. "No, I would like to give it to you." Jonathan leaned forward but he couldn't make his feet move. Instead he waited for her to come to him.

And this time she did.

Her scent of roses and plaster engulfed him, her head turned up as she raised the box toward him. "I'm sorry it has taken me so long to return a neighborly gift. I wanted to find just the thing."

Jonathan reached out and took the box from her, placing his hands just below hers. His index fingers grazed the smallest of her fingers, and even though she wore gloves, her eyes went to their hands and for a moment they both froze. The soft silk of her gloves begged him to lift that finger and slide his hand further up hers, but she stepped away before he had the chance to even decide if he was brave enough to do it.

He cleared his throat. There would be other times to hold her hand, and if the arrival of this gift meant anything, it was that those times were coming soon. "Should I open it now?"

She sucked her lips in, her head cocked slightly to one side. When she spoke, the edges of her mouth quirked up as if of their own accord. "Oh yes, please do."

Jonathan walked over to a side table and set the parcel down to untie the strings. Miss Duncan stepped to his side, her floral scent once again surrounding him, seeming so out of place in a hunting lodge built for men. He yanked on one end of the knot, expecting it to fall free, but instead the whole thing tightened.

Blast. He was so distracted by the fact that Miss Duncan was only inches away from him, and watching his every move, that he was making a fool of himself.

He could untie a simple knot. He attacked it with both hands, digging in with his fingernails to try and loosen the deuced thing, but he had pulled too hard and the cord was not budging.

"Do you need help?" Miss Duncan's voice was just over his shoulder and much too near his ear. He narrowed his eyes, forcing himself to concentrate on the task at hand and not the woman beside him.

"No, I am quite capable of untying a knot." His fingers weren't helping his cause. They were twice as large as they should be for the delicate, yet strong obstacle before him. He felt like a clumsy giant trying to embroider a handkerchief.

To make matters worse—or infinitely better but definitely muddling him even more—Miss Duncan leaned forward and her shoulder grazed his. "Because I could call for your servant, the one who opened the door. He seemed like a useful sort who could open a package for you."

Jonathan spun. "I am perfectly capable of—" He stopped. Miss Duncan was only inches from his face. With only the smallest of movement he could reach for her elbows and pull her to him.

She leaned forward and his breath caught. That was an invitation, wasn't it? To be so close and to lean in to him? He lifted his hand. He had thought he would need a few more weeks, but here she was now, standing in his lodge, mere inches away from him, and grinning in such a way he could see all the whites of her wide and open smile.

"You are perfectly capable of what?" she asked, the humor in her voice palpable. Who knew women could be this much fun?

The knot and the present were forgotten. He leaned forward and put her elbow in the palm of his hand. "I'm perfectly capable of a lot of things. Would you like me to show you?"

Miss Duncan raised an eyebrow at his hand. A small laugh escaped her mouth, or was it a sigh?

He lowered his eyelids and inhaled her scent once again. It must have been a sigh, for who would laugh in such a situation as this?

Just as he was about to lean down and claim Miss Duncan as his own in a way she surely would understand, suddenly she was gone. He opened his eyes to find her at the side table removing her gloves.

Was it wrong of him to try and kiss her when her gloves were still on? Had he breached some sort of etiquette?

But once she laid her gloves on the table she didn't return to his arms; instead she went to the package and started pulling at the center knot.

Jonathan ran his fingers through his hair. It made sense to open her present before kissing her, he supposed. He could wait a few more minutes to see what she had brought him first.

But Miss Duncan wasn't having much more success with the knot than he had. Her fingers were slender, not like his stout ones, but even she wasn't able to make much progress.

That gormless knot would be the death of him.

He reached around her and tried to pull at it as well, but she brushed his hands away. He had thought the silk gloves were heady, but the feathery touch of her skin set him on fire.

She was heedless to the torment she was causing him, though, her mind solely focused on getting that knot open.

"I've never seen a woman more determined than you."

A small chuckle, but her hands didn't stop in their work. "Yes, well, I was very much looking forward to seeing you open your gift."

"I don't mean with the knot." Her fingers stilled for a moment at that. "I mean in life." Her hands came back to life, but he could sense her listening, as if she was leaning closer to him, even though they seemed to have the same distance between them. "You have grown a business, sold a business, bought a home far from your own in order to make it yours. Those fingers, though half the size of mine, have done much more in their lifetime than mine ever will. It is daunting; *you* are daunting."

She gave a small cry and spun with a smile of triumph. "Got it!" With fingers at a frenzy she pulled away the cording that surrounded his present. "What was it you were saying? I missed that last part. Something about my fingers?"

Was she in earnest? "I called you daunting."

"Daunting?" She handed him the box. "Well, I am better at untying knots than you, so I suppose I can see that."

"No, I—"

"Would you please open your gift? I have most likely overstayed my welcome as it is."

"Overstayed your—" Why did he feel like he and Miss Duncan were having two separate conversations? Had he imagined everything up until this point? She did touch his chest during their very first meeting. Could it be that his nearness had no effect on her? He was the only one struggling to remain calm and collected when she was standing in his parlor mere inches away from him, smelling like something feminine and out of reach. "No, you haven't. You are welcome here any time."

Perhaps her present would provide a clue.

He lifted the lid and she leaned forward, her hands together at her mouth.

There was something...copper...inside.

And it appeared to have claws.

He set the box down on the table and reached in with both hands. What he pulled out was made of copper and stone and a lot of appendages. Too many appendages. What the blazes had she given him?

"Do you like it?"

Jonathan sputtered, trying to find the words. "I...do...I really do..." He turned the thing upside down, but that made it decidedly worse. "But what *is* it exactly?"

She clicked her tongue in disappointment, but he could sense something besides frustration in the sound. "A vase, of course."

"Of course," he repeated, pushing it farther away from his body, as if that might help it to be less hideous.

A pouting frown Jonathan wagered was a replica of a face Victoria would make overtook Miss Duncan's face. "You don't like it, do you?"

"No, I do. It is..." He struggled to find any word that could convince her he wasn't horrified by this...work of art. "Unexpected."

Miss Duncan's pout fell away and she smiled. "I thought you would like it. It reminds me of you, so I knew you must have it."

It reminded her of him? This thing he held by his fingertips? Which part, exactly?

Her eyes positively gleamed. "Where are you going to put it? I think the mantel would be an excellent choice. I know it is only you here, but that doesn't mean you can't decorate the place and make it more cheerful."

Jonathan eyed the thick wood mantel atop the oversized fireplace. In Miss Duncan's defense, it was bare. But, in the mantel's defense, the vase wasn't going to make anything more cheerful. He plastered on a smile. Miss Duncan had brought him a gift, she had visited his home, and if she wanted her gift left somewhere prominent in his home, then he was not going to deny her.

He strode across the room and plopped the thing directly in the center of the mantel, then stepped back. He tipped his head to the side, squinted one eye, then pursed his lips together. Would Miss Duncan think it strange if he drew the curtains? Dim lighting might be precisely what the vase needed.

Miss Duncan sighed deeply behind him. "It makes me happy to see it there. It truly does." He turned around and found her staring at the vase as if the last thing it needed was less lighting. Her mouth was curved into a smile, and her chin raised in pride. "Welcome to the neighborhood."

This had been his neighborhood long before it had become hers, but there was no avarice or mocking in her voice. In their previous interactions he had noticed some hesitancy in her manners, but now, he saw her as inclusive and devilishly hard not to want to spend the rest of the day with. It would be a break for him and Howard. They both had spent much too much time with one another, or, more often than not, alone.

"Thank you," Jonathan said.

"And now I shall leave you with your new vase."

Jonathan sputtered. He had waited weeks for this moment, and it was only to last a moment? He had thought...well, he had thought he might even get the chance to kiss her. And now she was leaving. "You won't stay for tea?"

"No." She turned and strode to the door. Her movement spurred him into remembering his manners and he followed her. Howard was waiting in the foyer. The door had been left open and the servant must have heard at least some of their conversation. How was Jonathan going to explain the vase to him?

Howard opened the door for Miss Duncan while Jonathan gave her a low bow and just as quickly as Miss Duncan had arrived, she was gone.

For a moment the day had seemed bright, but it was back to being gray again. The door closed behind Miss Duncan and Howard stayed where he was. Jonathan turned to head back to the library and Howard cleared his throat.

Jonathan spun back around. "What is it?"

"What is what, my lord?"

Jonathan hated it when Howard 'my lorded' him. "Why are you clearing your throat? Did you need something?"

"I suppose not."

"Brilliant." Jonathan continued on his way to the library.

"I'm just going to do some tidying in the parlor."

Jonathan paused again. Of course he was. And he wouldn't miss Jonathan's new decoration. But as he would see it eventually one way or another, he might as well see it now. Jonathan waved his hand behind him and continued on his original path.

However, when Howard's footsteps sounded on the foyer floor, Jonathan cursed and wheeled back around, jumping ahead of Howard and entering the parlor first. They both stopped just a few feet into the room. There was his new vase, in all of its armed and legged glory, standing like a creature rising from a lake or a cave to devour young maidens.

He blinked.

Was that what she had meant? He had risen from a pond in front of Miss Duncan, but he was no hideous beast, was he? He wasn't graceful like Oliver, but his experiences in ballrooms had shown him that a title and the protection that came with it were usually more important than an impeccable visage.

Not to mention the vase didn't have a visage at all. It was constructed entirely out of appendages. No, that couldn't have been what she meant.

Howard cleared his throat again.

Jonathan ran his fingers through his hair. "Out with it. What is it you are wanting to say?"

Howard shuffled back and forth on his feet. "Only that I think I understand why it took her so long to get you a gift in return."

"Because it was hard to find something so...interesting?" He couldn't call it monstrous in front of Howard.

Howard shook his head. "More likely because she must have had it shipped from…" His eyebrows furrowed. "Somewhere. I don't think they make vases like this in England."

Howard was undoubtedly right. Of one thing he was certain, and that was that the vase was decidedly not British. "I do not understand this woman, Howard."

"I do not understand that vase. Would you like me to move it somewhere less…visible?"

Jonathan closed one eye and squinted the other. He tilted his head back and remembered the look of joy on Miss Duncan's face as he had opened it. It wasn't so bad, actually, if you looked at it from far enough away. "No, leave it there."

"Are you certain?"

"Miss Duncan thought it should go there."

Howard nodded as if that explained everything.

And perhaps it did.

CHAPTER 12

SALLY CLOSED her eyes and rolled up the long strip of paper before setting it down on the floor. This empty room with tall windows was to be Victoria's sitting room, and while most of the other papers had not been to Sally's taste, this one, now that she was seeing it unrolled, was making her dizzy.

The sample she and Victoria had looked at together hadn't done this one credit.

She strode out of the room. She hadn't seen Victoria for over half an hour, which could only mean one thing: she was in the garden. Victoria had been spending more and more time outdoors the last few days. Since she was inclined to ask questions about the man in the hunting lodge when she was indoors, Sally hadn't minded doing a few things in the sitting room on her own.

Victoria's stamina and color had improved greatly with the sunshine, so it wasn't as if Sally was doing her any harm by allowing her so much time to roam free. But now she needed her help. There was no possible way they could hang those papers in the sitting room; the two of them would faint if they had to spend time there.

She started out of the room and then stopped and returned to retrieve the paper. Victoria would need to see it for herself. Sally strode out of the manor and stood on the balcony overlooking the garden. She saw Victoria in the statuary with Mr. Ashton, and—she rubbed her forehead and pushed her eyes closed tightly—Lord Farnsworth.

What in the world were those three doing in her statuary?

And when exactly had Lord Farnsworth met Victoria, and why hadn't she been told about it?

She stomped down the stairs, not caring that each time her foot landed on the marble it sent a shock up her legs. Had the three of them been speaking of her? Did Lord Farnsworth tell Victoria about the vase? Were they all having a good laugh at Sally, the crazy woman who laughed at the idea of giving such a hideous gift to a man?

Victoria's laughter pierced the air around her. Victoria had brightened when they worked together, but she didn't laugh like that. Before Sally had even fully entered the statuary, she couldn't hold her questions back any longer. "What exactly is going on here?"

Victoria spun in her chair. Wisps of hair had escaped the braids on each side of her head. Her eyes were bright and everything about her demeanor was different from who she had been in London. In London she had been a desperate, lonely girl. Here she was blossoming into a vibrant young lady.

And it wasn't the swirling wallpaper or the Sphinx statues that had changed her; it was spending time outside in the fresh air, being independent. At fourteen, Sally had already been helping her grandfather examine bolts of silk for imperfections, yet Victoria had never had much of a chance before now to even leave her own bedroom.

She took a deep breath and slowed her pace. Perhaps it was better to hold back judgment and see what exactly they had been doing with Victoria for the past few days.

"John and Mr. Ashton are teaching me how to box." Victoria's enthusiasm was palpable. It spread over Sally, and as the sunlight hit Victoria's dark braids, a deep understanding calmed the last bits of her anxiety.

This was the reason Sally had bought Greenwood Manor. This was where Victoria would thrive, and if it took two rather strange men to do it, she would not overreact.

But John? Who gave her permission to call Lord Farnsworth John?

"Lord Farnsworth, I knew you were an accomplished boxer, but I had no idea Mr. Ashton was also a pugilist."

Victoria snorted. "Who is Lord Farnsworth?" She turned to Lord Farnsworth accusingly. "Did you tell my sister you are titled? Sally, you can't believe anything he says. He calls me the queen of England."

Lord Farnsworth lowered his head and kicked his toe on the path below them. He could be contrite? Sally would have never guessed. He should be, though, to tell her sister his name was John, and on top of that, to teach her to box. She had never met a man with so few manners.

Victoria hadn't noticed the way he wouldn't look her in the eye. "I am sorry, Highness. I should have told you."

"You should have," Victoria continued. "And how could you pick the name Farnsworth? Didn't you know that was the name of the man who owned this house before we—" Victoria stopped, then swallowed. Her gaze shot back and forth between Sally and their pesky neighbor. "You *are* Lord Farnsworth."

Lord Farnsworth looked as if he had tasted something amiss. "I'm afraid I am." He stepped to Victoria's side. "Does that disappoint you very much? I'm not a typical lord. I do love to box and spend time with Mr. Ashton. Bernard doesn't care what title I have; I hope you won't either."

Victoria pulled back her head. "Did you just compare me to a dog?"

Now he was going to get it. Victoria's tempers were rare, but they were also magnificent. Lord Farnsworth squinted one of his eyes. "Y-yes." He stretched out the word as if he wasn't sure he should give the answer.

There was silence for a moment and then Victoria's shoulders relaxed. "You are lucky I like Bernard."

Sally threw her hands up into the air. She was the one who was supposed to be bonding with Victoria. Why was it Lord Farnsworth could tease Victoria and she would forgive him happily? Why did spending time with Lord Farnsworth make Victoria so happy? Why did no one take Lord Farnsworth to task? Her gardener loved him, Victoria was practically swooning at his feet; did no one else see through his charm? He was a lord. A baron. It was easy to be charming when every one of your needs had been met for your whole life. And when he actually ran into trouble then *voila*, he just had to sell a property and all of those problems disappeared. She took a deep breath. Hadn't she only just reminded herself to be happy for the situation she found Victoria in? But now that she was here, she could take over doing...whatever it was they were doing. Boxing? She could learn that. "Shouldn't you be heading back to the hunting lodge?" she asked Lord Farnsworth.

Victoria made a strange choking sound in her throat. "John, you live in the hunting lodge?"

Oh, dear.

Victoria spun her right wheel so she could face Sally head on. "John is Lord Farnsworth *and* the unattractive man from the hunting lodge?"

"Unattractive?" Lord Farnsworth's eyebrows bunched up like fabric pushed together on a table. This whole situation was getting out of hand.

"Oh, calm yourself, Lord Farnsworth." Did she really just say that? To a baron? "I didn't say you were unattractive, just that you were..." She struggled to know a better way to word what she had said. But there wasn't one. "...not handsome."

His eyebrows unfurled and raised high on his forehead. Every expression seemed to belie her declaration; no matter the contortions he put his eyebrows and forehead through, there was something compelling about his face, as if he could be a friend to trust in. But that wasn't the same thing as being handsome, was it? Mr. Harrison, at least by London's standards, was more handsome, certainly. Lord Farnsworth's hands went to his hips. "That seems to be roughly the same thing. I'll have you know, women all over town think I am handsome."

"Well, then, it shouldn't bother you that I don't." Heat ran up

Sally's cheeks. She was usually quite adept at twisting truths to her advantage. If she didn't get her blushes under control, it would only be a matter of time before Lord Farnsworth discovered that she did not indeed think him unattractive. She had only said that to keep Victoria from being suspicious. Sally huffed and said to Victoria, "How many men do you think would be running around Greenwood Manor? A baron, a hunter, and some boxer named John? It isn't as though we live in a city; we are miles from the nearest village."

Victoria leaned forward and in a voice that was soft like a whisper, and yet somehow also loud enough to carry halfway to the manor she hissed, "First of all, you never told me Lord Farnsworth was here; secondly, John *is* handsome." She gave the two men a smile. "Why would you say he was not handsome?"

Sally would not look at Joh—Lord Farnsworth. She slid her jaw to one side, teeth grinding. Heavens, but her sister's manners were starting to wear off on her. She would not think of him as John.

Lord Farnsworth chuckled. "Thank you, Queen Victoria. You make some very good points."

Sally finally dared to turn and face the men. "Oh, get on with your boxing lesson." She cleared her throat, wanting the attention off of her. "Did you say Mr. Ashton boxes as well?"

Lord Farnsworth winked at his old friend. "Mr. Ashton taught me everything I know."

It must not be much if Mr. Ashton had taught him. The man was one of the gentlest creatures she had ever met. Of course it wouldn't take much skill to teach Victoria a thing or two about boxing. Her eyes traveled back and forth between Victoria and the two men. How much of Victoria's change in countenance had been because of them and how much because of boxing? If she returned to London for the winter to spend some time with Mama, Sally would find her a proper teacher. It was rare for women to learn to box, but not completely unheard of.

"John says many young ladies take boxing lessons, but they aren't allowed to box. So they thought it would be all right to teach me."

That sounded exactly like the type of rule a baron would impress upon a young lady.

"Of course. Like you said, many young ladies take lessons, so I see no reason why you shouldn't. And some women *do* box, but likely not the women in a baron's circle."

"And do they box in your circle?" Mr. Ashton asked, eyebrows raised in surprise. "My grandfather regaled me with stories of Elizabeth Wilkinson and her career, but I certainly haven't heard of any reputable ladies boxing in my time."

No, she did *not* know any boxers personally, but she couldn't help but get her shackles up when ridiculous rules were placed on women. It made no sense to be allowed to learn to box, but not to actually do it. "I suppose I haven't either; I only meant to encourage Victoria. If she would like to box, let her box. But I won't have any silly ideas forced on her of what she can and cannot do with that skill."

Lord Farnsworth raised his eyebrows in surprise. "Really?"

"What? You won't teach her if she doesn't promise to not use the skills you are teaching?"

Lord Farnsworth furrowed his eyebrows. "No, I was only surprised you would allow her to continue."

"I have no objection to it."

Victoria pushed on the wheels of her chair and brought herself closer to Sally. Even in the few days she had been here, her arms were getting stronger. "You should try it too. John will teach you."

Sally huffed. "I'm certain Lord Farnsworth has better things to do."

"He doesn't," Victoria and Mr. Ashton said at the same time that Lord Farnsworth said, "I don't."

The three of them looked at each other and laughed.

So that was how it was. Sally had been slaving away putting up papers and rearranging rooms and stairs for Victoria while she had been having fun with these two. How had they become so close in just a few short days? Sally jutted her chin forward. "It just so happens I do have a few minutes. Mr. Ashton, could you teach me a jab or two?" She eyed Lord Farnsworth. "Who knows when it might come in handy?"

"Mr. Ashton is helping me, and honestly he is the better teacher. Since I am more advanced, I think John will have to teach you." Victoria smiled smugly at Lord Farnsworth. "Honestly, I'm not even certain why he is here for my lesson at all."

Lord Farnsworth turned to Victoria and gave her a frown, as if she had wounded him. Sally scoffed. It would take a lot more than a word to wound the type of man who would walk out of a pond with a woman watching. He was much too self-assured to allow anything she said to hurt him.

Lord Farnsworth leaned over Victoria. "I'm here teaching you to box, of course." He lifted an arm and swung it at Victoria. It was exaggerated and slow, but Victoria's reaction was not. Her arm flew up and blocked his fisted hand, causing it to land on the back of her chair just to the left of her head. Lord Farnsworth nodded and Mr. Ashton clicked his tongue in approval. "But if you don't appreciate my skills, then I suppose I can teach your sister to box."

Lord Farnsworth twisted and leaped toward her. Were they starting? Now? His movements were not exaggerated and showy like they had been with Victoria. She had no idea which fist he would strike her with. Without thinking of blocking like Victoria had, she pulled the roll of paper tight to her chest with her left arm and then slammed her right fist into Lord Farnsworth's middle.

He stopped, eyes wide and blinking. He didn't bow over or even bend at the waist to gain his breath. But when he did breathe, it was a little short. What had she done? Wasn't there a law against striking a lord? Everything had happened so quickly, she hadn't had time to think through her actions. He blinked again and then turned to Victoria. "It appears your sister has already been taking lessons."

Victoria laughed, the sound cascading around the garden. Her laugh had always been the same ever since she was a baby, bubbling out from her throat as if it couldn't be contained. Sally hadn't heard this full-bodied laugh for years. It might have even been worth risking a prison sentence for, but blast Lord Farnsworth for being the one to bring it out in her. That was Sally's responsibility.

Although, she had been the one to deck Lord Farnsworth, so

perhaps some of the credit could still be hers. "It is good to hear you laugh, Victoria. Should I punch Lord Farnsworth a second time? For not telling you his true name?"

"I told her my name."

She pulled back her fist and Lord Farnsworth was suddenly light on his feet, shifting his weight from one foot to the other. Sally had never seen a boxing match, for ladies of good standing were not allowed to watch them, but she had seen drawings of the men with their arms up and their feet positioned just like Lord Farnsworth's were now.

Was he actually a pugilist?

And a baron?

"But you didn't tell her who you were. In fact, when we first met, you didn't tell *me* who you were. I am starting to see a pattern here. Why would you be so unwilling to share who you are?"

The same expression of surprise he had shown after she hit him returned. His jaw clenched, and if she had been in the ring with him during an actual match, she would have turned and run. He was not dangerous, exactly, but not safe either.

"I share who I am."

"Not very willingly."

"People who share too willingly aren't to be trusted. And they aren't likely to be telling the truth, either. I haven't loved the name Farnsworth, it is true. It reminds me too much of my father." He turned back to Victoria and Mr. Ashton. "So, thank you for calling me John. I hope someday Miss Duncan will be friendly enough to do the same."

Victoria's eyes caught Sally's for a moment and then rested back on Lord Farnsworth. A smile grew on Victoria's face that Sally didn't recognize. It was not a smile of contentment, nor the smile she gave Sally when she was enjoying a nice meal. This smile reminded her of Lord Farnsworth's: mischievous and plotting. "I hope so, too."

Heavens, but she needed to get her sister away from that man.

If only he hadn't made Victoria laugh.

Mr. Ashton rested a hand on the back of Victoria's chair. "I'll continue to work with Miss Victoria here. Why don't you take Miss Duncan to the winter garden and work with her there?"

The winter garden would still have them in sight of each other, but she didn't want to be alone with Lord Farnsworth and his well-tailored clothes. "I see no reason why we can't do a lesson here all together."

"Miss Duncan—" Lord Farnsworth started.

"Call her Sally," Victoria piped up from her chair. "And you call him John; everyone else does."

"I will not." Sally straightened her spine. She was raising a hooligan. Sally couldn't go around telling a near stranger to call her by her Christian name, especially not Lord Farnsworth. "And he will not either."

Lord Farnsworth leaned down and placed his head near Victoria's shoulder but when he spoke it was not a whisper. "Not yet."

For the second time that afternoon Victoria snorted. It was not a lovely sound that rang throughout the garden. It was unladylike and embarrassing.

Perhaps it would be easier to keep Victoria to her rooms.

Sally gasped. That thought had not just crossed her mind. The world around her darkened and a crow left its perch behind her, squawking fiercely as it flew overhead. A force like a punch hit her in her middle.

Sally could not become Mama.

She swallowed her pride and took a long, deep breath. "Why would you have our lesson in the winter garden instead of here?" She nearly added "John," but she stopped herself. Calling Lord Farnsworth by his proper title did not make her like Mama; that was simply common decency.

But John did suit him. Even in all of his fine clothes, the casual way he walked and the way he always looked her in the eye didn't make him feel like one of the stuffy peers she tried to tell herself he was.

He seemed rather unremarkable, actually.

When he wasn't jumping in ponds, at any rate.

Lord Farnsworth raised his eyebrows as if he had heard her

thoughts. "You can't have the same lesson as Victoria. She is far ahead of you by now and will become quite bored."

A few days of boxing lessons had somehow made Victoria an expert? She opened her mouth to give a retort but stopped when she saw Victoria straighten in her chair with a proud smile on her face. That smile of Victoria's made Sally realize that she never wanted to surpass her sister in boxing.

Lord Farnsworth winked at Victoria and gave the air to her side a punch. In that moment Sally didn't see a gentleman or a lord. He was a man, and quite possibly a decent one.

She could take boxing lessons from a decent man in the winter garden. It might even be an enjoyable exercise. She could use a break from all the interior design—something she would have enjoyed more if *she* were the one picking the colors and patterns of the papers and rugs.

"I wouldn't want to slow Victoria's progress. Lord Farnsworth, I would be honored if you would teach me the first few things about boxing in the winter garden while Mr. Ashton continues Victoria's lessons here."

Lord Farnsworth was bent at the waist, still interacting with Victoria when she said it, and his body stilled for a moment before he stood straight and looked her in the eye. He had a question in his, a hesitancy that belied the ridiculousness of their situation. All she had done was offered to let him teach her. She fidgeted with the belt at her waist and then made herself stop. Sally Duncan was not a fidgeter. She could sit in a business meeting where the outcome could mean thousands of pounds for her company and not fidget. She would not allow the gaze of Lord Farnsworth to fluster her.

Sally had never been awed or intimidated by a man's position in life, and she wasn't about to start now. He was a lord, it was true. He was also a loggerhead who swam in ponds he only half owned.

Nothing to be flustered about. If only he would stop staring at her. "Well?" she said in hopes of getting him to move. "Shall we?"

He blinked and his half-smile returned. He swaggered over to her and held his arm out to escort her. He was back to being a peer again.

She breathed a sigh of relief. She might have been a bit thrown off by Lord Farnsworth looking at her like he was a man, but she could handle Lord Farnsworth escorting her to the winter garden as if he were an overly privileged lord.

Which he was.

CHAPTER 13

FIRST A PRESENT, and now Miss Duncan was inviting him to *do something* with her. True, it was a boxing lesson in full view of anyone in the house and not far from where Mr. Ashton and Victoria would be working on their boxing lesson, but still. In the past three days she had initiated contact twice. His first week here she hadn't at all.

Well, unless he counted her telling him to remove himself from the pond.

An invitation to leave shouldn't count.

Her arm was wrapped in his as they walked down the path toward the winter garden. How often had he walked this path with his mother? The roses and other parts of the garden weren't in bloom then like they were now, but the garden would always hold a sense of home for him.

And here he was walking it again, only this time with his future wife's arm about his. Everything was moving along even better than he had planned. Miss Duncan was still surprising him much as she had done on their first meeting. Life with her would never be lonely or dull, and her sister was a delight as well. Perhaps the struggles of his family in the past were all leading to this reward: a home that was filled with happiness. If his mother had found a spouse that had suited her, rather than being paired with his father, perhaps she could have been happy as well.

He had escorted a multitude of women at balls and even while on walks in the countryside, but everything about escorting Miss Duncan felt different.

It felt like triumph.

She wouldn't take a boxing lesson from him if she didn't like him at least a little bit. The wide round brim of her hat prevented him from seeing any part of her face, but he wished he could see her reaction to him. Just then, her fingers tightened on his arm almost imperceptibly. Something strange lit up inside him—a sudden intense feeling of possession. He wanted to make the woman by his side *his*, and only his, not in just a legal and written way, but in a real way. He wanted her to choose him, to give herself to him always.

It was a strange way to think about a woman he had only just met. He swallowed and increased the space between them. What was he to do with this growing attachment? He had always seen Miss Duncan as a woman he could grow to love. He glanced up at his mother's home. He had risked it on the chance that Miss Duncan would eventually agree to marry him.

But what if she didn't?

He would lose the manor and the young lady beside him. The world around him grew hazy and he blinked hard to clear his vision.

He was gambling heavily on the chance that Miss Duncan would accept his offer. When he had embarked on this journey, all he was risking was Greenwood Manor. Now that he had spent time here again, his heart had remembered everything that was associated with it—Mr. Ashton, the winter garden, and now Victoria and Miss Duncan.

A woman wouldn't want a man who was scared. He straightened and willed his breathing to return to normal. Miss Duncan would want a man who was strong, not one who was reduced to shaking at the thought of having everything he loved torn away from him.

They entered the winter garden and followed the path until it came to a small bower surrounded by dormant plants. Most of them were still green, but they would have no flowers until winter. Some spots were bare and brown where the plants lay hidden a few inches below the soil, waiting for the right moment to spring back to life again.

This corner of the garden was the converse to most traditional gardens. Each specimen here had been collected, planted, and loved for the fact that it was different from what was typically grown. Its beauty lay in its uniqueness.

Miss Duncan slipped her hand out from around his arm and glanced up at him, her wide mouth opened in a smile. His breath hitched. *Miss Duncan* a winter garden. It was no wonder he had immediately felt drawn to her. She was everything opposite of most of the women he had met. She was a businesswoman, straightforward instead of coquettish. She gave him gifts of the most unexpected nature. She teased him with terrible wallpapers and demolished staircases. Jonathan would always pick a winter garden over the common and generally loved rose garden. Its rarity and strength were its beauty.

"Are you going to teach me to box, or simply stare at me? You are usually more talkative than you have been today."

He blinked. Had he been staring? It was shaping up to be a strange day. "Do you already know me so well?"

Miss Duncan turned to look back at where they had come from. Victoria was laughing again. Victoria's laugh was like music. The hat was once again in the way of seeing her face, but Miss Duncan had to be smiling at her sister's laugh.

"Would you remove your hat?"

She spun and looked up at him once again. "And risk ruining my complexion?" Her eyes were wide in shock. He hadn't thought her so vain. But then the corners of her mouth lifted. "I jest. I don't give a fig about my complexion. Of course. I suppose I need to in order to box." She would need it for that, too. But he wanted to see her face, and even though he was only a few inches taller than she was, he didn't have a chance with that brim in the way. "Should I remove my gloves as well? I noticed you and Mr. Ashton weren't wearing any."

He nodded and Miss Duncan set down the long roll of paper she had brought with her to the garden. As she did so, a few inches of it rolled free.

It was a roll of paper for the walls, and it was rather hideous, black and white and swirling. "What was your purpose in bringing out the papers?"

"I wanted Victoria's opinion on them. I'm hoping to change her mind." She straightened and reached for the ribbons that held her hat in place at her throat. His hand moved to help her and then he stopped.

Was he really about to try to remove Miss Duncan's hat? To untie the knot that rested against some of the softest skin on her person? He swallowed and stepped back, placing his rough, ungentlemanly hands behind his back.

His heart began to pound loudly in his ears. When she was his wife he could help her with such things, and he would. Is this how all men felt about the women they would marry? Both fascinated and in awe?

Miss Duncan made quick work of the knot without his help and then pulled the hat off her head. Then she looked up at him.

He shook his head. He was staring again. What had they been talking about? Oh, yes...Victoria's opinion. "On the papers?"

"Yes."

"You are the one who bought the house. What do you think of them?"

"It doesn't matter what I think of them. I want Victoria to be comfortable. I want it to feel like home. I want to provide something that was made exclusively for her to enjoy while we are here, but I'm no longer sure any of us will enjoy those papers. Even for Victoria, they are too much."

The strange strangling feeling that had been growing in his chest tightened. Sally had done everything for Victoria: the stairs, the papers, buying the manor in the first place, everything. Sally Duncan was much more than her beautiful smile and her eye for fabrics. She was more than a businesswoman who would see the mutual benefit of a union between them. She was an exceptional woman and a loyal sister. Once again he felt the need to step away. He was the one who was supposed to be wooing her, not the other way around. Jonathan brushed up against the branches of a small evergreen bush to his side.

Buxus microphylla.

His mother had planted it. She had planted it for him. Every single flower that bloomed here in the winter was like Victoria's papers. He couldn't shake the feeling that this woman standing in front of him held the answers to questions that he had always been too afraid to ask.

"Does making something for her make you happy? If you never had any other enjoyment in life, could you take pleasure in just this home? In providing a place where Victoria can be happy?"

Miss Duncan chuckled. "Victoria and I don't always see eye to eye. But, yes, it makes me very happy. I wasn't really there for her when she was recovering from her surgery."

"She had a surgery? Did it help?"

"No." A haunted look passed over Miss Duncan's eyes. "No, it did not help. She was born with clubfeet, a bad case, one doctors had tried to fix with bindings, but that only ever helped and never cured them. She could walk, though; she could do everything, really, they just weren't pretty." Sally swallowed. "Mama wanted her to wear dancing slippers…"

"Oh." His response was inadequate. Completely inadequate.

"After the surgery we kept hoping that her feet would heal, but they only got worse, and then the bindings didn't help anymore. I wasn't really there for any of that, though. I was busy with Vermillion. It wasn't until someone mentioned how little time I spent with her that I recognized how I had neglected her. And Mama was never the same—the house had become a prison to both of them."

"So you bought Greenwood Manor."

"Yes. I sold Vermillion to do it. To go back to your question—was it worth it? Yes. Do you hear that laughter? It was worth it. The sale of the company got me not only the funds for the manor, but Victoria now has a dowry fit for a queen."

"It's a good thing she is learning to box, then."

"Yes, she is going to need it to fend off fortune hunters."

"Don't marry her off without consulting me first. I know most of the men of quality in London."

"Really?" She quirked one edge of her mouth. "And what are they doing running about with the likes of you?"

"They need someone to do their dirty work." He flexed his hands. They weren't the hands of a gentleman. Most of his knuckles had a few scars from practice or actual fights. He had mostly grown out of his tendency to settle problems with his fists, but he couldn't get his boyhood hands back.

Miss Duncan tipped her head to one side. "Will you be removing yours as well?"

Jonathan blinked, unsure of her meaning. "Pardon?"

"Your hat."

"Yes, of course."

He pulled his hat off his head and reached for hers so he could set them both down on the top of the *buxus* bush.

As soon as the hats were out of his hand, he tried to smooth down his hair. It had just enough curl in it to look quite disheveled whenever he removed a hat. He turned to see Miss Duncan staring at the top of his head.

Did it look that horrendous? "My hair is quite irredeemable, I'm afraid. It never stays put like it should."

Miss Duncan pulled her lips together as if she wanted to laugh. He used both hands to try to smooth his hair down again, but with no mirror he had no way to tell exactly where it was misbehaving. "You find my hair comical? Is it sticking up strangely somewhere? I can't have you distracted during your lesson."

Her eyes followed the line of his head. "I like your hair. Your comment before just reminded me how suitable it is to you."

"Whatever do you mean?"

"Only that I thought you would stay put in London when I bought this house, and when you didn't I thought at the very least you would stay put in the hunting lodge, but you have never stayed put like *I* think you should."

"You think I should stay in my hunting lodge?" He furrowed his eyebrows. He thought he had finally made some progress with her.

Once again her eyes made their way to Victoria and Mr. Ashton. "No, I thought that at first. But now, I think I may have been wrong."

Deep in his chest, his heart warmed. "I'm guessing that doesn't happen very often."

"It does not."

He shrugged. "It happens to me all the time."

Miss Duncan burst into laughter. Her laugh was similar to Victoria's, in that it rang throughout the garden and burst forth without restriction, but Miss Duncan's laugh had a husky quality that made him think about removing her hat again. His fingers would just graze the soft skin while he felt the vibrations on her throat.

He coughed. "Well, I shall try not to be hurt by your laughter."

"You are a grown man; you can handle it."

"Yes, I can. But I must admit there was one time I thought you quite wrong."

"Me?" she asked, as if the possibility was very unlikely. "What did you think I was wrong about?"

"The stairs, and the wallpaper, and the menagerie." The back balcony of Greenwood Manor was still unscathed by that particular plan. "Now that I think about it, you might still be wrong about the menagerie."

She scoffed. "I was never serious about the menagerie. I said that only to rile you up."

"Well, it worked."

"Of course it did. If I didn't know how to read a gentleman, I could have hardly made my business successful, now could I?"

"No, I don't suppose you could."

"And the stairs and the papers...you no longer feel that I am wrong about those?"

Victoria was laughing again. They both watched for a moment as Mr. Ashton feigned falling to the ground. He had used that same technique while teaching Jonathan to box. As an eight-year-old he had felt as mighty as a giant.

"You made the right choice on those." He said with a nod. "This is Victoria's home now."

Miss Duncan blinked rapidly for a moment, then cleared her throat and turned to him. "Show me how to punch someone so that they will fall like Mr. Ashton just did."

He smiled. "You forget yourself, Miss Duncan. Victoria is miles ahead of you. You don't get to start with learning punches."

"What?" She shoved his shoulder softly. The memory of her fingers toying with the fabric of his waistcoat during their first meeting flashed through his mind. She was so comfortable with him. Was she this way with all men? "I don't even get to learn one punch?"

He put a hand to his middle where she had punched him earlier. "I believe you are a natural at striking. Most people can hit someone if they really want to. We are going to work on something that may come to you less naturally: footwork."

"Ah," said Miss Duncan. She now comprehended the true reason she was taking her lesson separate from her sister, other than the fact that Victoria had seemed to want to get the two of them alone.

Bless her.

"Boxing is like dancing. You have to remain light on your feet, always ready to pivot and turn in another direction if needed. Your knees should always be bent and ready to push to either side." He stood on the balls of his feet and bent at the waist, his arms instinctually raising to put his hands in a position to either block or land a blow. "Bend at the waist like this, arms up, and watch the person in front of you. That is the first lesson in boxing: how to move, and how to stand. Victoria got to skip all of these lessons. She has the distinct advantage of being very hard to send to the ground. But you, my dear, must start from the beginning."

The "my dear" slipped out without thinking. He had never taught a woman to box before. Victoria was a girl, which was very different. Miss Duncan hadn't seemed to notice, though—a fact that didn't disappoint him. It was as if calling her by an endearment wasn't astonishing to her.

Miss Duncan nodded her head and bent at the waist. She lifted her skirts slightly so he could see her feet moving about in the small bouncing steps he had illustrated.

"Yes, that is good. You are a natural, just like your sister. Now, stop holding on to your skirt and put your hands up like mine." She did as he said. He wasn't sure why she had agreed to take a boxing lesson, but now that she was here, he could see that she was enjoying it. The slight wind pulled at the few curls that had escaped her coiffure.

"Like this?" she asked. She was still dancing around, bouncing softly from foot to foot. Her arms were up but bent at ninety-degree angles instead of being out more in front of her.

"Almost." He stepped forward, conscious of his rough hands, but she would have to see them at some point. Her eyes followed his movements like a deer watching a hunter. He adapted to that philosophy and moved slowly so as not to scare her. He engulfed her small fist, not much larger than Victoria's in his thick, scarred hands. Hers were softer than the silk of his favorite waistcoat and just slightly cooler than his hands. "Do you favor your left or your right hand?"

"Right," she said so softly he nearly missed it.

He gently moved her hand up higher, taking her elbow in his other hand and positioning it to a wider angle. He then did the same with her left arm, only leaving that one slightly lower. Stepping away, he surveyed his handy work.

Her form was good. "Have you ever seen men box?"

"Definitely not."

"The actual striking of one's opponent comes in bursts. Until one of them makes the decision to attack, usually the two men will dance around each other, looking for a moment of distraction or an opening."

"Like I was dancing before?"

"Yes."

Miss Duncan kept her arms raised as he had shown her. She narrowed one eye just as he had seen many sparring opponents do. But on her, it was different. She was most likely trying to be intimidating, but he was more charmed than anything. He kept the line of his mouth straight. The last thing a boxing student wanted was to not be taken seriously. He began circling to his right and she followed.

"Bright girl."

Her lips spread in a grin. "I can't allow you to find an opening."

When she spoke her arms dropped slightly. He stepped in, closing the distance between them, and placed a soft jab onto her shoulder—a touch only, just enough to let her know she had let her guard down. She raised her arm to block but she was too late; all she could do was push his arm aside and away from her.

"You dare strike a woman?" she asked in mock affront.

"I do not dare. That is why I simply tapped you."

Miss Duncan took two quick steps forward and he threw himself to his left to avoid her. She grinned at his avoidance of her. "I don't plan on holding back."

"I wouldn't want you to, but you will have to find an opening first."

"You don't think I can?" Her left arm was dropping, leaving open a hit to the body. He stepped in, but she was more prepared this time and took a quick step back. If he hadn't been pulling his punches, he might have been able to land that one. Instead his hand met only air.

Miss Duncan's soft laughter was so out of place in his world of boxing that he landed flat on his left foot. If she hadn't been so delighted with herself about missing his jab, she could have caught his kidneys with a quick hook. But she hadn't noticed him losing his rhythm. He stepped away and went back to his defensive stance once again. "Well done."

She grinned. "Thank you."

"You could have capitalized on my missed hit, though. There is a reason why the blows come in bursts. Once one person strikes, there are usually all kinds of openings to look for."

"But you haven't taught me hitting yet."

"What is this? The great Sally Duncan, former owner of British Vermillion Textiles is making excuses. I wouldn't have thought you capable of it."

Her eyes narrowed and this time it was not in a charming way. He knew that look: pure determination. Miss Duncan wasn't going to be satisfied until she had landed at least one solid punch.

Come to think of it, it was still charming. Not only that, but her determination worked significantly in his favor. Not much more than an hour had passed when Victoria and Mr. Ashton made their way to the winter garden. Miss Duncan dropped her arms from her fighting position.

"Have you already finished your lesson?" Miss Duncan asked, looking reluctant to end the lesson without having landed a punch.

"It is starting to get dark. And Mr. Ashton is getting tired of me landing punches."" Victoria looked fairly smug at this announcement.

IT WAS STARTING to get dark; how had he not noticed? Miss Duncan turned to Jonathan. Her eyes darted over him: stomach, arms, jaw, shoulders; all the places she had tried unsuccessfully to hit him. Finally she met his eyes. "We'll continue tomorrow, then." It wasn't a question.

She picked up the hideous paper and returned to the house with Victoria. When they were a good distance away, Mr. Ashton placed a hand on Jonathan's shoulder. "We may have opened Pandora's box teaching these two young ladies to box."

CHAPTER 14

Over the course of the next week Jonathan sparred with Miss Duncan every afternoon, save only one drizzly day. She and Victoria would always come out together talking about their latest project in the home, but without fail Miss Duncan ended up with him and Victoria with Mr. Ashton, a situation he had no desire to change.

Miss Duncan was usually the winner with verbal sparring, but sometimes he managed to unnerve her and get in a witty jab of his own. On those rare times when she couldn't think of a quick retort, she'd purse her lips and turn away. But she didn't always turn away in time, and more than once he caught a glimpse of the smiles she tried to hide.

With the physical sparring, he definitely had the upper hand. She was a quick study and had made vast progress over the week, but he had too much experience dodging jabs, uppercuts and hooks for any of her blows to reach her intended target.

Besides, she had an enchanting tell. When she made up her mind to take a swing, she would narrow her eyes just before her arm moved. With that forewarning, even her improved skill and speed hadn't been enough for her to land a jab.

He had considered allowing her to hit him. It wouldn't be difficult to move too slowly out of the way. but he knew no matter how well he covered his allowance of an opening, Miss Duncan would see through him. Not only that, her determination to land a punch kept her coming each day.

Would she even show up again once she had bested him? This afternoon was similar to all the others, with Victoria and Mr. Ashton in the statuary while he and Miss Duncan continued their lesson in the winter garden. They danced around one another. She circled to the left, then slowed and crossed her left foot in front of her right and began circling the other way. He held her gaze as they moved about, waiting for her to make the first move.

Finally he changed his stance—not much, but enough to allow her an opening. She saw it, ignored it, and continued circling. He raised an eyebrow and stepped closer, tightening the circle as they continued dancing. She did the same and suddenly they were too close. Neither of them would have to step to throw a punch. It was a position he would never allow himself to be in if this were an actual fight, but with only a few feet keeping them apart he could truly study her face. Her eyes returned his gaze, but now one eyebrow was raised as if in challenge. Different moves kept playing in his mind—different ways he could topple her without so much as breaking a sweat, but instead he found himself circling and waiting, waiting for the telltale narrowing of her eyes to indicate she was going to throw a punch.

And there it was. She pulled back her right arm slowly enough he could have landed a blow on her chin, but instead he waited to see what she would try. She jabbed her fist forward, aiming for his waist. With her intent so obvious, he sidestepped out of the way. She grunted in frustration, once again leaving the delicate skin of her cheek open. He was going to have to take that shot at some point, but touching Miss Duncan's face? It was too intimate, surely.

She went for him again, this time with her left hand, which was smart of her. If he was completely untrained he might have missed her movement, but once again he stepped away and blocked her punch with his arm.

She tried three more times to hit him—once on the belly and twice aimed at his face, but she never landed anything. Her breath was coming rapidly, and a few more tendrils of her hair had fallen out. Miss Duncan lowered her head slightly, a sure sign she would be going for his body next.

She swung. He sidestepped and this time he didn't hesitate. He had ignored this opening for days. He gently brushed his thumb along her cheekbone in a quick smooth movement, and on the way back caught the tendrils of her hair. The soft curl slid through his fingertips, silken like the petals of the flower she had granted him in the garden.

He shouldn't have done that. The tips of his fingers tingled from the contact. He was supposed to be teaching her boxing, not finding excuses to feel the soft curl of that delicate hair just behind her ear.

Miss Duncan stepped back and stopped dancing.

His heart, which had been beating wildly, stopped. Had he offended her completely? Was she disgusted with his ungentlemanly behavior? What if she wanted to stop their lessons? He would have to resort to chasing Bernard over to her property in hopes of getting a glance at her again.

She tipped her head to one side and examined him. She touched her hair. "I just need one moment. I have a few pins that are irritating my head while I dance about."

He hadn't thought of that. Her skirt seemed quite cumbersome and he did wonder how she was so light on her feet while wearing all the garments that ladies did. On top of that her head had grown uncomfortable. Men did have some advantages besides strength when it came to boxing.

He put his hands down and waited for her to adjust the pins.

A long lock of dark hair cascaded down Miss Duncan's back. Jonathan sucked in a breath. She moved her fingers to another part of her head, and a few more thick locks fell nearly to her waist. Each time she removed a pin, she would slide it onto the belt she was wearing on her waist. She wasn't readjusting the pins; she was removing them.

How exactly was he supposed to concentrate on boxing if Miss Duncan's hair was down?

Blasted smart woman. She had seen exactly how distracted he was by those few small tendrils and now she was going to take full advantage of that fact.

"Lord Farnsworth." She still had her hand in her hair, even though more than half of it was now free from the intricate styling.

"Yes." Why was his voice hoarse?

"I'm so used to having my lady's maid do things like this that I'm not good at it myself. I can't seem to find one pin." She turned her back to him. "Do you mind removing this last one?"

He swallowed hard. That seemed like a very bad idea. He glanced up at the balcony of the house. No servants were outside, but what if one of them was watching through the window? Mr. Ashton and Victoria were still in sight, but they were busy working on jabs. "You want me to act as your lady's maid?" He pretended to be affronted. Better to pretend jest than to pull that last pin from her hair.

Her hair was dark—very dark, but it still managed to shine in the sunlight. When it fell from her coiffure, it fell in long, curling waves. A small part of one side was still up and his fingers itched to help her and see it join the rest of her hair.

But that was a task for her maid. Or perhaps someday for her husband.

Oh.

He stepped back.

"Lord Farnsworth?" She craned her neck around to see what he was doing. "Don't be silly, you look nothing like my maid. Now stop moving backward and help me with this last pin so we can return to our lesson."

Was he being silly? He stepped forward, but the closer he got to that hair of hers, the more certain he was that he was not being silly—not at all. Undoing that hair would be extremely intimate.

She was impatient with his slow progress and with a huff stepped over to him. "The last pin is somewhere above my left ear, but I can't seem to find it. She spun and leaned her head back so that the top of it was only inches from his. "Do you see it?" she asked.

His hands shook slightly as he raised them to the top of her hair.

He could still leave. He could claim that Bernard needed to be fed or that he needed to tell Mr. Ashton something...anything. But he forged ahead. In a matter of weeks, something as mundane as taking a pin out of his wife's hair would be no strange thing.

He may as well become accustomed to it now.

His fingertips were less than an inch away from her, but he couldn't actually make them close the distance. Miss Duncan leaned her head back farther, and suddenly his lack of movement didn't matter, for she had caused his fingers to land on top of her head.

His fingers were encompassed by her rose petal hair. He didn't dare move for fear he would end up running his hands down the length of her hair, following every twist and turn until his palm lay empty at her waist. He swallowed, then took a deep breath, closed his eyes and willed his hands to remain where they were.

"A little to the left," Miss Duncan said as if he were merely positioning a piece of furniture or hanging a painting on a wall. Ah, yes, his hands were in her hair for a reason, and it wasn't the reason that was flashing through his mind at the moment. He pressed his fingertips around in her hair trying to find that last remaining pin. It had to be in there somewhere. Her hair couldn't have stayed up if it wasn't. Just when he was about to give up and tell her to find her own blasted pin, his fingertip bumped a thin rounded object just at the nape of her neck.

He grabbed the pin between his thumb and finger and carefully tugged. He had no sisters and his mother hadn't ever asked him to help with her hair. Was he even doing this right? He didn't want to hurt her.

"I did it," he said and held up the thin metal pin in triumph. The last of her silken hair tumbled down and swung into position like the last leaf of autumn joining its comrades on the forest floor.

Miss Duncan spun and slammed her fist into his stomach.

"Oof." He doubled over, breath gone. Miss Duncan snagged the pin from his hand and placed it on her belt to join the others.

She raised an eyebrow and leaned over him, a smug half-smile on her face. "I told you I could land one punch. I suppose today's lesson is over now."

Jonathan held out a hand and straightened. His abdomen still smarted, but it wouldn't for long; he had taken much worse. Still, her strike had caught him unawares and it had been solid. Miss Duncan had more talent for boxing than he had assumed. "This lesson is far from over, and you didn't win. In order to win, you have to play fair."

"Didn't I play fair?"

"You distracted me with your hair." She furrowed her brows and lowered her chin, giving him a look that screamed he was a nuisance to women. "Pin." He added lamely. "You distracted me with that hair pin."

She pursed her lips together. "And that is an official rule? An opponent cannot ask you to remove a pin from their hair?"

"Of course that isn't a rule. Who would make such a ridiculous rule?"

"So I won then." This time she raised both her eyebrows as if what she wanted most in the world was for him to contradict her. She was ready for another war, and this one wouldn't involve fists. Intellect was her strength just as his was his fists. He would not win in that battle—not against Sally Duncan.

"Fine, you won."

The smile that sentence brought to her face made him second-guess his decision to marry her. No woman should want to win against her husband quite that badly.

But that smile also solidified something in his heart: Sally Duncan would always keep him on his toes. He would be dancing about in circles trying to keep abreast of what she was planning and then she would distract him. She would easily distract him, for the longer he spent in her presence, the harder it was for his mind to concentrate on anything else. And while he was caught off-guard by the softness of her hair or the different hues of her eyes, she would hammer him in the gut, and then give him that deuced smile.

And he wouldn't even mind.

Jonathan's breath came up short, and it had nothing to do Miss Duncan's blow.

He wanted Miss Duncan as a wife.

He was not prepared to feel so...so...whatever it was he was feeling.

Her hair was still down and it shone in the sunlight behind her. Her eyes glistened with merriment and a hand at her slender waist seemed to embody her confidence and joy in this moment.

He took a step back.

He could devote his life to putting that look on her face and he would consider it a life well spent. Miss Duncan was enchanting and their boxing lessons had put him solidly under her spell.

He undid the button on his jacket.

"What are you doing?"

"This match just got very serious. You can't expect me to spar with such a worthy opponent while wearing a jacket."

She narrowed her eyes, but with her hair falling down her back it wasn't as though she could complain about him being improper. He finished unbuttoning his jacket and pulled it off, one sleeve at a time. Miss Duncan's eyes followed his every movement. Is that what he had looked like when she had let down her hair?

The two of them were in very serious trouble.

"I have enjoyed looking at the vase you gave me every afternoon when I take my tea."

"Is it still on the mantel?"

Jonathan dropped his jacket to the ground next to Miss Duncan's hat and gloves. "Of course it is. Your taste is impeccable. I wouldn't go against your decorating advice."

She smiled and started circling around him again, her hair trailing behind her back. Taking off his jacket might not have been enough. He tugged on the knot of his cravat. For now he would simply loosen it. If she landed another hit, he would remove it as well.

"I'm glad to hear you are enjoying it."

"I have another gift for you."

Miss Duncan stumbled slightly, but he didn't take advantage of the moment. "Is it another squirrel?"

"It has been in the back of my wardrobe for three weeks, so I sincerely hope not."

"When will I be receiving it? Will it be a parting gift for when you finally leave?"

"Why, Miss Duncan, when you put it that way it makes me feel as though you don't want me here."

"I didn't realize when I bought the home a baron would come with it."

He stifled a laugh, because...well...she wasn't far off. At least he hoped so. She noticed his distraction and tried to hit him with her right hand, but he blocked her. "It isn't a parting gift. I'm just waiting for the right moment to give it to you."

"Why does that make me very worried?"

"I have no idea. Thus far our gifts to one another have been given in extremely good taste."

The smile on her face broadened and he took the opportunity to jab his left hand forward and brush it along her chin. Her eyes flashed and she jumped forward and flung out her right hand, but he was already out of reach.

Boxing, he decided, should be a prescribed method of courting.

CHAPTER 15

WITH SALLY'S hair streaming out behind her, she climbed the back staircase of the manor. She hadn't been able to land any more punches after her first. Lord Farnsworth was above letting her win, a fact which made landing even one solid strike more pleasurable, even if it had taken her a week to do it. The last time she had felt so exhilarated was when she had managed to convince Henry Poole on Savile Road to buy his fabric exclusively from British Vermillion textile.

The first order of business, besides putting out a highly superior product, was to always look for preferences in those she was trying to negotiate with. The second was to look for their weaknesses.

Apparently her hair was both to Lord Farnsworth.

She reached the balcony and resisted the urge to turn around and see if he was still watching her. Based on the fact that her hair was still down, she assumed he was. She couldn't go into the house with her hair down to her waist.

She quickly grabbed a pin and started pulling up sections of it.

In a few minutes it would be up.

She smirked. Perhaps she should have asked the baron to help her put it up as well. What would he have thought of her?

She tore out beautiful stairs, papered walls with disastrous designs, and now asked the man to act as her lady's maid. She closed her eyes as she put in the last pin. The way he had watched her hair as it fell...

An odd feeling in her stomach made her eyes flash open. She leaned back against the balustrade and blinked.

Lord Farnsworth was a baron. She could not develop feelings for the man.

Mr. Harrison had explained to her, very patiently, that a businessman like her grandfather could leave his worldly goods to a granddaughter, for none of it was entailed. It was easy for him to shrug off a lack of sons. But Mr. Harrison would be a baron, and a baron needed heirs; otherwise everything would go to his cousin, and heaven forbid that happened.

She pushed herself off the balustrade and turned to see Lord Farnsworth still looking at her. She jerked her head around and made her way into the home. It didn't matter that Lord Farnsworth was a baron. It wasn't as if he was courting her; he was simply teaching her to box.

Mrs. Hiddleson was repositioning a vase in the grand drawing room. Blast. Had she seen the boxing lesson? Mrs. Hiddleson turned, her face bland. "Ah, Miss Duncan, were you out with Miss Victoria?"

"Yes."

"And is she enjoying the gardens?"

"I believe she is, very much so."

Mrs. Hiddleson smiled and smoothed down her apron. "It is so good to have a family here again. The home sat empty for far too long."

Why, though? Why had Lord Farnsworth spent ten years away from Greenwood Manor only to come here now, when it was no longer his? "Mrs. Hiddleson, I don't mean to pry, but do you know why the previous owners never visited?"

"Well, they did come, or rather..." Mrs. Hiddleson stopped and looked about the room as if someone could be listening. "The house was always occupied up until Lady Farnsworth's death, and after that…" She stopped again, then leaned forward. "I think both Lady Farnsworth and this home were just not grand enough for Lord Farnsworth. He never visited it after she died."

Not grand enough? The manor had twenty-four rooms. What did the other Farnsworth estates look like?

This room, with wall-to-wall windows overlooking a garden and a pond, was not grand enough? Her bedroom with floor-to-ceiling windows was not grand enough? The stunning marble staircase at the front of the home was not *grand* enough? No wonder Lord Farnsworth had given her such a shocked look when she said she was replacing them with cement.

If the manor hadn't been grand enough before, it certainly wouldn't be now.

Mrs. Hiddleson must have seen the look of disgust on Sally's face. "Lady Farnsworth loved this home. It had been in her family for generations. She was always happiest when she was here."

"I suppose she didn't get to live here often, then, with a husband who felt it was beneath him."

Mrs. Hiddleson chuckled and shook her head. "Lady Farnsworth wasn't one to mind what her husband thought. She lived here as much as she pleased. I shouldn't talk about my previous employers, but both of them were prideful, only in different ways. While Lord Farnsworth still needed Lady Farnsworth, he made efforts. All that stopped, though, once…"

"Once what?" She shouldn't be prying. But something had gone on in this house and she needed to know what.

"Once he had his heir." Mrs. Hiddleson shook her head. "He didn't ever need to condescend to apologize after that. Lady Farnsworth never really had her husband back after the young master was born."

Sally's stomach twisted.

Would she never learn? She didn't belong in this world of heirs, pride and reputations. Mr. Harrison should have taught her that.

He had taught her that. She'd had a strange moment with Lord Farnsworth during one of their boxing lessons, but nothing more.

Perhaps it was time she stopped the lessons. Just until he left for London. She and Victoria could continue them again with Mr. Ashton once Lord Farnsworth was gone. That would be the end of that.

Whatever *that* was.

CHAPTER 16

AFTER WATCHING Miss Duncan in all her glory ascend the stairs of Greenwood Manor, Jonathan returned to Mr. Ashton and Victoria. He pretended to watch them work, but in reality there was not much else he could do but relive that moment when Miss Duncan's last hairpin was released.

Heavens above, she was beautiful.

Victoria pulled one of her punches and turned to Jonathan. "Are you thinking about my sister?"

Thinking about her? He was fantasizing about her. But he couldn't quite admit that to her little sister. "Should I not be?"

Victoria pursed her lips together and tilted her head to one side, then the other. "I suppose I will allow it."

Jonathan tried to hide his grin at this young woman's blessing, but he couldn't. "Does she ever speak about me?"

"Yes, she says we should prepare for our boxing lesson, and when she is really feeling talkative, she mentions that you never let her hit you."

"I mean besides speaking of boxing. What about before we started our lessons?"

"I didn't even know who you truly were until Sally started coming to the boxing lessons. Suffice it to say, she never mentioned you."

Victoria was a mean young lady. She could have pretended that they had spoken of him, and spoken of him positively at that. It wouldn't be hard. That wasn't Victoria's way though. She was honest to a fault and it was one of the reasons he admired her.

"She never spoke of the man she bought the manor from?"

"Him? Yes, I suppose she did mention him once."

"That *him* is me."

"Yes, I know that now."

"And did she mention the man living in the hunting lodge?"

"Yes, she did mention him."

"Also me."

"I see your point."

"And what did she say?"

"She said she bought the manor from a baron named Farnsworth, and she wanted to give a vase to the unattractive gentleman who lived in the hunting lodge..."

That unattractive comment still stung. "That is all?"

Victoria simply nodded. Did Miss Duncan feel nothing for him?

Would she take boxing lessons from a man she felt nothing for? Would she allow him to touch her hair? He needed to bring Victoria with him for their next lesson so she could see that Miss Duncan was not indifferent. She felt something for him. He was certain of it.

"However," Victoria said. Jonathan leaned forward, his heart in his throat. One positive word from this little miss and he would offer marriage to Miss Duncan now. He had come here with that intent, and other than the few times he had misunderstood what exactly she was trying to do with the manor, he had never been disappointed in his choice of spouse. Every interaction with her had solidified in his mind that he had made the correct choice. "Sally was nearly engaged before, and she almost never talked about him. So perhaps she doesn't talk about men she likes."

She was nearly engaged? His mind went blank and then exploded with hope. "Wait, you think she likes me?"

Mr. Ashton chuckled behind his hand.

Victoria smiled. "We saw you two. You weren't so far away that we couldn't see your lesson. Tell me, why exactly did my sister's hair end up loose?"

"It was a distraction. A good one." It was still a distraction.

"And why did she need a distraction?" Mr. Ashton asked.

"So she could land a punch in my abdomen."

Victoria laughed. "She likes you, John. I think she likes you quite a lot."

He turned to Mr. Ashton. "What do you think?"

"Well, I'm inclined to agree with this young lady. She either likes you or…"

"Or what?"

"Or she *really* wanted to hit you."

Oh, she had certainly wanted to hit him. The look of joy on her face when she succeeded was something he would never forget. He tipped his head to one side. "You don't think it could be both?" Mr. Ashton and Victoria threw back their heads and laughed. "What? It could be both, couldn't it?" This was his life on the line, his mother's manor on the line. He needed to know if he had any hope.

Victoria settled. "I think you are right. And that is what's so funny. I think she does like you, and I also think she was very happy to have landed a punch." She grinned. "I must admit I relish any chance I get to have the upper hand on either of you. It doesn't mean I don't like you. It simply means I respect your skill and I like the feeling of proving myself to you."

"Are you certain?" Jonathan's chest started to tighten in anticipation. He was ready. If he proposed now, they could be married in a few short weeks. He would be able to move out of the hunting lodge and into Greenwood Manor, the only place that had ever felt like home. And together he and Miss Duncan would make it even more their home.

Children, laughter, boxing lessons…they would have it all.

"I wouldn't say I was certain," Victoria said. "But I am quite confident, and not just because of your boxing lesson."

Confident. That was enough for Jonathan. It was time to start a new life, this time with Sally Duncan in it. "What else makes you think she might like me?"

"When she was giving you the vase, there was this look in her eye —happiness, joy, excitement, I'm not sure what exactly, but when she told me you weren't handsome, I had the very distinct impression she was lying. Why would she lie about that if she weren't at least a little bit interested in you?"

Miss Duncan thought him handsome. He spun on his heel and marched toward his lodge.

"Where are you going?" Victoria called after him.

He turned at the waist but didn't stop walking. "I'm going to ask your sister if I can become your brother."

Victoria's face wrinkled for a moment and then realization dawned. "Now?"

Jonathan threw his hands in the air. "Yes, now!"

"The manor is that way," Mr. Ashton blurted out.

"I have something I need to fetch from the lodge."

"But I wasn't certain." Victoria's voice had a squeak in it he didn't recognize, as if she was fearful for the first time since she had met him.

Jonathan shrugged as he turned back to the lodge. "I am," he called out behind him.

He had never been more certain of anything in his life.

CHAPTER 17

SALLY'S HAND hovered above the handle to the drawing room door.

What on earth could Lord Farnsworth want now? She had only just left him in the garden. Perhaps he was finally returning to London and had come to take his leave. She would be able to continue renovations without his interruptions. A twinge of regret spiked in her chest but she pushed it down. She had grown accustomed to having him nearby, but all along she had been hoping he would leave soon.

Hadn't she?

Victoria would be sad to see him go, but she could continue her lessons with Mr. Ashton. Sally would continue to join her. Her few lessons had proved quite entertaining, and she might have a talent for it.

She wouldn't take advantage of her hair the next time, though. That had been a silly mistake.

She pulled open the door to find Lord Farnsworth pacing in front of the fireplace, a small package in his hand. Oh dear, had he brought her a gift? What would it be this time? What exactly had he told her about it? Only that it had been sitting in his wardrobe for weeks, which meant it couldn't be in response to the vase.

That could have been disastrous.

He turned at the sound of her footsteps and stepped toward her. Something was different. His eyes scanned her face, stopping as they often did at the curls at the nape of her neck. There were likely more of them than usual since she had pinned her hair up on her own.

She had left the door open behind them, but the room suddenly felt confining. She could leave. She could jump out the door and call out that she had forgotten something and could he please come back when Victoria was done with her boxing lesson.

But she didn't.

"Would you like some tea?"

He stepped closer, making the room grow even smaller. He chuckled low and quietly. "Now you ask me that? No, I haven't come for tea." He eyed the door behind her, as if willing her to close it.

Not likely.

What in the world did he want?

"Did I forget something in the garden? Or does Victoria need something?"

"No, Victoria is still outside. I am certain she will return shortly."

"Would you like to wait for her so we can all have tea together?"

"I didn't come here for tea."

Oh.

She was done beating about the bush. Whatever Lord Farnsworth wanted, he should come right out and say it and not just stand there looking at her as if she was some sort of Viking warrior ready to behead him at any moment. "Then, what did you come here for?"

"You."

What? She put a hand to her middle. Did he realize what he sounded like when he said something like that? If a servant were walking by, they might misunderstand him. "You mean you came here to speak to me?"

"Yes." He threw back his shoulders and stood like a soldier. "And no."

Something deep inside Sally woke up—a demon of fear she had buried since breaking off her engagement to Mr. Harrison. She had agreed too readily and too soon to that engagement and she would never do that again. Perhaps that was not why Lord Farnsworth was here, but his choice of words and the way he eyed the door sent her scrambling to find a place of safety. She couldn't marry Lord Farnsworth. She barely knew the man. She wouldn't marry any man until she knew not only from his words, but also from his character, that her daughters would not feel like disappointments in the eyes of their father because he wished for sons. It might take years for her to trust a man enough for that, and Lord Farnsworth had the deck stacked against him, for he was a baron. How could a baron *not* care about producing heirs? His father certainly had.

Sally closed her eyes. She had been having such a pleasant day. She never would have guessed it could turn courses so completely.

MISS DUNCAN, or Sally as he must certainly call her now, had both hands behind her back, and seemed not to understand his silent pleading for her to shut the door. But that was no matter; once he asked her to marry him, all would be settled. They could shut the door then.

If she said yes.

Her eyes were wary, but that was only because she didn't know what it was he had come to ask her. Victoria felt she liked him, and his father, for all his faults, had always assured Jonathan that any woman would be happy to marry him in his position. Miss Duncan was wealthy, for sure, but even she must see the advantages to marrying a baron.

Besides, there were much worse men who could ask for her hand —old ones, poor ones, men with no hair. He swallowed. Better to just get this over with and move to the part where they got to shut the door and enjoy being engaged.

"Miss Duncan..." What exactly should a man say to a woman in this situation? "From the moment I first saw you, you have surprised me in so many ways."

"Then why do I feel like *you* are about to surprise me?"

"Perhaps I am...but I hope...my surprise is as pleasing to you as yours have been to me."

"Lord Farns—"

"Please, call me Jonathan."

"I cannot."

"After today, I hope you will."

"Stop."

"Miss Duncan, I want to marry you."

Her shoulders sagged and she let out a breath of frustration. "I told you to stop."

"Why?"

"Because I don't wish to marry you, and I hoped to save us both from the embarrassment of your asking. What in heaven's name were you thinking?"

She didn't want to marry him? He blinked for a few moments, trying to let her sentence sink in. He stepped forward again, this time with his hand outstretched. She kept both her hands behind her back and raised her chin. What had he expected her to do? Take it? Lord Farnsworth dropped his hand, his brow furrowed. "Why wouldn't you want to marry me? I'm young, I think I'm pleasant at times, and I'm a baron, even."

"You're a blockhead. I'm not even sure I like you."

"But wouldn't you like to be a baroness?"

"Not at the price of being a baron's wife. The things that are important to barons will never be important to me."

"I don't know how you could know that."

"Do you pretend to know what is important to me?"

He floundered. He had just proposed to the woman; he should know what was important to her. After a split second of scrambling he had it. "Victoria. Victoria is important to you."

Miss Duncan's shoulders dropped at that. He had guessed correctly. Miss Duncan had turned her life upside down for her sister; she had bought and renovated a manor for her. He would have to be a blockhead indeed to not know that her sister was the most important person in her life.

She rubbed her hand over her face. "If you know me so well, then why didn't you stop speaking when I asked you to?"

His eyes went to her hair. A pit formed in his stomach as the reality of what she was saying settled deep into his bones. He would not be shutting the door to the drawing room, and he would never again help her with her hair. He had asked too soon. He would be returning to London alone. "I didn't stop because I want to be engaged to you. I've wanted it for some time."

"See!" She was back to being rigid. "What *you* wanted. And you never stopped to consider *my* feelings. I would rather pluck chickens for a living then come home to a man who disregards me. When I marry, if I ever do, it will be to a man who at a bare minimum respects me enough to listen to me."

She would rather pluck chickens? He squeezed his eyes shut. Had she ever plucked a chicken? Jonathan hadn't, but he couldn't imagine it was a pleasant experience. But that was her point, wasn't it? Being married to him would be extremely unpleasant. "You don't want to marry me?"

"No." She stepped back, her face stoic. "The thought has never crossed my mind."

He was losing her, just as he had lost Mother, and now her manor as well. Something deep inside him cracked. He bit down on his lip. He would not mourn Miss Duncan, not like he had Mother. He would not spend his nights crying himself to sleep with no one nearby willing to comfort him. He had come here because he wanted the manor. And, well, he had gambled, and he had lost.

This would not break him. Four weeks was not enough time to fall in love. Love had never even been a part of his equation.

"Well, that is fine, then. We won't get married. It was a silly idea, one that doesn't really bear thinking about at all."

Miss Duncan winced at his words, but he knew better than to think his words had caused her harm. "Then why in the world did you propose marriage to me?"

In a matter of moments, Jonathan had gone from the excitement of finally having a family again to the reality of knowing he was returning to London alone. Those days at Eton before he had learned to adequately express his hurt came back to him. He was alone, he was hurt, and he was about to lash out, not with his fists, but with words. "I wanted the manor." It was harsh of him, but it was true. If she hadn't bought Greenwood Manor, he never would have thought to marry her.

Miss Duncan took in a deep breath and sucked in her cheeks as if she were trying to control her tongue. "Well, I want the manor as well, and in this I have the advantage, for it is mine. Now leave before I have Mrs. Hiddleson throw you out."

He stepped forward, bringing him within arms' reach of her. And yet, he would never have cause to bridge the gap between them and reach out to her again. "Do you honestly think Mrs. Hiddleson could throw me out?"

Miss Duncan's breath was coming fast, her hands fisted to her sides. At any moment she was going to use what few lessons he had taught her about how to pummel a man. Would she be so angry if he hadn't made at least some impact on her?

He leaned forward. His world had shifted so drastically in the past three minutes, he struggled to comprehend it. He would ask one last time, and then he would never see Miss Duncan again. "You don't like me at all?"

She bent at the waist and brought her face closer to his. "You have been nothing but a nuisance. What in the way I have treated you in these past few weeks makes you believe I have cared for you in the slightest?"

Victoria's admission that Miss Duncan looked at him differently than any other man came to his mind. "You look at me in a way…" How did Victoria phrase it? He had believed her. But Miss Duncan's eyes were sparking now not with interest, and definitely not with love. He couldn't rightly tell her she looked at him in a way that had spurred him on when she was shooting daggers at him now. "I have caught you staring at my chest."

"You asked me to marry you because you want my home and I look at your chest sometimes." She threw her hands up in exasperation and stepped away from him. He missed her nearness already. What the devil was wrong with him? "I admire your tailor, then. He is skilled at constructing waistcoats and jackets that fit your form well. I would like his name and address, actually. I might hire him for some work."

Jonathan's shoulders fell. His chest was the final arrow in his quiver. He had nothing else to recommend him. She didn't care that he was a baron, her interest in his physique was more business than pleasure, and she would rather pluck chickens than share a home with him. The only thing she wanted from him was the name of his tailor.

He stomped over to the small writing desk and threw down the present he had bought for her in London and pulled out a sheet of paper from a drawer. He grabbed a pen and dipped it in the inkwell, ink splattered on the page, but he hardly cared. Hands shaking—from rage or disappointment, he hardly knew—he scratched out his tailor's name and address. Setting down the pen, he grabbed the paper and marched back over to her, holding it out. "I will give it to you now, for no doubt we will never have cause to see each other again."

Her chin lifted high and she took the paper from his hand. Her finger grazed his thumb as she took it. That would be the last time they touched. There would be no more boxing lessons. She would never again demand he leave her pond. This was their last transaction, and it was done with pride and anger. "No doubt," she replied.

There was nothing more to do but leave and never come back. His thumb tingled in a way that begged for him to reach out and grasp her hand fully, ask if he could start again, not with a proposal, but with questions and gifts and hopes of courting her slowly. But it was too late. As usual, something he loved was being ripped from him, and there was nothing he could do about it.

One last time he let his eyes wander over her face. He would never graze a thumb along her jawline before pulling her to him.

He cleared his throat and spun on his heel. He couldn't be in this room another moment, not with Miss Duncan looking so lovely and yet so unattainable. He strode to the door but then stopped. He put his hand on the doorframe and took a deep breath. The library. He wanted just a few moments in the library.

He needed a chance to say goodbye to the memory of his mother and the stories she had told him there. The library had been the brightest spot in his childhood, the one time he was together with both his mother and his father, even if his father was simply a painting on the mantel.

He didn't turn to look at Miss Duncan; he couldn't. "There is one thing I would ask even though I have asked far too much of you already."

"I will hear what it is." Her voice was quiet but firm. He swallowed, for if she didn't allow him this one pleasure, he knew it would break him.

"May I have just a few moments in the library?"

Lord Farnsworth's head was bent and his voice low. He wanted to see the library, but why?

She couldn't see his face, but everything about the way he was standing in the doorway felt vulnerable. His hand slowly slid down the inside of the door frame as he waited for her answer.

It would be no trouble to let him spend a few minutes in her library, except then she would know he was still here in her home—the home he had wanted badly enough to propose to a woman he openly admitted to not loving.

She hated that his admission of wanting her for what she had and not for who she was hurt her pride, but it did. And she couldn't help but want to hurt him in return. In this moment, he had given her just that chance.

"No," she said.

His reaction was immediate. He didn't rage or swear, or spin around and demand to know why. His hand simply dropped from the door frame and his shoulders slumped. He didn't act surprised, though. It was as though he was expecting her answer.

Immediately her stomach hardened. She was going to be sick. She needed him to leave so she could lie down and give her body a moment's rest. Sally was a businesswoman; she knew how to be hard. But this was different. She didn't know how, exactly, but she was being cruel, and a small part of her hated herself for it. How much had it cost Lord Farnsworth to ask to see the library after all she had said to him? Still, she would not change her mind. Everything would go back to as it should be as soon as Lord Farnsworth was out of her life. She could go back to her plans. She and Victoria would be happy here, on their own. Why had he shown up today and put a sour note on this home that should have only brought her and her sister happiness?

"Why did you choose today, of all days, to ask me?"

He turned to her then, his eyes full of anguish, but he forced a corner of his mouth into a smile. "Victoria told me you were happy today. And I foolishly thought that might have been because of me. I've left your present on the writing table. It looks as though it has turned out to be a parting gift after all." He ran a hand through his hair. "I'm sorry if I have ruined your mood. I shall be gone from the hunting lodge by tomorrow morning. Will you tell Victoria goodbye for me?"

And then he left.

CHAPTER 18

SALLY SAT ALONE in the drawing room and stared at Lord Farnsworth's present for a long time before she dared to stand up and approach it.

She ripped open the paper and a note fell to the ground. In her hand she held something made from a delicate fabric: Vermillion fabric. She recognized the weave and the pale yellow design as soon as she saw it. It was one of the first she had helped her grandfather sell before she had taken over the company. It was a strong, sturdy cotton, not like the silks her company produced now.

She lifted the fabric and shook it out to see what exactly he had sent.

It was a dress.

But not one for her.

With shaking hands she picked up the note from the floor and flopped back down on the sofa.

Lord Farnsworth had gifted her with a beautiful, well-made dress meant for a three- or four-year-old girl. He had to have known what fabric this was. If she were to search all of London, there couldn't be a single item of clothing she would want more than this dress.

It was something to dress her daughter in, a garment that would carry with it stories of Grandfather and his trust in her. It was a dress that would hold power, and it was meant for a little girl.

Tears clouded her eyes as she forced herself to unfold and read Lord Farnsworth's note.

For a little girl with dark curls and a smile for everyone. For our daughter.

How could he have left her with this? Didn't he remember what he had written inside? Sally was suddenly sick. Her stomach ached and her limbs couldn't manage to stay still. Her arms tried to rest at her sides, but then they were behind her head or pressing against her stomach.

What had she done?

Lord Farnsworth had never, not once, spoken of heirs. She had tried him and found him guilty without ever consulting him on the subject. And then he writes her a note and mentions a child they could have together, and it is a daughter?

A daughter with hair like hers.

What had she done?

Perhaps he hadn't left yet. Perhaps she should run and find him and tell him to give her more time. Perhaps she had finally found a man who would see life as her grandfather had—where all their children would be cherished, no matter if they were daughters or sons. Why hadn't he given her more time?

She stood and wiped her eyes and went to a mirror that hung next to the door to check the condition of her hair.

After the day she'd had, it was a disaster. But it was dark and curly, just as Lord Farnsworth had written. She blinked rapidly. What would be happening right now if she had said yes?

First of all, he would have kissed her. She hadn't missed the way his eyes had gone to the door. He had wanted it closed. He may want the manor, but despite what he had said about not wanting her, some part of him did.

And some part of her had known it. Why else would she have used her hair as a distraction for him during their boxing lesson?

But marriage?

They hardly knew each other. It was ridiculous. And Lord Farnsworth was ridiculous and she was right to reject him outright, even if that meant that she had spent the last hour in a trance looking at a package she hadn't dared to open instead of...

Well, instead of kissing Lord Farnsworth.

The truth of the matter was, no matter how enjoyable it would have been to be engaged to the man, even if he was someone who would love and appreciate their daughters, she would have always wondered why he was so smitten with her. And because she had told him no, he had admitted he wasn't. He was smitten with her house. And for some reason he was smitten with her library.

She strode from the room, then nearly ran down the hallway. She needed to find Mrs. Hiddleson and learn what exactly it was about the library that held so much sway over him.

She found Mrs. Hiddleson in the kitchen speaking to Cook about food orders. Not wanting to interrupt, she waited just outside the open door. Cook caught her eye and stopped talking. Mrs. Hiddleson turned her head to find Sally there. With a nod to Cook that seemed to say *we will continue this later,* Mrs. Hiddleson came to Sally's side.

"What can I help you with, Miss?"

Sally couldn't talk about it in the kitchen. She turned and started walking away, and Mrs. Hiddleson followed her.

"May I ask what Lord Farnsworth was after?" Mrs. Hiddleson asked. "He didn't seem himself today. He couldn't sit still. He acted just like that every time he and his mother celebrated his half-birthday. He was always bouncing about wondering which flavor of cake Cook had made for him."

Lord Farnsworth had grown up celebrating his half-birthday? How very different the two of them were. Even though her mother had enjoyed celebrating her children's birthdays, Sally had plenty of friends who never took much note of what day their birthday was, let alone their half-birthdays.

Still, she needed to answer Mrs. Hiddleson's question. But how? "He wanted to see the library."

Mrs. Hiddleson was walking slightly behind her, so Sally turned her head to see the older woman nodding as if that made perfect sense. "Ah, that would explain it."

Why? What was so special about the library? "Why would he be so excited about visiting the library?"

"Well, I suppose it isn't my place to say."

"I didn't let him in the library, Mrs. Hiddleson. And I could tell he was hurt by it. I've half a mind to allow him to, next time he asks, but I would like to know why."

"You didn't—" Mrs. Hiddleson stopped mid-sentence. It obviously wasn't the housekeeper's place to question her employer, but still the question hung in the air. "I suppose it is so far in the past, and with both his parents gone, it wouldn't hurt anyone to talk about."

"No, it wouldn't, and what is more to the point, it may help me understand Lord Farnsworth better."

"Poor thing." Mrs. Hiddleson mumbled softly under her breath. "I don't think the young master would like me telling..."

"He is no longer your employer. I am. And while I cannot force you to tell me, I would appreciate it, and I don't know that Lord Farnsworth would mind. We are, after all..." She stumbled over the word. "Friends."

"You are friends?"

"Yes."

"But you didn't allow him in the library."

Sally gritted her teeth. She needed a reason that would make sense to her housekeeper. "I am a woman living alone in the country. I cannot allow a man to roam about the manor; it could do terrible things to my reputation." Sally didn't care a fig for her reputation, not now that she had no business to worry about. But at last Mrs. Hiddleson seemed to understand.

Because what kind of woman would deny a man entry to a library just because she was in a foul mood?

A vindictive one.

"I suppose that makes sense. But you really should allow him some time in the library. If you are worried about rumors, I can show it to him when you are out of town. Poor boy. Every night his mother would read to him in that room."

Sally's mother had read to her, but she didn't hang her hopes on revisiting those times.

Of course, her mother was still alive. And she had had years of memories with her to overshadow the ones of her being read to.

"That is why he wants to visit the library?"

Mrs. Hiddleson looked to her left and then her right as if a servant or someone else could have come upon them and overheard what she was about to say. They were nearly to the library. Sally hadn't even realized that was where she was leading Mrs. Hiddleson. "It is more than that. The young master only visited here in the winter, when his father was sitting in parliament."

"I believe I heard him say something of the sort. And during the summer the family would be off to one of their other homes."

"Not the whole family."

They had reached the library. Sally opened the door and stepped in. It was a beautiful library with floor-to-ceiling shelves filled with books. An oversized fireplace was the focal point across from them as they walked into the room. Mrs. Hiddleson closed the door behind them and then leaned forward. "After their first few years of marriage, Lady Farnsworth never left with them. And her husband never set foot in Greenwood Manor. They would pass that boy back and forth like a shuttlecock, never seeing each other in the process. I never heard what it was that tore that family apart, but it wasn't good, and it never healed, and even after her ladyship died, Lord Farnsworth wouldn't allow the boy to come back, not even to look at the place."

Sally reached for the door handle behind her and held herself upright. She should have waited to ask. This was too much in one day. She had already hurt Lord Farnsworth; she didn't want to hear any more about his past. There was nothing she could do about it now. She couldn't write to him and ask his forgiveness, but perhaps she could catch him before he left. Her mind raced. It wouldn't take her more than five minutes to walk to the hunting lodge. Surely he hadn't left yet.

She could tell him to come see the library before he left, and also tell him he didn't have to leave. She couldn't agree to marry him, not without knowing him better, but he didn't need to leave.

Mrs. Hiddleson was still talking. For all her hesitancy, it seemed once the dam was broken there would be no pulling back the water. "There used to be a portrait of Lord Farnsworth, Lady Farnsworth, and the young master above the mantel. It was a large portrait, and though I never saw him smiling while he picked up his son, he was smiling in that portrait. One night I was passing by the library while the young master and Lady Farnsworth were reading and I heard her say, 'Here in the library, we can always be together. The three of us, whenever we come here, we are all together: your father, me and you. And your father...he is smiling.'"

Sally closed her eyes. She had been wrong about Lord Farnsworth. Terribly wrong.

"Thank you, Mrs. Hiddleson." She turned and pulled on the door handle. She had to try to reach Lord Farnsworth before he left. Of course he could spend some time in the library. She wasn't cruel, or at least, she hadn't been until today.

"So you will let him see the library the next time he stops by. He is always stopping by. If I didn't know better, I might say he was taken with you."

Another dagger to her heart.

"Yes. Thank you for telling me, Mrs. Hiddleson. Had I known of his past, I would have allowed him some time here. Now, if you will excuse me, I just remembered somewhere I need to be."

Mrs. Hiddleson stepped away, giving her more room to open the door. "Of course."

Sally kept her steps moderated while she was in sight of Mrs. Hiddleson, but as soon as she turned the corner, she lifted her skirts and ran to the back of the house.

She threw open the glass door that led to the balcony and ran down the steps. Was it really only a little more than an hour ago that she had climbed these same stairs while Lord Farnsworth watched her?

Why couldn't the fool man have told her at least a little bit about himself before proposing?

The ridiculous idea of banking everything on the fact that she would marry him simply because he was a baron—didn't he see his own worth?

Mrs. Hiddleson's 'poor boy' echoed in her mind. A boy who was passed from parent to parent, never truthfully having a home or a safe place. He didn't know his value.

And whatever value he thought he had had just been debased by her harsh rejection.

She ran through the garden, past the winter garden where they had boxed and Lord Farnsworth had slid his fingers down her hair. The way he had held his breath each time another lock of hair would tumble down to her waist had given her such a feeling of power. She had thought only to lord over the poor man, and then she had judged him for using her.

Sally came to the statue in the middle of the garden and started around the curved path, only to bump into Victoria on the other side of the statue.

Victoria clapped her hands at the sight of her. "Sally!"

"I can't speak now, Victoria. I'm sorry, I will be back in just a moment."

"Are you going to Lord Farnsworth's lodge?" Every nuance of Victoria's voice was edged with excitement. "Did he ask you, then?"

"Yes, he asked me."

Victoria sat back in her chair, obviously satisfied. "I like him so much better than Mr. Harrison. Mr. Harrison hardly ever said a word to me when he would visit."

Sally rubbed a hand down her face. She liked him better than Mr. Harrison too. Mr. Harrison had done everything properly and in order, but it still hadn't ever felt right. Lord Farnsworth had rushed and bumbled about, but it had never felt wrong—not until he proposed. But would things have been different if she hadn't been disillusioned by her first engagement? It didn't matter, really. "I told him no, Victoria. I hardly know the man."

Victoria's mouth hung open. "You told him no? But…"

"But what?"

"You seemed so happy when you were with him."

There it was again—the comment that had sent Lord Farnsworth rushing over to propose. "Things like this take time, Victoria. A man and a woman are often happy when they first meet. It is exciting, and perhaps there's some pull toward one another, but marriage is for a lifetime. You have to investigate and get to know each other better before making such a monumental decision. You must understand that."

"But he loves you."

"No, I don't think he does. How could he? There has not been enough time for something like love to develop."

"Maybe not everyone takes as long as you do for things like that. I've only known him for a few weeks, and I can tell you, I like him better than any other man I have met." Victoria's face grew slightly red. "Not for me, of course; I've always known he liked you. When he talked about you his eyes would light up. It didn't make me like him less, I'll tell you that. I think every man should be in love with my sister."

"Oh, Victoria, of all the silly things to say."

"Well, it is true."

"Regardless of what is true, he is leaving and I need to speak to him before he does."

"He is leaving?"

"Yes."

"Because you rejected him?"

"Yes."

Victoria pushed her wheeled chair to one side, making room for Sally to pass. "Go talk to him. Tell him you need more time, and that you don't fall in love as quickly as he does."

"That is not—" Sally started, but then she wasn't sure what she was going to say. If she allowed him to visit the library, would he stay longer? Would it be appropriate? How would he even court her? Mrs. Merryweather had left not long after bringing Victoria here. Sally had no chaperones, and there were no balls or teas to attend. She brushed a lock of hair out of her eye. If Lord Farnsworth wanted to court her, he would find a way to do it without all those things. As it was, he might not want to.

Sally sped past Victoria. Whether he stayed or not would be his choice. The main thing she needed to do was to make certain he saw the library before he left; otherwise she would have a very hard time living with herself.

She ran past the rest of the garden and the pond. She was now on Lord Farnsworth's property. It was silly for the property to be split so. Honestly, a marriage between the two of them would make sense as far as property lines went. Everything could be combined into one estate again.

She shook her head. She still hardly knew him. And he had come here for the manor, not for her.

The path was less worn after she left the pond behind her, but she could see that Lord Farnsworth or one of his servants had recently cleared some of the overgrowth away from the path.

It didn't take long before the path opened up to a clearing, and the two-story lodge stood in front of her.

It was quiet.

She stopped running and listened, her breath and heartbeat loud in her ears. She heard nothing but the sound of birds—no horses, no men stomping around and packing.

She rushed forward, hoping she was wrong.

She knocked on the heavy wooden door and was met with silence.

She was too late. Lord Farnsworth was gone.

CHAPTER 19

"I DON'T KNOW what else to do with you, Farnsworth. Getting you drunk was my last resort."

Jonathan looked up from his cup. He had been staring at the amber liquid in it for the past half hour. If Riverton had wanted to get him drunk, he was failing miserably. If that was his plan, he should have picked some shady alehouse, not the Horse and Hound. "Your last resort for what?"

"To get you over that trip to Greenwood Manor. I finally understand why you never visited. I don't remember you being this depressed at Eton after your time there as a child."

Well, at that time his mother had been alive.

And he hadn't had his dreams of a wife and children running about the manor squashed before they could even completely form.

He gritted his teeth together. Now he was lying to himself. His dreams had formed. They had been complete with dark, curly-haired daughters, for heaven's sake. No, he hadn't simply dreamt of marrying Miss Duncan, he had planned on it, and planned on it so fully, that he wasn't simply disappointed in her rejection. He was lost.

A vision of a dark, foreboding future empty of any family opened up before him every morning. It was the same future he had faced before meeting Miss Duncan, but now it weighed on him like a collapsed tunnel, stealing away his light and his ability to breathe.

Riverton had no idea what that kind of emptiness did to a man. He had enough family to populate half of Scotland.

"Greenwood is gone."

"What do you mean gone? Was there a fire?"

"No, I sold it."

"You sold your mother's estate?" The way he said it made Jonathan sound like some sort of unfeeling wretch.

He might be a wretch, but he was far from unfeeling. Unfeeling would be easier.

"It was Oliver's fault. He put the idea into my head. It did save what is left of my father's estates, but I feel so blasted empty without it." That was the truth, even if it wasn't simply the home he was missing.

"It is gone, then? All of it?"

"I kept most of the lands, and a hunting lodge."

Riverton slapped him on the shoulder. "That isn't so bad, then. Let's plan a hunting trip. What kind of game are we likely to get in Dorset?"

Jonathan swirled his drink. "The only game I ever had luck with was squirrel."

Riverton was already nodding his head, a smile on his face as if the trip was fully planned and the two of them were already on their way. His smile dropped and his eyebrows pulled together. "Did you say squirrel?"

Did Riverton honestly think he knew anything about the sport? "Have you ever seen me hunt?"

Riverton's face sunk. His happy hunting trip must have been evaporating before his eyes. He sighed and looked down into his drink. "Come to think of it, no."

"That is because I don't. And it is only thanks to a blessed miracle and a muzzle full of bird shot that I got even that one small animal."

"Even in all my days of hunting, I've never bagged a squirrel. Seems to me it would take some talent. Or at least a very lucky shot."

"Can it be lucky if it took hours of shooting to hit something?"

A chair dragged behind them; whoever was sitting behind them must be leaving. They might as well leave too. If Riverton's plan was to get him drunk and make him forget about Greenwood Manor and everything he had left behind there, it was never going to work.

Jonathan pushed his liquor away from him and shoved his hands against the table, but before he could stand, a heavy hand landed on his shoulder. "Did I hear Family Man say you shot a squirrel?"

Jonathan slid his lower jaw to the right. Only one man in London called Riverton Family Man. He had enough on his plate tonight. Did he really need to deal with Chatterton on top of everything else? Jonathan crossed his hand over his body and flicked Chatterton's hand off of him, then rose.

"His name is Lord Riverton." Chatterton had his regular goons with him. Robert Gowen and Mathew Harrison flanked him on each side, both with stupid grins on their faces. "And you know it. And yes, I shot a squirrel, but not on my first try nor my fiftieth. I'm better with my hands than with a weapon...a fact you well know." Jonathan nodded toward the scar on Chatterton's left cheekbone.

"Ah, Flower Boy. You never did understand, did you? Using your hands isn't the way a gentleman fights."

"Then you must be a true gentleman. Every time I've seen you try to pick a fight, you don't know how to throw or even block a punch."

Bowen lurched forward, but Chatterton's arm shot out and held him back. "We aren't going to start some pub fight like riff-raff."

"Not with Farnsworth, you're not," Riverton said, still sitting with his neck craned up and a guileless grin on his face. "He would pummel all three of you. I might have the chance to land a facer or two—you know, for old time's sake—but he would have you on the floor before you even knew the fight had started."

Jonathan pulled his hand back. If he was going to prove his friend right, he needed to get this fight started right away. Chatterton wouldn't know what hit him. How long had it been since he had been in a good, old-fashioned brawl?

Too long.

A deep part of him that had been sleeping ever since he left Greenwood Manor awoke and rose to the surface. He was still alive.

Jonathan rocked back on his heel and then thrust his fist forward. But something barreled into him from the side. Arms snaked around his middle and sent him crashing to the floor. His head hit the dark floor of the pub and he spun to see who had taken such a cheap shot.

Oliver.

Who had invited him? Oliver righted his spectacles. "We aren't at Eton anymore, Farnsworth."

Chatterton had stepped back, away from where he had been standing, his eyes wide. "Looks like I caught you on a bad night."

Jonathan shoved Oliver off of him. "If it weren't for Oliver, it would have been the perfect night."

Chatterton bent over him—a dangerous position when all it would take was a jerk of Jonathan's hand at his cravat to send his head crashing into the wooden floor. "Most of us have grown up and left these childish things behind us."

"Really, Chatterton? You have never left your childish game behind. Not once."

Chatterton's face drained of color. He swallowed and straightened, then turned on his heel.

"Well, that was a disaster," Riverton said with a smile that belied his sentiment. He put a hand out to help Jonathan up. "But at least you got a bit of your spark back. You'll be back to your old self in no time." After Jonathan was standing, he lifted Oliver as well. "Good to see you Oliver, but a few minutes later would have been much more fun."

Oliver brushed the dust from his trousers. "It seems to me I arrived just in time."

Oliver was an interfering oaf. He was the reason Jonathan was in this mess in the first place, and now he had denied him the one spot of entertainment he might have enjoyed in weeks. Jonathan punched him in the shoulder harder than he needed to.

He owed him a sore shoulder at least.

CHAPTER 20

"MUST YOU SIGH QUITE SO DRAMATICALLY?" Sally was trying to read and the sound of Victoria's heavy boredom made it quite difficult to ignore her own.

"There is nothing to do now that it is so cold outside."

"You may still go outside. Take a scarf and a blanket for your lap."

"I know I *can* go outside. I have already today, but I can't stay out as long as I used to. Besides, Mr. Ashton doesn't like to say it, but I can see that this cold weather hurts his joints. We have to keep our boxing lessons short."

If Mama heard her two daughters talk about boxing lessons, she would have a conniption. Yet the types of lessons she would encourage for them, like embroidery or watercolors, never seemed to make Victoria smile.

Sally was sure to get an earful about Victoria's freckles, though. Victoria wouldn't box with her bonnet on, and Sally wouldn't stop her for such a silly reason.

"We could redo some of the papers in your wing." The fish papers were worse on the wall than they ever had been in her sample book. It had only been a few months since they were put on, but Victoria might be getting tired of them even sooner than Sally had expected.

She could hope, at least.

"We only just papered everything there, and it is just how I like it."

"Well, what do you propose we do?"

"Most families with estates still spend their winters in London."

"You *want* to go back to London?"

"It would be different now, wouldn't it? You would be there, and you wouldn't be working all the time. Perhaps we could go to the theater or watch a real boxing match."

"Victoria." Sally gave Victoria her sternest look. "I am more indulgent than Mama, but never assume that means I don't know what is appropriate or not. You are not allowed anywhere near a boxing match. It isn't just I that would keep you away. No one would let you anywhere near it. Women simply aren't permitted to watch them."

"Most women also don't own businesses, but you did that."

"That is very different from a boxing match. What we do with Mr. Ashton is simply instruction. A real match will be full of blood, blackened eyes, and a ruined reputation if you were to be seen at one."

"We could dress up as men and see one. No one would know."

"You want us to don breeches and face moustaches and show up at a match and hope no one notices?"

"You don't think that would work?"

Sally tried to picture her delicate sister dressed as a man. She definitely should not don a mustache if she tried. If anything she might be able to pass herself off as a boy, but not a man. "You are far too pretty to be mistaken for a man. We would be caught immediately. And can you imagine Mama's reaction?"

Victoria scrunched her face together in distaste. "All right."

If Victoria actually tried to go to a boxing match, Mama wouldn't allow Victoria and Sally to live together anymore. Being kept prisoner in one's room was more acceptable than being seen where one shouldn't be.

"But I suppose a musicale or two wouldn't hurt."

Victoria straightened. "Do you mean it?"

"Of course. It's about time we visited with Mama anyway."

Victoria pushed her chair over to Sally, grabbed her arm and hugged it. "Thank you."

"I must confess, I didn't think you would be so excited to return to London. You do like it here."

"I love it here. Thank you for making such a wonderful home for us. But I am ready for a bit of entertainment. It has been rather dull ever since..."

Victoria stopped, but Sally knew what she was going to say: since Lord Farnsworth left. It had been two months, and she had yet to hear a word from him. Twice a goose had landed in the pond and swam about and both times, for an instant, she had thought perhaps it was a man swimming there. But it was only a goose. Of course. He had no reason to return. He came once in ten years, and it could well be another ten years before he came back again, if ever.

She had contacted his solicitor, just once, to ask where she should send a box of things she had discovered in the attic. He had told her to send them to his office and he would see to it that Lord Farnsworth received them. And that is exactly what she had done. As close as he had been while he was here, she didn't have the address of his London home.

It was a good reminder that she hardly knew Lord Farnsworth. It was easy to romanticize a man when he wasn't around to prove her wrong. She and Lord Farnsworth wouldn't have suited each other as husband and wife. They were so very different.

But it wasn't as if marrying Lord Farnsworth was an option. After all, she had told him no, and that was that. A woman only got one chance at a proposal. Men were proud things that wouldn't stoop to asking twice.

Which was why it was good she had made the correct decision.

Lord Farnsworth may not have grown up spoiled in the ways she had assumed, but he still was incompetent with money, and that was a flaw she wasn't willing to forgive, not when her grandfather had worked so hard, rising from almost nothing to build wealth. She couldn't turn that wealth over to a man who would squander it on things of no use. It might seem to Lord Farnsworth that she had unlimited resources, but after buying and renovating the manor, most of the remaining money had gone to Victoria's dowry.

What had he thought more important than keeping his mother's manor? His clothing was impeccable, but surely he didn't spend enough money on clothing to bankrupt all of his estates. Sally closed her book. It wasn't as if she were reading. "I'll go speak to Mrs. Hiddleson about preparations to leave."

Victoria smiled. "Thank you. It will be nice to be back in London. Perhaps we will see some familiar faces."

Sally groaned. Mama hadn't exactly taken Victoria along on social visits. The only person of note that Victoria knew was Lord Farnsworth.

"I doubt we will see him. Don't get your hopes up."

"Who?" Victoria's eyes were wide with innocence.

Sally simply shook her head. She had never met Lord Farnsworth when she was in London previously, and there was no reason she would meet with him now. After all, their only socializing would be for Victoria's benefit. It wasn't as though Sally would be participating in the balls and soirees of the Season.

CHAPTER 21

SALLY HAD NOT COUNTED on her mother's meddling ways.

"I'll not have you visiting London during the Season and not attend at least three balls."

"Mama, we didn't come for the Season. We came to see you."

"And you have seen me. Now you must show me your ball gowns from last year. We shall see if we can make them over while we wait for more to be made."

That was how Sally ended up at the Harwoods' ball with Mama, wearing the same dress she had worn when Mr. Harrison had proposed. It was the only one Mama had deemed suitable and still fashionable.

With her arm in Mama's, Sally scanned the ballroom. Please, let Mr. Harrison *not* be at this ball. Thank the heavens she hadn't told her mother of Mr. Harrison's proposal. If she had, she would still be engaged, or perhaps even married by now.

Mr. Harrison would be a baron someday, and there was no chance Mama would have let that opportunity pass her by. By the same reasoning, she would have made Sally marry Lord Farnsworth as well, but Victoria was the only one who knew about that proposal.

Mama was scanning the ballroom, no doubt looking for her

165

friends. She grabbed Sally's arm and propelled her to one corner of the room, where a group of three matrons stood speaking rapidly to each other.

Oh, that she had somewhere else to be.

The crowd parted to her right and Mama froze. Sally turned. Mr. Harrison was here with his two closest friends, Lord Chatterton and Mr. Bowen, but he had left the two of them behind and was quickly approaching Sally.

"Mama, come, we must visit with your friends." Sally pulled her mother's arm in the direction they had been heading, but she didn't budge. Instead, a smile the size of the bow on the front of her gaudy dress bloomed on her face.

Merciful heavens, Mama knew. "Mr. Harrison," she said. "What a *surprise* to see you here this evening."

Mr. Harrison raised his thick eyebrows and gave her a dashing grin. "A surprise, indeed. And you have brought your lovely daughter this evening. A pleasure, Miss Duncan." Mr. Harrison gave her a low bow, much deeper than the eldest son of a baron should have given the daughter of a merchant.

Oh, but he was charming. And he knew it.

"Mr. Harrison." Sally gave him a short curtsy. She would not say it was nice to see him. It was not nice to see him. She had hoped to never see him again.

"I would be honored if you would dance the supper set with me? Unless that dance is already taken."

The only way to refuse was to say that she was not dancing this evening. Mama would be furious, but really...the supper dance? Not only would she have to dance with him, she would have to endure him at supper as well. She opened her mouth to refuse him. She had come to the ball, but it didn't mean she *had* to dance. But Mama was faster. "Sally has not yet been asked. She would be pleased to dance with you."

Mr. Harrison nodded, his smile jumping back and forth between the two women. Sally ground her teeth together. Had he told Mama of their past? *He* was the one who had asked to keep their engagement a secret. *He* was the one who had postponed telling anyone. *He* was the one who had hoped to have Victoria settled in a home somewhere before the wedding.

He had no right to tell Mama. Especially now that there was no engagement.

Sally gave him the slightest of nods. At least the supper dance was still hours away. She would put it out of her mind for the moment. She pulled her mother in the direction of her friends, suddenly anxious to hear all of the London gossip she had missed while in Dorset.

"How can you accept a dance for me?" Sally hissed once they were out of earshot. "I do not want to dance with Mr. Harrison."

"You would go the whole evening without a single dance, simply to deny one man the pleasure of dancing with you?"

"If it is that man, then yes, I would."

"What do you have against him? He has visited me twice while you were gone, and I believe he has a sincere interest in you."

So she didn't know everything about Sally's past relationship with Mr. Harrison. That was a mercy, but there was no way to answer Mama. Sally had thought him to be all that was amiable and good in a man. She had known he was attracted to her money, but she had put that thought aside, for she was also attracted to him for some of his worldly capabilities.

If she told her mother the reason she had cried off their engagement, Mama would have Victoria put in a home immediately. The last thing Sally wanted was for her to believe that Victoria was a stumbling block to Sally's marriage.

"I will dance with him tonight, but you must stop visiting with him. I have no interest in him."

"No interest in him?" Mama stepped away from her so that she could look Sally up and down. "The man will be a baron. Your father was a merchant, your grandfather as well. How could you not be interested in him?"

"Titles don't hold the power they used to. Soon it will be the merchants who hold the power in London."

"And do you have any wealthy merchants asking you to dance this evening? Show me a few and I might be persuaded to look at someone besides Mr. Harrison."

"Mama, I didn't come to London to be married off. I am happy living in Dorset with Victoria, and I will not marry until we are both well and settled there. I would ask you to kindly stop trying to partner me to any young man of importance."

Mama's head darted up and a false smile sprung to her lips. They were only a few feet from her friends, and it wouldn't do for the two of them to be seen arguing.

Sally spent the next twenty minutes hearing everything that had happened in London since she had been gone, and by everything, she meant everything scandalous. When one of her mother's friends introduced her son to Sally, she was quite relieved to have the chance to leave the group, even if it meant dancing with a man who smiled at her a bit too brightly.

Sally shoved down her pride and smiled back at him. She shouldn't ruin Mr. Brook's evening simply because hers had already been spoiled. When the music of a Schottische started and her feet found the familiar rhythms, she relaxed and allowed herself to remember how much she liked to dance. Her life in the country had come with much exercise in the form of long walks, but other than boxing, nothing had gotten her heart beating like dancing did.

Mr. Brook's eyes were bright by the time the set was over, and her eyes were probably shining as well. He thanked her happily and led her back to her mother.

After that, she never had another break from dancing. By the time the supper set came around, her feet were starting to ache. If she were at home in Greenwood Manor, she would already be abed. Here, the night was still young. After supper there would be even more dancing and entertainment.

She wiggled her toes inside her dancing slippers, hoping to relieve some of the pain, just as Mr. Harrison came to claim his dance. Mama handed her off happily.

The first dance in the set was a polka quadrille. She wasn't sure she had the energy, but they were already halfway across the floor before she could speak.

"I am feeling quite—"

"Fatigued. I am certain you are; I haven't seen you without a partner all evening."

"You have been watching me all evening?"

"You are hard to miss in that stunning gown." Please, oh please don't remember which gown this was. "I find it hard to believe it a coincidence that you would wear that gown tonight. Did you do it intentionally?"

"That depends on what you mean. Did I intend to wear the gown my mother claimed was my only suitable gown? Then, yes, I suppose I did do it intentionally."

"But that purpose had nothing to do with me?"

"How could it, when I had no idea you would be here tonight?"

"But you may have hoped."

"I hoped for nothing." They took their position with three other couples. Sally didn't greet them right away, as she needed to make certain Mr. Harrison understood her meaning. "My position has not changed since the last time we spoke."

Mr. Harrison was more polite than she, for he gave each of the other couples a courteous bow before turning back to her. His gaze bored into hers and he laid a hand on top of the one she had laced through his arm. "Have you not considered that perhaps my position has?"

Sally furrowed her eyebrows. What could he mean by that? Was he referring to his position on Victoria or his feeling about producing heirs? Did it matter? He had already shown his true desires for what he wanted. She wouldn't accept him now simply because he couldn't get what he wanted unless he bent to her wishes. The music started and she hastily turned to the other couples without bothering to truly look at them. She curtsied to the couple at her right, and then the couple across from her. She never made it to the couple to her left, for when she looked up from her hasty bend, her gaze locked on familiar, deep brown eyes.

169

Lord Farnsworth.

Lord Pond-Swimming Perfect-Dress-Giving Pugilist Farnsworth was dancing this polka quadrille with her and Mr. Harrison, and his eyes were so dark they almost appeared black. He was not happy to see her. Not one whit.

Thankfully the couples on either side started off the dance, for there was no possibility she could have stayed on beat to the polka while knowing Lord Farnsworth was dancing only a few feet from her. The other two couples frolicked about to the bouncing tune while Sally and Mr. Harrison looked forward. Mr. Harrison smiled stupidly while Lord Farnsworth's partner, a petite young lady, grinned back at him.

Lord Farnsworth and Sally simply stared. There was not even a hint of a smile on his face. At times his eyes would shift to Mr. Harrison, but for the most part they stayed steady on her. How could she have been grateful to not lead out the dance first? Moving around the room would be so much better than having to simply stand there and look at Lord Farnsworth.

He looked the same, only...smarter? His hair was meticulously styled and his clothing tailored to perfection, as always. He held himself stiffly in a way he had never been stiff at Greenwood Manor. But he was also, somehow, achingly beautiful—like a marble statue that one was forbidden to touch. In the months she had spent away from him, he had become more fiction than fact, a fantasy that had happened so long ago she wasn't certain it had happened at all.

But he was standing in front of her now, and the line between his eyebrows was a testament to the fact that Lord Farnsworth had indeed proposed marriage to her, and she had haughtily refused him.

And then denied him entrance to her library.

The dancing couples returned to the start position and Mr. Harrison's hand tightened about her own. Obviously unaware of the turmoil raging between her and Lord Farnsworth, Mr. Harrison led her forward. Lord Farnsworth and his partner jaunted forward as well, until Lord Farnsworth was only inches away from her.

They all spun around and for a few sweet seconds, Sally looked outward, away from any of the couples in their set. The moment was short-lived, however, for Mr. Harrison's hand landed on her waist and he pulled her close to him as he spun her about. She tried to pull back her shoulders, but she couldn't dance and pull away from him, so she simply let him lead her in the way he wanted. Her eyes slid to Lord Farnsworth again. He was holding his partner at the waist, but kept a respectable distance between them. His gaze was dark, but at least for once he wasn't looking at her.

They returned to their original positions only for a moment and then she and Mr. Harrison bounced forward. Sally put her hand out and Lord Farnsworth grabbed it. She was expecting his grasp to be soft and noncommittal, but instead it was firm and warm, even through their gloves.

For a few brief turns she danced with Lord Farnsworth's hand in hers. The ballroom around them seemed to fade and she was back to their boxing lesson, where their steps were different, but the circles around each other were the same. Lord Farnsworth had been smiling then. He hadn't looked like a man ready to pummel someone. If she weren't so focused on Lord Farnsworth's hand in her own, she might have laughed at the contrast. Who frowned when dancing and laughed when boxing?

Lord Farnsworth did.

How could one man be so drastically different from any other she had met?

Lord Farnsworth handed her back to Mr. Harrison, and the ballroom came back into focus. She was not boxing with Lord Farnsworth in the garden of Greenwood Manor; she was in London dancing with another man.

For the rest of the dance, she and Lord Farnsworth never again touched. They danced toward each other, but never again together. When Mr. Harrison's hand went to her waist for the last time and they spun out of their quadrille formation and away from Lord Farnsworth, even though the space should have relaxed her, her breathing suddenly became short.

The dance ended and her whole body went weak. The edges of the room grew dark. Mr. Harrison's hand about her waist was the only thing keeping her standing. His fingers dug into her flesh and his other arm grabbed her elbow. "You are fatigued." His eyes were full of concern, but all she could do was blink back at him. She could not speak. "We will sit out the next dance. Let me get you some punch."

The last thing she wanted was punch; her mind was hazy enough as it was. But she followed him to the refreshment table. He poured her a glass, but she didn't even have the energy to lift her hand to take it.

What had happened to her? She was Sally Duncan. She didn't have fits of the vapors, nor did she swoon over some man.

Mr. Harrison set the cup back down and glanced around the ballroom. "Let's get you some fresh air."

It was the first thing he had said that made sense to her. He steered her away from the table and whispered a few words to a servant, who pointed him in the direction of a doorway. In a few steps they were out of the ballroom and in a corridor. A few groups of people had made the same egress from the heat and noise. Mr. Harrison moved her until the corridor opened up to a small sitting area with four doors leading to rooms.

The seats were all taken by guests.

Cursing, Mr. Harrison strode to one of the doors and opened it. Sally peeked in. A library.

And it was empty.

Mr. Harrison, still helping her remain upright, propelled her into the room and dropped her onto a sofa. Even in her exhaustion she checked behind her. He had left the door wide open.

Mr. Harrison was a good man.

He didn't like Victoria enough for her to marry him. But he was a basically decent human being. With that thought in her mind, she leaned her head back on the sofa and closed her eyes. Sally wanted nothing more than to lose herself in a few minutes of sleep. She had been dancing for hours—her chance meeting with Lord Farnsworth had taken her last grains of strength and she simply needed a moment's peace to process it all.

Even with her eyes closed, she could hear Mr. Harrison pacing in front of her.

His footsteps stopped. "Should I call your mother?"

He should. But the last thing she wanted was to speak with Mama.

With great effort she lifted her head. "No, I am simply overtired, that is all. Thank you for allowing me to sit this dance out."

"I didn't feel that I had a choice. Not unless I wanted to carry you around the dance floor like a ragdoll."

Sally scoffed. Mr. Harrison was jesting. She hadn't thought he had a sense of humor. She smiled back at him. "You would have had to marry me then."

Mr. Harrison stilled.

Sally rubbed her eyes and sat up straight. She needed her wits about her. "I'm sorry, I shouldn't have said that—"

"You broke off our engagement." His jaw clenched.

"It was hardly an engagement. You didn't even dare tell your father."

"I told him last month."

Sally suddenly felt very awake. She sat forward. "What? Why? We weren't even engaged last month. That was months after our broken engagement."

Mr. Harrison dropped down on one knee, his face now level with her own. "Miss Duncan, I know there were misunderstandings during our previous engagement. I will tell you all. Then I hope you will give me another chance."

"Mr. Harrison—"

"No, let me speak." He cleared his throat. "As you know, I come from a long and proud line of ancestors. My sixth-great-grandfather was given the title of Baron Bridgewater, and we have lived prosperously from that time forward. But these last few years have proved hard on many old families. Times are changing and I knew—I could foresee—that our family needed to do something drastic to continue our long traditions."

Something drastic? He meant marrying a merchant's daughter—

even worse, a merchant herself. Mr. Harrison was being sincere, but his sincerity was not moving her in the ways he hoped.

"Mr. Harrison—"

"I'm not finished. You see—I knew, but my father wouldn't have understood, not when I first proposed to you, at least. But the last few months have changed him. He has come to understand exactly what our family needs. No matter your birth or even your sister being in the condition she is in. our family needs you. I need you. Miss Duncan..." He took her hand in his. "I ask you to be my wife. I will not hide it from anyone; we will tell my father straight away. I won't ask you to put Victoria in a home. She can live with us. She can even be there when people visit."

Sally's stomach grew harder with each of his words. She pulled her hand away from his. "Ask me, then," she said, her voice icy.

Mr. Harrison's face beamed. "Miss Sally Duncan, will you consent to be my wife and the next Baroness Bridgewater, mother to our sons —" But not daughters. Why did he never, in all their talk of children, mention daughters? "—when the time comes?"

"No."

His hand fell from where he had rested it on the sofa beside her. "No?"

"No, Mr. Harrison. You are going to have to find some other heiress to propose to—one with less pride than I have."

"But..."

"I said no. There are plenty of women with money who *want* a title. I don't want a title, and I don't want to be married to a man who will *sometimes* let my sister be a part of our family."

Mr. Harrison frowned. "That isn't what I meant. That is the opposite of what I meant."

"And what if I had a daughter? In all your talk of children you have only ever mentioned sons."

"If we have a daughter, or daughters even, that is fine, I won't blame you for it. There will be plenty of time for a son or two, even if we do happen to have daughters first."

A flash of pale yellow fabric seemed to cover the outside edges of the room. Lord Farnsworth had wanted a daughter. He had never once said anything about heirs, or sons. He had looked at Sally, and seen small versions of her running about Greenwood Manor. He had planned for her, looked forward to her, hoped for her. He had bought her a dress made out of her grandfather's fabric.

Sally shook her head. "It doesn't matter anymore. I don't want to marry you regardless of anything you just said. Please, move on from this idea of yours and find another young lady."

His head drooped and his shoulders sagged. He took in a deep breath and then released it. "I have looked, you know. It is just…"

"Just what?"

"You are comelier than all of them."

Sally furrowed her eyebrows, tipped her head to one side, but he was not in jest. She fell back on the armrest of the sofa and laughed.

How had she ever agreed to marry this man?

CHAPTER 22

JONATHAN KNEW THAT LAUGH. He had been searching everywhere for Miss Duncan. Blast him for taking his eyes off her after the last dance; he should have followed her immediately. He sped down the corridor until he came to an open section. There were a few couples sitting on the chairs clustered about, but none of them were Miss Duncan and Mr. Harrison.

Mr. Harrison.

Of all the Mr. Harrisons in the world, *he* was her Mr. Harrison? That man was more entitled than anyone he knew, save Lord Chatterton. And he would be a *baron*. She had told him she didn't want to be a baron's wife. Obviously, that depended on the baron. He shook his head, but it wouldn't clear.

Her laugh had definitely come from somewhere around here. There was one open door to the left side of the corridor. He strode toward it. As soon as he stepped foot in the room his world darkened.

Mr. Harrison knelt at the feet of Miss Duncan and Miss Duncan wiped a tear from her eye. He stopped, unable to move further. What was he doing? If Miss Duncan wanted to engage herself to Mr. Harrison, she had every right to do so. She would still own Greenwood Manor and she would bring her husband there. They would walk

176

about the winter gardens and laugh with Mr. Ashton and every night... He shook his head again, his hands fisted at his sides. He should leave. He needed to leave.

Instead he strode over to one of the bookshelves and picked out a random book, then situated himself on a chair and opened it.

Neither said a word until he turned his first page.

"Farnsworth?" Mr. Harrison asked.

Jonathan took his time looking up from the page, as if he was engrossed in what he found there. When he finally did look up, Mr. Harrison was no longer kneeling. He was standing with both hands on his hips. "Ah, Harrison. How is your father?"

"How is my—" Mr. Harrison sputtered. "He is fine. He is always fine." Mr. Harrison looked down at Miss Duncan, but she didn't make eye contact with either of them. "Did you not see us when you came in?"

"I saw you."

Mr. Harrison waited. But Jonathan would go to the devil before he offered any more explanation than that. *Yes, I saw you, and I am in love with the woman who is about to become your wife, so I couldn't help but interfere.* How well would that go over?

"Perhaps we should leave, Miss Duncan. It seems Lord Farnsworth wants to read."

Miss Duncan was still. "I'll stay," she said softly. Jonathan jerked his head up. The room was no longer oppressive. She was going to stay...with him. "I'll find you at supper when I am feeling better." The room darkened again. She would still be supping with Mr. Harrison. She most likely wanted to tell Jonathan to stay away from her while she was in London.

"Are you certain?"

Jonathan looked heavenward. "The young lady said she would stay."

Mr. Harrison looked back and forth between the two of them, and then slowly stepped backwards to the door.

Jonathan counted in his head to twenty after he was gone, then threw the book to the floor, rushed to the door, and closed it. He turned on Miss Duncan. *"That* is your Mr. Harrison?" He pointed to the door. *"That* is the man you were engaged to? He is almost as much a baron as I."

Miss Duncan stood from her seat but steadied herself with a hand on the arm of the sofa. Was she feeling ill?

"How did you know about that? No one knew about that but—"

"Victoria," he answered. "She told me on the day I..." He stopped. He couldn't finish the sentence, and she must know exactly what he was about to say. "Have you agreed to be his wife? Or did I interrupt you before you could answer him?"

Her chin jutted forward. "I answered him."

An icy cold settled in his chest. He had known that Miss Duncan would marry someday. She wouldn't remain unattached simply because she wouldn't attach herself to him. But so soon? It was only three months ago that he had asked her to marry him.

Of course, she had felt nothing for him, so for her, there was nothing to move on from. She hadn't envisioned them together as man and wife like he had so many times—so many times he had begun to believe the wheels were already in motion at the time of his proposal.

"Do you expect me to congratulate you?"

"No."

"Good, because I will not." He turned and put his hand on the door handle. There was nothing more for him in this room. He had already known he would never get another chance with her; just because he had to witness the truth of it didn't change that.

A rustle of her skirts told him she was moving closer. "You should not congratulate me because there is nothing that needs congratulating. I am not engaged to Mr. Harrison, nor will I ever be."

He dropped his hand. Slowly he turned around. "You are not engaged."

"No."

He searched her face for a sign, or a look to show him that her feelings for him had changed since they last met. But how could they?

She had claimed not to know him then, and she could not know him any better after months of not seeing each other.

Her hands fidgeted at her waist. "I refuse to marry someone who wants me for my wealth rather than for who I am."

He clenched his jaw. "And you include me in that."

"Should I not?"

"What do you want me to do, Sally?" Her name slipped from his lips as naturally as he sidestepped around a punch. "Do you want me to open my heart to you again? Confess that I have done everything I can to sear the memory of your smile from my mind, but I cannot? I know some would call you a hard businesswoman, but I never saw you as cruel."

Her face went white and she turned away from him.

He should leave. Ever since he proposed, the only thing the two of them could do was hurt each other.

But his feet stayed firmly rooted in place.

She placed a hand on the side table next to the sofa she had been sitting on. "I was cruel to you. I was. And I'm sorry. Your gift…was beautiful. I shall treasure it always."

"Sally?" Could her feelings have changed?

"Two generations ago, my family had nothing." Her voice was soft, barely above a whisper. "My grandfather built a company with his bare hands, and he didn't do it so his granddaughter would syphon it away with her husband's greedy spending habits. I might believe you when you say you don't want me for simply my home or my money, but my family…my family worked too hard to gain what we have to see it squandered away by a baron who doesn't know how to manage his finances. Even if I wanted to, most of my family's fortune has gone toward the manor and Victoria's dowry. I can't take it back from her now."

That was why they couldn't marry? This was a very different reason than the one she had given him previously. He inched closer to her until he was standing directly behind her. She must have known he was there but she didn't step away. He reached for her elbow and softly turned her to face him.

Her eyes were wet with unshed tears. "Miss Duncan, do you not hate me anymore?"

A shaky laugh caused her lips to turn up. "I never hated you. I only wanted to hate you." Her gaze moved to his mouth and it took every ounce of his will not to pull her to him and cover her mouth with his own. They had no agreement; in fact, she had only just told him she couldn't marry a man like him. "May I ask you a question?" she asked.

His hand slid from her elbow down to her wrist. The way she had turned, she was practically in his arms. "Of course." She could ask him anything.

"If I offered to sell you your mother's home, would you take me up on it?"

He closed his eyes and dropped her hand. She knew the answer. "I could not."

"You don't have the resources."

"No." He opened his eyes. She was looking at him with eyes that didn't show remorse or love, but pity. She pitied him for the financial position he was in.

"And if you had had the money when I rejected you?"

"I would have begged you to sell it back to me."

"Yes, and then I would have nothing that you wanted—not your mother's house, and not my wealth either."

"That doesn't mean I wouldn't want you."

"It doesn't matter, though, does it? If I marry you, who is to say you won't find yourself in a similar position in a few short years? Even the fortune I've gained through selling my family's company wouldn't last forever."

He wanted to deny it, but he had been in Oliver's office only this morning. His estates were bleeding money, and the only way he could run them without a loss would be to raise the rents on the tenants.

They would starve.

He had no right to do that, not as a man of honor, nor could he ask Miss Duncan to put her family's wealth to such a lost cause.

He hoped the price of grain would rise in a few years to a point where his lands were profitable again, but it was only a hope. He had no guarantees. "It seems you know my finances well."

"There isn't anything you could do to curb your spending? Couldn't you try to live more frugally?"

Live more frugally? As a youth, he had loved fashion and fabrics. He had visited clubs and gambled. But those things had been easy to give up. The servants he had let go one by one as soon as they had found employment elsewhere. He kept only a skeleton staff at each of his estates, and he would even give up Howard and dress himself once the man could find a suitable position.

The sale of Greenwood Manor had allowed him to make repairs that had needed his attention since he had inherited. Much was still left in his coffers, but each month the amount grew smaller. He would either need to raise rent or let one of the estates run to ruin in order for him to truly break even each month. Neither of those options would lead to more food on his tenants' tables.

Her eyes searched his, and she must have seen his answer. Her shoulders dropped. Had she hoped he could deny it? "Then I suppose there is nothing to do but say goodbye." He swallowed. His hand went back to her elbow and she turned more fully to him. In a motion he had only dreamed of, she let her head fall forward and lay on his chest. Her hands clutched at the lapels of his jacket. "I'm sorry I didn't let you see the library." She sighed and relaxed into him. "Anytime I am in London, you are welcome to go there and see it. I have told Mrs. Hiddleson as much."

Anytime she was in London, but not while she was there. Then this truly was goodbye. He wrapped his arms around her and nestled her head under his chin. What a cruel pleasure, to hold her in his arms when he knew he would never do so again. "I'll do that." He spoke into the dark silk of her hair.

"I'm glad I had the chance to see you again." Her voice was muffled in his shirt. "I didn't want you to think back and remember me as being shrewish."

He laughed. That was definitely *not* how he had looked back on their time together.

Neither of them moved. The moment they separated, their relationship would be over. Jonathan pulled her closer and inhaled her scent. She smelled differently here in London. Her hair was perfumed with rosewater. He liked it, but he had also liked it when it had smelled of sunshine and glue from the papers she had been putting up at Greenwood Manor.

Miss Duncan was the first to pull away. She kept her hands at his elbows as she leaned back. "Goodbye, Lord Farnsworth," she said, and then leaned forward and kissed the side of his mouth.

She dropped her hands and stepped away, but the world stilled and he could not let go of his grip on her arm. "Miss Duncan, wait." She paused, then turned back to him. Her gaze lowered, fixed at a point just above the buttons of his waistcoat. "I didn't get the chance to say goodbye to you yet."

Miss Duncan's eyes raised, first to his, then lowered to his lips. She cleared her throat. "You did not."

"And may I?" He swallowed, his eyes straying to that mouth of hers. Her smile had been the first thing to draw him in; it seemed fitting that a kiss would be the last thing they shared together. "Say goodbye to you?"

She took in a deep breath, her chest rising and falling, then her eyes closed slowly. "Please." A fire lit within Jonathan. She reached for his elbow and squeezed. "And make it memorable so that I might relive it long after tonight."

Jonathan may not ever have lands that produced income, he may never be the responsible man who could give Miss Duncan the life she deserved, devoid of financial burden, but giving Miss Duncan a memorable kiss goodbye?

That he could do.

He reached for her chin and lifted her head until he could see her face. The only light in the room came from the fire and a few scattered candles, but even in the low light, he could see the smattering of freckles just below her eyes. His thumb traced the softness of her lower lip. Everything about Miss Duncan was achingly beautiful. He had spent the last three months determined to rid his mind of her. He was certain this kiss would rip out the last remaining bits of his sanity. He didn't care.

Even if he spent the rest of his life tormented by the next few moments, he would not give them up. Not for his peace of mind. Not even for Greenwood Manor.

Sally swallowed and the movement only served as a reminder of all the places he had dreamt about placing his lips—her throat, her eyes, that spot at the base of her neck where tendrils of hair seemed to always rest.

He had dreamed of a long life with her, but this stolen moment in the Harwoods' library would be all he could ever have. He wouldn't waste it.

He lowered his head not to her mouth, but to the crown of her head. His lips touched the curls that were piled together there. Since the moment she had walked into Oliver's office, her hair had fascinated him. It was so dark, and yet it managed to shine. He leaned back and once again tipped her head up towards his. She wasn't smiling, but somehow she was still welcoming and she wasn't welcoming just anyone, she was welcoming him. This time, he could wait no longer. He dipped his head and caught her lips with his own. She wrapped her hands around his neck and responded with a sigh, sinking into him. His arms went around her waist as if they belonged there, and they did. They truly did. If only he had been born a person without responsibilities, without men counting on him to keep their livelihoods intact, she would have married him, even had he not had a penny to his name. She would have married him even if his name meant nothing to anyone in the world. He could feel it in the way she folded herself into him. Sally would have loved fully in a way he had only dreamed about being loved, but she couldn't sacrifice all that her family had gained for love. She could marry a man with nothing. But she couldn't marry a man with less than that. She was much too sensible for that.

He loved her even more for it.

He deepened the kiss and her response was to deepen it as well. She stepped forward into him with the strength of a woman who had run a company, papered a whole manor, and boxed daily in the garden. He had never felt more wanted. He found himself stepping backwards while she continued to press into him. Something caught him from behind at his knees and he landed with a plop on a side table.

Sally's eyes were dark, but the sight of him fallen and sitting so indecorously brought a spark to them. "Lord Farnsworth, what are you doing down there? I wasn't nearly done with you."

He stood and stepped around the side table, then pulled Sally toward him. "I believe I was the one who was supposed to make this memorable. I am not done."

Jonathan rested his forehead against hers and then lifted his mouth to each of her eyes, kissing each lid, and for each kiss he left a blessing: a blessing of love, that she would someday find a man worthy of her, and that she would love fully, and forget him. He didn't speak the words, for if he did he would have to acknowledge the fact that he shouldn't be holding her in his arms now. As a gentleman he should have left her long before this.

His fingertips grazed the velvety skin of her throat, and his lips followed, kissing the hollow of her neck. Sally gasped but only pulled him closer to her, giving him the confidence to move to the base of her hairline just behind her ear. He grasped a soft curl between his thumb and forefinger and kissed that as well. Even here, with her hair perfectly coiffed, some of the stubborn hair had managed to come loose.

"Sally." He lay his forehead on her collarbone. His voice was hoarse. "I don't know how I am going to say goodbye to you."

A soft laugh reverberated in her throat, sending vibrations down his fingertips. "You seem to be saying goodbye very well."

"I'm a cad."

"No." She shook her head and he buried his under her chin. "I kissed you first."

So practical. So forgiving. "I love you, Sally Duncan. The most devastating loss in my life will always be you."

This time she didn't laugh; she made a sound in her throat like she was in pain. He needed to stop this, and stop it now. It was one thing for him to always wonder what might have been, but he had no desire to cause Sally the same affliction.

It was time to leave.

He dropped his hands and, feeling as though he was ripping apart his soul, he stepped back. Suddenly bereft without her in his arms, the air left his lungs. He was empty and hollowed out in every way.

Sally leaned toward him again, but if he accepted that invitation, he didn't know how he would ever have the self-control to step away from her again—not now that he knew what it felt like to hold her. "I have to go, Sally. I have to." Her hands lifted and then froze. The room stilled. "Do not reach for me again, unless you are willing to marry me no matter my financial position."

Ever so slowly, her hands dropped to her sides.

Her gaze fell to his feet, creating perfect crescents of dark lashes on her cheeks. "I'm sorry."

He stepped back once again, needing to be out of her reach. "You are making the right decision." He pasted a smile on his face. "The last thing I want is to siphon away Victoria's dowry. If I want to risk money, it will be my own funds. I won't let that spark I see in your eyes now turn into resentment."

He took a deep breath, steeling himself for what he had to do next, and then he passed by her, stopping for the briefest of seconds to return to her the sweet kiss she had given him, at the corner of her mouth, and then he strode out the door. The last place he would touch Sally would be on her mouth. It was fitting, for it was the first thing that had drawn him to her.

SALLY FELL backward until she came to rest against the bookshelf a few feet behind her. She grabbed the shelves with both her hands. She would not go running after Lord Farnsworth. She would not.

His kisses, though. She closed her eyes and for the first of what she was sure would be many times, she relived how it felt to have his fingers in her hair, his head bent and pleading on her collarbone, and his lips, careful and worshipful, on her throat. How could he share such kisses and not desire to work through his financial troubles together? But he hadn't asked that of her, he had only asked that she marry him no matter what.

Could she do that? Could she give up everything she had worked for, and everything her grandfather had worked for, so that Lord Farnsworth could come home to Greenwood Manor and make her laugh every day? Would Victoria be willing to have a Season without her dowry? She would; she had never counted on it in the first place.

It would be so simple.

But she couldn't.

Her head fell back, pushing a handful of books deeper into the bookcase. How was she supposed to go back to Greenwood Manor now? That would always be Lord Farnsworth's home. Every winter the winter garden would bloom and she would be reminded of that poor boy's mother who had planted every plant in it to bloom for his arrival.

And the library?

She stumbled over to one of the chairs. How would she ever visit her library again? She glanced around at the neat and orderly shelves surrounding her. How would she visit any library, for that matter?

Her head dropped into her hands. She shuddered and swallowed a sob. At least she had apologized. She could go back to Greenwood Manor with her head held high, knowing that at the very least he would know he was welcome to come see the library.

It was a small victory, but the only one she had gained tonight. Everything else was simply lost.

CHAPTER 23

"Oliver." After a sleepless night, Jonathan tore through his solicitor's door only moments after nine o'clock. He nodded to the client sitting in front of Oliver's desk and proceeded to address his friend. "I need a way to make money. What are gentlemen investing in lately? I need something foolproof."

Oliver pulled off his glasses and stood. "I'm with a client."

The man at his desk shrugged his shoulders. "I wouldn't mind hearing your advice either."

Oliver massaged his eyes with one hand and then motioned for Jonathan to sit. Jonathan took the seat next to the older gentleman. They shook hands but didn't exchange names.

"First of all, what money do you have to invest?"

"Everything I earned from the sale of Greenwood Manor, minus what I will need in order to keep my other estates running for the next three years. If I cannot solve those estates' problems in the next three years, then I'll plant different crops or find another way to make more income off of them."

Oliver nodded as if that was a sensible decision. Jonathan pulled back his shoulders. Sensible—that was what he was. That was what he needed to be. He couldn't allow Sally to marry some boring good-with-money sap, when Jonathan could learn to be just such a boring good-with-money sap himself.

Only he wouldn't be boring, and he wouldn't be a sap. He would be married, and anything but bored living with Sally and Victoria at Greenwood Manor.

Jonathan leaned forward. "I need to earn enough interest to keep all my properties afloat and save enough money to buy back Greenwood Manor."

"In order to buy back the manor, Miss Duncan would need to be willing to sell it to you."

"I will talk her into it."

"You haven't seemed overly capable of talking her into anything thus far."

Jonathan snuck a glance at the man next to him. He raised both his snowy white eyebrows, and a grin spread across his face. Perhaps Jonathan would have been better off to wait until Oliver was through meeting with this man. He faced forward again. "Let's simply assume I can talk her into it. How long will it take? And what is the best manner of investing?"

Oliver pursed his lips, pulled out a sheet of paper and started some calculations. "Nothing is certain about investments, you understand."

"I understand."

"You should only invest what you can stand to lose," the man sitting next to him said.

"I understand that, as well. Which is why I will be withholding the money I need." He turned back to Oliver. "With the sale of Greenwood Manor, my expenses have gone down. I am operating at a deficit, but it is much smaller than it was when I had to maintain Greenwood Manor as well."

Oliver nodded but didn't look up from his paper. He knew that already, of course. Jonathan's foot tapped a staccato beat on the floor as he waited. Finally Oliver looked up.

"There isn't a safe and expedited way to earn income from investments. All of this takes time, but if invested properly, I can see to it that your overall investments increase from year to year. Railroad mania threw the whole system apart, unfortunately. There was a time when I could have doubled your money in the railroad, but I've seen many men lose significant amounts of their fortunes in it in the past year."

"No railroads, then."

"There isn't really an investment to be had in the railroad anymore. I only say that to warn you against investing anywhere that guarantees a quick and easy rate of return."

Jonathan nodded. He was fine with it taking some time. He could be patient.

"Well, you have enough money to diversify with both foreign and domestic endeavors, so you should be able to cover the costs of your estates in the next year. The following year you should be entirely in the black, and you could start saving to buy Greenwood Manor."

Jonathan swallowed. One year until he could *start* saving for Greenwood Manor? Exactly how patient was he going to have to be?

Oliver scratched a few more numbers on the paper in front of him. "If my calculations are correct, I would say conservatively you should be able to come up with enough capital to buy Greenwood Manor in roughly thirteen years."

Jonathan sagged into his seat. Thirteen years. He could be patient, but thirteen years? There had to be another answer. He needed to find a quicker way. "I must admit I am disappointed by that number. The way Riverton talked last time I met him, money was just pouring in with his investments."

Oliver put his glasses back on. Never a good sign. "Riverton has more to invest than you do."

Ah. Of course he did.

Thirteen years. Investment would have to be only part of his solution. "What are pugilists making these days?"

Oliver's eyes widened, and in his half-inch thick glasses the result made it look as though his eyelids touched the brows above them. "You want to actually become a pugilist?"

Jonathan shrugged his shoulder. "You're the one who made me realize it's the only thing I am good at."

Oliver shook his head. "That isn't true."

"It feels true."

Oliver pushed his papers aside and leaned forward. "You are a good friend, Farnsworth, and that is immeasurable. I will find you some very good investments. I'll talk to Riverton and see if he has anything new that is safe and is producing well. We very well might get that number down to ten years. Not many people can earn enough in investments to buy an estate in ten years. You should count yourself lucky."

The white-haired man seemed to agree. But then he leaned over in his chair. "I'd pay a good deal to see a clean-cut gentleman like yourself in the ring with the likes of The Tipton Slasher."

Oliver furrowed his brows. "There is a reason gentlemen don't become pugilists."

"It would mess up their pretty faces," the older man said.

"No." Oliver frowned, and then tipped his head to one side. "Well, perhaps that and the general aversion to pain, but it doesn't pay well."

The man beside him sat up in his chair. "The Tipton Slasher is proposing 200 to 500 pounds a side if Bendigo will fight him. The Slasher wants the purse and the championship belt."

That was no small amount of money. A few fights of that caliber could change his fortune.

Oliver grunted. "He is offering that to Bendigo, and Bendigo has the belt, which is what he is really after. How many matches did both of them have to fight in order to get to that level?"

The older man shrugged.

Oliver turned to Jonathan. "It wasn't one or two. And each match comes with serious risk of bodily injury. You have no heir. It would be irresponsible to take on such a dangerous prospect, not to mention the fact that no one will want to strike a peer of the realm."

The old man coughed.

Oliver looked to the ceiling and let out a breath of frustration. "No pugilist is going to want to risk the *repercussions* of striking a peer of the realm. If they did you serious harm there could be significant consequences. Money makes money, Farnsworth. You simply have to give the investments time."

Ten years if he was lucky. Jonathan's shoulders sagged. The weight of being alone for what felt like a lifetime settled heavily on him.

There was no getting around it—Sally would be married by then, and he had no right to ask her to wait anywhere near that long. He ground his teeth together. Oliver knew what he was talking about; he always did. "I'll sign whatever I need to sign. Let's start the investment procedures."

Ten years was at least a sliver of hope, and he would take even a sliver at this point.

CHAPTER 24

"WILL you be spending any of the Season in London this year?" Mr. Sterling tapped the top of his knee, a nervous habit. His tea would be cold by now. He had been visiting with Sally and Mrs. Merryweather for the past half hour and had barely sipped from his cup. Did he even like tea?

"Yes, Victoria and I will. Last year we visited for a few weeks, and it was good to see Mama."

Mr. Sterling furrowed his eyebrows. He lived in Weymouth and owned two popular stores in town. He had started visiting Sally three months ago, and when it became apparent his intent was to court her, Sally had invited Mrs. Merryweather to come live at the manor and act as chaperone. He was a good man, and serious. From all accounts, his businesses were running at a great profit. Sally's head wanted to like the man.

Her heart was as lukewarm as his tea.

Mr. Sterling's hand stopped its incessant tapping. "You must miss your mother. Does she not visit Greenwood Manor?"

"She came in the summer, but during the Season she prefers to remain in London. If nothing else, she likes to pressure me into coming there and participating in society, even if it is only for a short time."

"But she must see there is ample society here in Dorset. I hope I have provided some in the past months."

"You have, and I thank you."

"I hope you won't leave without letting me know."

Mrs. Merryweather set down her empty cup. "I will make certain you are informed of Miss Duncan's departure."

Mr. Sterling made a few more comments about the wealth of society Weymouth provided, but Sally struggled to follow his conversation. Was it time to go to London again? If she did, would she find Lord Farnsworth there? Would they dance?

If they had another chance to be alone, would the outcome be any different?

It had been a year and he hadn't ever come to visit, not even to see the library. One word from Sally to Mama about him and Sally could at least have news of him. Had he found an heiress to remedy his financial woes?

"Miss Duncan." Mrs. Merryweather interrupted Sally's thoughts. "Mr. Sterling is taking his leave."

Sally jerked to attention. She had been uncommonly rude, and it wasn't the first time. It was a wonder Mr. Sterling still visited. She bade him farewell, then excused herself to Mrs. Merryweather.

Victoria had spent the morning out of doors. She was most likely in the library now. Sally opened the door to the library slowly so as not to startle her.

Victoria sat with her legs up on the sofa, her wheeled chair nearby. Mama would have had a fit of the vapors had she seen Victoria so casually draped on the red velvet cushions, but it settled Sally's nerves to find her so comfortable. Victoria finished reading the page she was on and then looked up. "How was your visit with Mr. Sterling?"

How was it? "Uneventful."

"So he hasn't asked to speak to you alone yet?"

"No." She wanted to deny that day was coming, but unless Sally started being more forceful in her responses to him, it eventually would. If he weren't exactly the type of man that she had pictured marrying after she ended her engagement to Mr. Harrison, she would have said something to discourage him last month.

"Do you ever think of John?"

"John?" She meant Lord Farnsworth. But it was ridiculous that Victoria called him by his Christian name. Even Sally didn't call him that, and she had kissed him. She had held his head while he rested it on her collarbone, and she had traced the lines of worry from his brow. Sally cleared her throat and straightened her shoulders. "John who?"

Victoria shook her head and her eyes went to the heavens. "Lord Farnsworth. The man who practically lived here a year and a half ago."

Why was Victoria bringing him up now? They hadn't spoken of him in months. "Ah, yes, the man I bought the manor from."

Victoria snorted in a very unladylike manner. Perhaps she needed to spend time with someone other than the gruff gardener. She narrowed her eyes at Sally. "The man I was hoping you would marry and make my brother."

"Why did you want me to marry him? You didn't know him any better than I did."

"That is easy—he made you smile."

A knot of pain that she hadn't felt in at least six months twisted her gut. "I smile."

"Not as much as you should. He made you laugh, too. He made you laugh and smile. I never saw you happier than when you were plotting to make his life a bit more miserable."

"*That* is why you thought I should marry him? Because I laughed when I was coming up with ideas to frustrate him? That is certainly nothing to build a relationship on."

"Maybe not for ordinary people."

"Are you implying we are not ordinary?"

"Oh, Sally, of course the two of you aren't ordinary. He is a baron who taught me how to box. You owned a very successful business and gave it all up so we could live here together. Ordinary people don't do things like that. And you would be bored with an ordinary man."

"What do you mean I sold the business for you? I wanted this manor. Vermillion was an amazing amount of work."

"Vermillion was the other thing that made you smile. You didn't sell it so you could live in the country. You sold it for me."

"I've never regretted it." Sally padded her way to the sofa, lifted Victoria's feet, and sat down with Victoria's legs on her lap. "You have blossomed here, and in ways I never would have guessed."

"Is it very bad of me to be grateful? I missed you when you were working so much. But I do know you loved it."

"Can you believe it? I love you more."

"I know. But you can do it again if you would like. It wouldn't be grandfather's business, but you could start another."

"Once you are married, I plan to."

"You don't need to wait for me to be married. That day may never come."

"Do you want to marry?"

Victoria set the book down on the side table next to her and swung her legs to the ground. "I don't know. I don't want a husband who feels sorry for me."

"Then don't marry one who will."

Victoria scoffed. "That man will be hard to find. It isn't as though there is a world filled with men like John and Mr. Ashton."

There she was again, mentioning Lord Farnsworth as if he were still part of the estate. "There are. There really are." But Mr. Sterling wasn't one of them. Sally would have to turn him down the next time he came. It was cruel of her to keep his hopes up. There was a time when she might have seen him as a suitor, but now that she knew men like Lord Farnsworth were out there—men who could make her smile and laugh and be wonderfully *unordinary*—the very ordinary Mr. Sterling was no longer enough.

How could a fifteen-year-old understand her heart better than she did? She was bored enough as it was; she didn't need to add a boring man to her life, no matter how fiscally solvent he was.

"I think they might be hard to find, though," Victoria said.

"Are you saying the two of us aren't up to the task?"

Victoria laughed. "No, I know you will accomplish anything you set your mind to. I only wonder if perhaps we shouldn't have let John slip through our fingers."

The sun outside the windows went behind a cloud and the room darkened. "Victoria, do you mean for you?" It would make sense, providing Lord Farnsworth hadn't married. Victoria's dowry was large enough to tempt a man who had financial troubles.

Victoria made a face like she had eaten fish that had been left out too many days. "Ew. No. I meant for you, of course."

The knot at the back of Sally's neck loosened. She hated to disappoint Victoria, but at least she wasn't going to pretend like she would be happy if Lord Farnsworth were to join the family as her brother. "Well, it has been a year and he hasn't even tried to contact me, not even to see this library."

"Why would he want to see the library?"

Sally tipped her head to one side and shrugged. "He thought I was going to turn it into a menagerie."

Victoria burst out laughing. "You told him you were going to turn this beautiful room into a menagerie?"

Victoria's laugh had always been the contagious kind. Sally snickered and pointed at Victoria. "It was your fault, you know, with that fish paper you picked out. How else was I to explain it?"

Victoria bent at the waist, her shoulders shaking uncontrollably. "You are going to blame my fish papers for the fact that you told that poor, besotted man you were going to build a menagerie in his home."

Sally stilled at the word *his*. Victoria's laughter, short as it was, stopped. Greenwood Manor would always be his home. It didn't matter how many atrocious papers they lined the walls with, both of them would always feel like it was his.

"Perhaps it is time we redid the library."

"With fish paper?" Victoria smiled, but it was too broad, the moment of laughter was gone, and no amount of fish paper would bring it back.

"No, probably not."

"I think what you did to the library last year before we went to London was perfect. It doesn't need to be redone."

It was perfect, and it had been the least expensive of all of her projects. More elbow grease had been required than anything else. But the truth of the matter was, that library was the heart of the home, and as long as it remained as it was, the heart of the home would be his. "Maybe next year. If I find just the right carpets."

Victoria seemed to read her thoughts. "Maybe, but there is no rush. Take all the time you need."

Sally stood from her chair. She didn't excuse herself, but simply walked away. All the time she needed? It had been a year, and nothing had changed other than the fact that she grew more and more certain Lord Farnsworth had forgotten about her. After all, she had to spend every waking hour in his home. He had nothing of hers to keep her on his mind, and lived in a town full of heiresses who would be happy to trade their wealth for a title.

If he hadn't married by now, it would be quite astonishing.

She nearly made it to her room, ready to throw herself on her bed when she stopped, turned around and headed toward the garden. She was tired of waiting for the newspaper with no news of Lord Farnsworth. She had seen the way he had interacted with Mr. Ashton. Even if he didn't write to Sally, he would have written to his old gardener, wouldn't he?

Sally marched through the house and then the garden until she came to the path that led to Mr. Ashton's cottage. She stopped for a moment when her foot sank into the soft gravel of that path. What was she thinking, begging information from her gardener?

She shook her head and continued onward. Mr. Ashton would not think less of her simply because she was asking after an old friend of his. She would simply have to begin the conversation with something else, and then ease into her questions about Lord Farnsworth. She could do that. If she was natural about it, he wouldn't suspect anything.

She rapped on Mr. Ashton's door. Sounds of shuffling inside

informed her he was there, but he didn't open the door. What was taking the old man so long?

After what seemed like an eternity, he pulled open the door. "Miss Duncan?" His eyebrows raised in surprise. "Is everything all right in the garden? Do you need something?"

This was the perfect opening to ask him a completely reasonable question. "Have you heard anything of Lord Farnsworth? Victoria has been speaking of him, so I was simply curious. In the last year, has he contacted you or sent you any news?"

Sally forced her face to remain still and not grimace. So much for easing into the conversation. At least she had mentioned Victoria. That had to help a bit, didn't it?

Mr. Ashton chuckled. His eyes shifted to his living room and the door on the other side of it. She hadn't ever been inside Mr. Ashton's cottage; they had only ever spoken outside. "Why don't you come in?"

"You have heard of him, then? How is he doing?" What answer was she hoping for? Was he as miserable as she was? Was he well? Neither thought brought her joy. Him being miserable brought her perhaps the slightest bit of satisfaction, which most likely meant she was a horrible person.

"I think he is doing quite well, actually. I have heard from him."

"Quite well? What do you mean by quite well? Is he to be married?" She grimaced. Had it been so long since she was in a high stakes conversation that she had forgotten how to negotiate at all?

Mr. Ashton chuckled again. "It is my guess that he hopes to be."

The room went dark. She reached for the side of the door to steady herself. She shouldn't have come. She turned on her heel to leave, but Mr. Ashton reached forward and grabbed her elbow. "Come in and sit down, Miss Duncan. I have more I can tell you."

More? Did she want to hear more, like who the woman was and what she looked like? An evil part of her hoped she was rich as a king, and as ugly and mean as a pockmarked boar. Mr. Ashton led her gently to a chair, then seemed to change his mind and instead guided her to a settee. After she sat down, he took the chair. "Tell me what you know of Lord Farnsworth's finances."

His finances? The only thing she knew is that they were bad, and he didn't feel that he could change his ways enough to improve them. "He had to sell a home to me, so I know they aren't good."

"They weren't; you are right about that. Now, I know plenty of people who wouldn't complain to have his financial problems, but the fact of the matter was, the money coming out of his estates was not as much as the money going in, and he didn't know how to fix that."

"And his extravagant taste in clothing couldn't help."

Mr. Ashton raised an eyebrow. "I'm not sure I've seen him in anything new since he came to stay here a year ago."

"You've seen him? He has visited you, and he never even thought to stop in and see me and Victoria?"

He was silent again. He shifted in his chair and pulled at the collar of his shirt.

"*He visited Victoria?*"

Mr. Ashton jumped up from his chair and put a finger to his lips.

"Why are you shushing me? No one is here."

Mr. Ashton's brow furrowed, the lines deepened to crevices, and his eyes flashed to the room at the back of the house.

Her heart froze. The shuffling before Mr. Ashton let her into his home, the way his eyes kept nervously returning to his bedroom door, could only mean one thing: someone was here. And there was only one person Mr. Ashton would hide from her.

Lord Farnsworth.

He was in this cottage right now. He had most likely spoken with Victoria earlier. Surely their topic of conversation in the parlor was not by chance. Lord Farnsworth was not on Victoria's mind simply because he was always on her mind like he was for Sally. Victoria had *seen* him.

She put both hands to her sides and gripped the settee as if her life depended on it. "He is here."

"Now, Miss Duncan, don't get ahead of yourself."

"He is here and he doesn't want to see me."

"I highly doubt that. In fact, he was just speaking to me about the possibility of seeing you."

"He was?" Her voice came out as a squeak. What was wrong with her? She smoothed down her dress as she debated running out of the cottage and back to her room. If he had truthfully wanted to see her, he would have come to Greenwood Manor, not to Mr. Ashton's cottage.

"He was. He simply wanted me to explain something to you first, so that he wouldn't have to." Here it was—the news she had been waiting over a year to hear. Lord Farnsworth was getting married and he wanted Mr. Ashton to tell her so he wouldn't have to. Mr. Ashton leaned forward and patted her hand. "First of all, I want to go back to my original question about his finances."

Lord Farnsworth was in this cottage. Only a door stood between them and Mr. Ashton wanted her to sit down and talk about Lord Farnsworth's finances? Why couldn't he tell her himself? She had never thought him a coward.

Sally stiffened her spine, determined to get through this conversation as an uninterested third party. "They aren't good."

"They haven't been, but he has been working hard and things have been changing for him."

"He stopped buying such expensive waistcoats," she said loudly enough and with enough bite that he would hopefully hear.

"His trouble was never about waistcoats. It was about the price of grain and decreasing the rents for his tenants because of it."

"Decreasing the rents? Why would he decrease rent if he was also getting lower prices for grain?"

Mr. Ashton clicked his tongue. "John knows those tenants. Some of them spoke more to him than his father did while he was growing up. The decrease in grain prices has most tenants moving into cities for work, but he didn't want to force them to make that choice, so he lowered his rents. He is a good man, Miss Duncan. It is a hard time to be a baron with a conscience, is all."

Her stomach sank. All this time, she had wasted a whole year thinking he was frivolous and not worth dwelling on. But *that* was the reason he was bleeding money? Because he wanted to make life affordable for his tenants? She would have married him if she had known. Surely he must have known she would have married him. Mr. Ashton didn't seem to notice her distress. "Well, things have gotten better and he has come into some money—not much, mind you, but he is certain soon it will be more and, well…" He shifted uncomfortably. "Blast it. *He* should be the one telling you this. He doesn't want to play the part of martyr because of his tenants, is all." His eyes flashed to a paper on the table and he sighed a sigh so deep she could have built a well around it. What was on that paper? She stood and rushed over to it, grabbing it before he had a chance to stop her.

Her eyes caught hold only of the first line. A proposal to buy Greenwood Manor. She blinked. Why would he want to buy the manor?

Mr. Ashton grabbed the paper from her hand. "Don't look at that. Not without him explaining it."

She grabbed it back from him and crumpled it without reading any further. "I will never sell him Greenwood Manor, and you can tell him that." She raised her voice loud enough that Mr. Ashton wouldn't have to tell Lord Farnsworth what she had said. He should have heard it loud and clear from where he was hiding.

She spun on her heel and dashed out of the door.

There was only one reason to buy the manor, and only one way he could possibly afford to. Mr. Ashton had just told her his financial situation was not good but that he hoped it would soon improve. That meant he would soon be getting married. Jonathan had found a woman rich enough to allow him the luxury of buying his mother's house back. "Miss Duncan!" Mr. Ashton called out behind her, but she didn't turn around "John, get out here, you idiot. I told you I shouldn't be the one to speak to her. She has run off."

Where could she go? She lifted her skirts and let her legs fly. The months of country walking had done her good. When she reached the end of the path where it branched out to different sections of the garden, she turned, almost as if pulled toward Lord Farnsworth's hunting lodge. It was where he would least expect her to go. She stormed down the path and ignored the tearing of her skirt as she passed the pond on her left.

"Sally?" *His* voice rolled over the evening air and pierced her heart. He was coming this way and faster than she had hoped. She wouldn't have time to make it to the lodge; somehow he had guessed she had come this way. The early evening sky was just starting to darken. If she found a good hiding place he wouldn't be able to find her. She kicked off her shoes and hid them under a log, then before she could think better of it, she walked directly into the pond. Icy cold shocked her into realizing how ridiculous she was being. What was she going to do? Hold her breath underwater while he passed by?

The sound of Lord Farnsworth's feet on the path neared. "Sally," he called out again.

It was too late now. She had no time to put her shoes back on, nor could she run away barefooted. Holding her breath would have to be the answer.

She took a few more steps into the water. Her foot came down on a sharp pebble and she bit her lip to keep herself from crying out. Her skirts pooled about her as she went deeper into the murky pond. How much farther would she have to go in order to duck under the water and remain unseen? Just a few more steps should do it.

"Sally, what in heaven's name are you doing in the pond?"

She didn't turn, but kept walking. And why not? He had done the same to her. Of course, he had a huge advantage—he could swim. She would have to stop soon or her skirts would pull her under anyway. But not yet. She wasn't even in up to her waist yet.

"Come out. I need to talk to you."

"I don't need to talk to you," she called out behind her.

"What are you doing in our pond?"

Our pond. She shook her head. There was no *our* pond. He wanted to buy Greenwood Manor and live here with his new wife. And she would let him, too, even though she had declared to Mr. Ashton that she wouldn't. She couldn't possibly live here, reminded of him every day, while knowing he was married to someone else. "Going for a swim."

"When did you learn to swim?"

"I haven't. But I thought perhaps today would be a good day to start."

Lord Farnsworth groaned and then, after a few short grunts—pulling off his boots—the splash of his feet hitting the water sounded behind her. She spun around.

Rather, she tried to, but she was now waist-deep and her clothing wouldn't cooperate. Instead she reeled backwards, turning around only enough to see Lord Farnsworth practically running through the water. She flailed her arms, pushing up as much as she could from the surface, but the pools of her clothing hampered her every movement, pulling her farther out into the pond.

Lord Farnsworth cursed and dove headfirst into the water. Sally's legs kicked out in front of her and she sank down into the water until her shoulders were wet, but just before her head went under, Lord Farnsworth's strong arm wrapped around her waist and pulled her to him.

She was instantly warm.

His face was dripping, his hair plastered to his forehead. It was not at all how she had imagined seeing him again. He muttered something under his breath that sounded an awful lot like *demmed fool woman*. His curse brought her back to her senses and she pushed against him with all her might. "Get away from me."

His fingers dug into her waist but the force of her panic still managed to make him reel backward. She slid out of his grip and back into the water.

Immediately she lost her footing and slipped back down into the water. When the cold water hit her face, her lungs froze. Once again a strong pair of hands pulled her to her feet.

"Stop fighting me and tell me exactly what you think you heard in Mr. Ashton's cottage."

His hair was still in his face, but he wouldn't let go of her in order to brush it out of his eyes. Droplets of water streamed down his cheeks. She wanted to brush back his dripping locks, but she had no right to. Instead she wiped her own forehead and eyes. She had tried escaping him, but had only ended up soaking them both, and he could move faster than she ever could in the water. She had wanted at least a few minutes to process what Mr. Ashton had said; a few minutes to compose a calm, business-like manner. Instead, she would now have to hear him confess that he was marrying someone else and agree to his terms about the manor while water ran down his face and his hands were firmly wrapped around her waist.

He was right. She *was* a demmed fool.

Sally cleared her throat and threw back her shoulders. She could be a businesswoman anywhere, even dripping wet in a pond. "Mr. Ashton told me you were planning on getting married, and I saw that you want to buy the manor back. That is fine. I haven't particularly enjoyed living here of late."

Lord Farnsworth risked her escape and brought one hand up to his eyes, wiping away the water and hair that had covered them.

"You haven't liked living here? It doesn't suit you?"

She loved the manor. It would break her heart to leave it, but since he had left, it hadn't been the same. "I thought it would, but..." She couldn't continue. Her voice cracked and if she had to lie to him about a silly reason Greenwood Manor didn't suit her, she would likely end up crying. Extremely unprofessional.

"Did you look closely at the offer?"

"No, but I don't need to. I'm sure whatever you have offered would be reasonable, and I will take it."

"You are certain? Even without looking at it?"

"I think I know you well enough to assume you would be fair to me."

He put his free hand back around her waist and held her firmly. Whatever he said next, it wouldn't be good. "I offered you one pound."

She slapped her hand upon the water. "A pound? First you torment me for weeks, then you ignore me for a year and now you offer me one measly pound for my home—a home I have put hundreds of pounds into, I'll have you know. Do not be cruel, Jonathan. I will sell to you, but you will have to ask your fiancée to advance you some money. I will not sell for a pound."

"I don't have a fiancée."

Why was he being so stubborn? This wasn't a time to stress about semantics. "The woman you hope to make your fiancée, then." Jonathan released her waist one finger at a time, waiting for the smallest fraction of a moment to ensure she wouldn't try to escape before allowing the next finger to lift. When his hand was free and she still hadn't run off, he brushed away the water dripping down her cheek. Sally lifted her chin. "I'll have you know, those aren't tears. It is only this pond water has gotten into my hair and—"

"Sally—"

"You shouldn't call me that, you have no right to call me that—"

"Sally, will you advance me some money so I can buy this home for what it is worth?"

Sally pushed him away. "I didn't say you should ask me, you dolt. I said you should ask your—" She stopped struggling. "Wait, what do you mean?"

"I came as soon as I had a pound of profit. I've invested, I've introduced some new improvement to one of my estates, I've done everything I could to make my income equal to what it takes for me to keep what is mine. I *wanted* to offer you a fair price for Greenwood Manor, but that would have taken ten more years and I didn't want to wait that long." His thumb stroked the base of her jawline. "Living without you for a year has been torture enough."

The pond water was starting to addle her brain. Lord Farnsworth was here to ask her to marry him? "Your estates and investments are no longer operating with a deficit?"

"They are not." He stepped closer to her, the little sunlight that was left in the sky reflecting off the surface of the pond, thousands of specks of light offering hope and laughter when she had gone much too long without it. She focused on that bouncing line of light while her world shifted.

She was about to be very, very happy.

She leaned forward, placing her mouth only inches from his. "I am exceedingly glad to hear that, Lord Farnsworth—"

"Jonathan."

"Victoria and Mr. Ashton call you John."

"Well, that is what everyone at Greenwood Manor called me, but my friends and my father always called me Jonathan, before I became Farnsworth, at any rate."

"Well, John." She was a part of Greenwood Manor, so she would call him John. Her lips went to his ear. "I will not sell you the manor for a pound. It is worth much more than that."

He didn't step away, but twisted his head so that his mouth was next to her ear. "But if we marry, it will be yours anyway."

"Still." She traced a line down his waistcoat, touching each of the buttons. "I'm not such a bad businesswoman as that."

He caught her hand over a button and held it there. "You want me to wait nine years and offer for your hand then? When I can afford it?"

She stepped back, but not far, for her hand was still kept prisoner. "Heavens, no. But I cannot in good conscience sell you this home for a pound. What if we don't marry? What then?"

"Oh, I will marry you, Sally. But I cannot marry you while you own this home. You will think that is the only reason I did. You will have to trust me to marry you after I buy the manor."

His thumb was stroking the back of her hand. Very distracting. This could in fact be her most difficult negotiation yet. "No."

His face fell, and this time she did lift a hand and brush a lock of dripping hair away from his head. "Your offer is a terrible offer. I am not a young woman who has never seen a contract before and I won't be swayed by your sweet words and that torso of yours that is decidedly wet and most tempting to wrap my arms around." His head lifted and he tipped it to one side, listening. "I will, however, trust that if you marry me now, it will *not* be because I own the manor. If you are willing to accept the terms of my agreement, then you may consider us engaged."

His eyes scanned hers. "That is it?" She nodded her head. "That is all I have to do? You do know all of London will think I married you for the manor."

"I don't think all of London will think that much on—"

Both his hands went back around her waist and he pulled her to him, stopping her words with a kiss.

She laughed but the sound of it was muffled by his mouth. He responded with a laugh of his own and, using his powerful arms, lifted her up and partially out of the water. He deepened the kiss and attempted to spin her around, but her dress weighed so heavily in the water that he only managed to make them tip to one side. He gave up on the spin and instead pulled her closer to him.

Sally's hands went in his hair, grabbing fistfuls of it and pulling him even closer to her. His fingers slid up her back, pinning her to him, but the movement unbalanced him and his legs were suddenly kicking in the water to find purchase on the mud below them. With a laugh in her throat, she shoved him down into the water, following him under with all her heart.

They came up sputtering, and this time she didn't hesitate to wipe away the water from his eyes. He returned the favor. Even wet, his fingertips felt warm against her eyelids.

She closed her eyes and leaned into his ministrations. "You spent an entire year getting your finances in order?"

"Yes." The light pressure of his lips on her forehead caused lights to flash beneath her eyelids. "It was a very long year."

He wrapped her in his arms and rubbed his hands up and down her back to warm her. They needed to get out of the pond, but being held by Jonathan made it impossible to want to move. If she held very still, perhaps her legs would no longer feel numb.

Jonathan was more responsible, though. He kept one arm about her waist and propelled them to the shore.

His cheek was clean shaven, and the water gave his hair the slightest of waves. She reached up and traced the very corner of his lip with her thumb. "You could have told me, you know. You let me think you wasted away your money on fine shirts and whatever else barons typically waste money on."

He squeezed her shoulder. "I wanted to explain everything to you. But it wouldn't have changed anything. You deserved a man who didn't squander your family's wealth. I couldn't raise my rents. If I had, my tenants wouldn't have been able to afford it. I wanted to come to you without that burden."

They stepped out onto dry ground and Jonathan once again enveloped her into his arms. She wrapped her arms about his chest, her fingers only just grazing each other on his back. Every one of his breaths pulled her fingers apart. She would never get tired of the sturdiness of him. She leaned her head back and looked up. "But you weren't willing to work for ten more years so as to pay me what my house was worth."

He shook his head with a look of horror on his face. "One year was bad enough. There is a limit to my patience. I was lost without you."

"I will be sure to remind you of that whenever you leave for a long hunting trip."

He raised his eyebrows. "You think *I* will go on hunting trips?"

"That is what you were doing most of the time I have known you."

"True, but I was hunting you. You must know that. What reason would I have to go hunting now?"

"Not hunting then, but whatever it is husbands do when they are off with friends."

A smile burst out on his face. He straightened his back and raised an eyebrow. "Husband. I like the sound of that."

"Well, then, future husband." It did have a nice ring to it. "There is something I want to show you. Will you come with me to Greenwood Manor?"

"I will come with you anywhere, but not quite yet."

Sally raised her eyebrows. What exactly did he need to do before then? They were both quite wet and it wasn't a warm evening...

John folded her into his arms once again. When his lips met hers, their soaked clothing was forgotten.

This... She sighed into him. She could wait to show him the library for this.

CHAPTER 25

JONATHAN PULLED at the lapels of the borrowed dressing gown, but try as he might, the blasted thing wouldn't stay closed until they reached a few inches above where he had cinched it together at his waist.

He wore one of Sally's butler's shirts as well, and although he had gotten it over his head and had managed to push his arms through the sleeves, the fabric strained against his chest and upper arms. He couldn't leave the spare bedroom like this.

A soft knock sounded at the door. It must be a servant coming to fetch him.

"Tell Miss Duncan I will wait for my clothing to dry, or my trunk to arrive, and then I will join her."

"It is me." Sally's voice was soft and quiet from the other side of the door. He took the two steps over to it and rested his forehead on the oak panels above the handle. Hearing her voice, husky and low, so unlike the lilting voices of London, was a pleasure he had denied himself much too long. "I want to show you what I have done to the library."

He took a deep breath. "Did you really tear out the shelves?" It would be fine if she had. Greenwood Manor was already transforming into a new home, and as long as he could share it with her, it didn't matter what she had done with the library.

"Open the door. I think we should see it together."

She must have done something drastic if she didn't dare tell him what it was. Most of what he had seen of the house had been tasteful, but his one glance at a corridor in the east wing had confirmed some of his worst fears. Sally had let Victoria run amok in some of the rooms. The library might have fallen prey to her whims as well.

He undid the latch. If Sally saw him in the ridiculous clothes her servants had found for him, she would understand his need to stay exactly where he was. Sally pushed on the door and he allowed it to open only a few inches.

Her broad smile nearly made him throw open the door and join her in the corridor. It was a smile for him, simply because he was there. Her gaze wandered downward to the taut linen shirt he couldn't quite cover. Her eyes widened and her smile changed from open and friendly to a half-upturned smirk. "You know all this time I have been giving credit to your tailor for your well-fitted clothing, but it turns out ill-fitted clothing becomes you just as well."

He opened the door wider. "You must see why I need to await my own clothes."

She licked her lips and then pulled them together tight as if it was all she could do to stop a laugh. Sally wouldn't take her eyes off his deuced chest. She tipped her head to one side. "You are decently covered." Once again she swallowed what must have been a gleeful laugh. "Come with me. It isn't as though we will run into anyone from Town. It is just us, Victoria, and the servants. And Mrs. Merryweather is here to act as chaperone."

"I am covered." He scoffed. "I wouldn't say decently."

In a movement hidden as well as any trained pugilist, her hand flashed into the room and grabbed a hold of him by his forearm. "I'm going to read to you in the library, and I'm not going to wait for your clothing to do it."

"With Mrs. Merryweather acting as chaperone?"

"Heavens, no. I only meant the fact that she is here as a chaperone should provide London with some relief. I'm not inviting her into the library."

He could have stopped her. It wouldn't have taken much force to plant his feet and stay where he was, but he allowed Sally to drag him out of the room. Despite her assurances that they would cause no scandal if they were seen, each time they crossed an open space or a corridor, Sally glanced about hurriedly before continuing.

Every corner of the house was familiar, yet different. Sally had put her tasteful touch on many of the furnishings. Everything was clean and bright, and there seemed to be twice the number of sconces, providing light to every nook and cranny.

It had never been so light in his childhood. It had been the brightest of his homes, but it didn't shine like it did now.

He would thank her for every change she made, even if what she had done to the library was atrocious.

They reached the door of the library and Sally stopped. "Close your eyes."

He did. And then he waited. The door didn't open. He cracked open one eye. Sally wasn't opening the door. She had stepped back and was simply looking at him. He pulled on his lapels "What are you doing?"

"I was just thinking...perhaps Wickers could give you that shirt. I think it fits you rather well."

He narrowed his eyes. "It doesn't fit me at all."

Her gaze finally rose to meet his. "I know."

He shook his head. Heat permeated his neck, which was ridiculous. Wasn't he the one who was supposed to make *her* blush? "Please open the door."

"Are you sure you don't want to close your eyes for a few more minutes?"

"Minutes? How long were you planning on ogling me?"

She shrugged, her mouth still turned up at one corner. It was a simple movement of her shoulder, and yet that one movement, so comfortable and open, confirmed what he had known about Sally from the first moment she had smiled at him. She was not one to shut anyone out—not strangers, and certainly not loved ones.

He sighed. "All right."

"All right, what?"

"All right, I will close my eyes and you can ogle me. But only for three minutes. That is positively my final offer."

Sally's laugh echoed through the corridor. Her golden brown eyes sparked with fire as she clapped her hands in victory. "I'll ogle you in the library. Come on."

She pushed open the door and Jonathan stepped backward. He had not been prepared for this.

Everything was the same.

But it was all better, somehow. The wood was polished to a brilliant shine. Every window covering was opened. Furniture sat in the same position it always had, and the material of each chair and sofa looked to be the same texture and color he remembered. But the fabrics were too unblemished and new to be the same.

Sally had completely redone the library without changing a thing.

He stepped into the room and walked over to the deep red velvet sofa that sat in front of the largest of the fireplaces. Above the mantel hung the picture of his family—mother, father and him, all standing together and smiling. Here in the library was where mother would read to him, his head in her lap as she reminded him that here, in this room, they were always happy.

"I should have sent you the painting. It was boxed up and I only found it a month or so after you left. I sent you everything else we found. I thought you might return for this one."

"No, don't apologize, this painting always belonged here."

"That is what Mrs. Hiddleson said." Sally came up beside him and intertwined her fingers into his own. "I really, truly am sorry I didn't let you come here that day."

Jonathan pulled on her hand and wrapped it about his waist, then unlaced his fingers and placed his arm around her shoulders, pulling her into him. "Because it has led to this day, there is nothing to forgive."

Sally leaned her head against him. "I thought you only wanted me for the manor. I thought it was the reason behind all of our interactions."

"You weren't wrong, Sally, even though I was fascinated by you from the first moment I met you. I wouldn't have proposed had you not owned Greenwood Manor. But when I left, you were the one I missed—not the house, not our pond, not even the library. If we would have married then, we would have been happy—I've never not been happy with you around—but neither of us would have known how much I needed you."

"You need me?"

He wrapped both arms around her, curling her into his chest. "Like air."

"I need you too. You have brought me sunshine in a world full of work, the scent of Rose du Roi on a day full of rushing about. You bring me joy, and I don't want to lose that again."

Heat rose to the back of his neck and it wasn't from embarrassment. His fingers made their way up her back and then her neck until they reached the softness of her hair. "I love you, Sally. You—not your house and not your money. You."

"And I love you...*and* your chest."

Jonathan laughed, then lifted her mouth to his. He had a family again. And this one he would never lose.

EPILOGUE

SALLY OPENED the door to the library. John sat reading one of his books, most likely something to do with fertilization and crop rotation. Keeping his estates running at a profit was still an everyday battle, but in the six years they had been married he had managed to make a profit every year, even if only a small one. A fire burned brightly in the oversized fireplace. The portrait of John's family still hung above it. On each side of the mantel sat a vase, both equally horrendous.

John had bought Sally the second one on their first anniversary.

Evelyn's little hand was curled into Sally's. She glanced up at Sally with excitement beaming from her eyes. Sally tiptoed into the room, but didn't pull Evelyn in with her. "Evelyn has something to show you."

John's head turned and a smile lit up his face. "She does?"

"Yes, but it's a surprise. So you must close your eyes."

John narrowed his eyes, but he didn't close them. "Evie, are you out there? Do you really have a surprise or is Mama going to do something unfortunate to your father?"

Evelyn's free hand covered her mouth, but a snicker still escaped. "It is a good surprise, Papa."

And it was. Evelyn was four, and petite for her age, but today when Sally had pulled out the little dress John had given her during his first proposal, it fit their daughter perfectly. The yellow brought out the gold in her light brown hair.

"Fine, I'll close my eyes, but Evie, don't you let Mama sock me in the jaw."

Another snicker.

Sally bent low and grabbed both of Evelyn's hands. "I would never sock your father. Not unless we were exercising."

"Boxing?"

"Yes, boxing."

Evelyn nodded. John had already started to teach her a few boxing movements. Each afternoon when Sally had finished her correspondence with Vermillion fabrics, she and John would run out to the garden for a daily bout. Sally was usually able to land a few blows, but her hair somehow always ended up coming undone—a fact that annoyed her maid to no end.

"Are your eyes closed, Papa?" Evelyn peeked around the door.

"They are." John put a hand over his eyes to prove it.

Evelyn pulled her hands out of Sally's grasp and ran into the room. She stopped in front of the sofa and twirled. "Open!"

John's eyes opened and he sucked in a breath. "I know that dress."

"Grandpa made it."

"He made the fabric." Sally corrected her. "That is Vermillion cotton. We don't make much of that anymore."

Vermillion had tried to go back to cotton after she sold the business. They had done well enough with it, but silk had been the material that had brought Vermillion out of obscurity, and after two years of trying to go back to her grandfather's roots of cotton, the executives called on her and asked her to help reestablish her silk contacts.

Which she happily did, for a fifteen percent share in the company. Vermillion had blossomed again. She was worth every penny.

"Did you know I gave that dress to your mama?"

Evelyn's eyebrows furrowed. "But she is too big."

John laughed and scooped her up around the waist. "I gave it to

Mama so she could give it to you, before you were even born. I think it might be why she fell in love with me. Wasn't Papa smart?"

Sally came up behind John and rested her chin on his shoulder. "He was very smart. I definitely fell in love with him when he gave me that dress."

"You shouldn't have told me no, then." John hefted Evelyn onto his hip and placed a kiss on Sally's forehead.

"You didn't let me see it until after you left."

"Excuses."

"By the way..." Sally ran her fingers through Evelyn's hair. "Victoria is coming to visit next week."

John stiffened. "Is she bringing that husband of hers?"

"Now, John." Sally tipped her head in Evelyn's direction. "Be nice."

"That's easy for you to say. You didn't grow up with the man."

"I didn't, but he has been nothing but pleasant with Victoria, at least once they settled everything. I think he is lovely."

John frowned, a crease forming between his eyebrows. "Victoria sure seems to think so."

"Most wives do think that of their husbands."

"Not all wives."

"Happy ones."

"What do you think, Evie?" John propped her higher up on his hip. "Is your mama happy?"

"Of course. Grandpa's dress made her happy today."

"I'm the happiest wife in the whole of Great Britain, John. You should know that."

Jonathan turned and wrapped his free arm around her waist. "I do know that. Thank goodness I decided to sell you this manor."

"Thank goodness I was in the market for one."

Sally reached up and placed a kiss to the corner of his mouth. It had been the first place she had ever kissed him and she never tired of it.

And John never let her get away with just that kiss. He set Evelyn down and then wrapped both arms around her shoulders and dipped her low to the ground. Evelyn squealed but that only made the devilish gleam in John's eyes shine brighter. "I never would have forgiven you had you bought some other man's manor."

"You never would have heard of it."

"That…" He kissed her nose and then pulled her upright. "…is the scariest thing you have ever said to me, Lady Farnsworth."

"I will never mention it again."

They settled together with Evelyn on the sofa and Jonathan cracked open his book. "One should always take care to limit the risk of fire when farming—"

Evelyn's nose wrinkled. "Not that one, Papa."

"Really, John."

"What? Would you rather read her a book about sericulture?"

"No, she doesn't want to learn about silk. Evelyn, go get one of your books off the shelf. Papa will read whatever you want." Evelyn jumped off the couch and went to the section of the library that contained children's stories. Sally settled closer into Jonathan's chest. She never imagined when she had stepped into Mr. Beechcroft's office that day that she would end up warmed in front of a fire with a husband beside her and a young daughter frolicking about in a dress made from Vermillion fabric.

Life was full of surprises. Her surprises had brought her more joy than her well-thought-out plans ever could have offered.

ALSO BY ESTHER HATCH

ACKNOWLEDGMENTS

This book has been an amazing learning experience for me. I never would have dared to write and publish it without the example of so many of my writing friends.

In no particular order, here are the wonderful authors who have helped me through the process of publishing, and shown me through their example how to write beautiful books and basically run a business at the same time: Kasey Stockton, Martha Keyes, Sally Britton (yep, Sally is named after you, as you well know), Deborah M. Hathaway, Mindy Burbidge Strunk, Jen Geigle Johnson, Ashtyn Newbold, Heather Butler Chapman, Anneka Walker, Bridget Baker, and many, many more. You are all an inspiration to me.

Mindy and Anneka, thanks for all the early help on this one. We are all busy writing, but I'm grateful we take the time when we can to help one another. April Young and Lisa Kendrick, you saved my bacon and the likeability of the main two characters. I will send you my next book sooner. Alice Patron and Paula Anderson, thank you for reading and Paula for last minute crunch-time help.

Krista White, your insight has been both eye-opening and heartwarming. Thank you for your time and your devotion to ensuring I had a small understanding of what life might be like for Victoria. I have a lot more plans for her, and your encouragement has made me brave. Truly, thank you.

The cover for this book is (in my humble opinion) amazing. When I had the idea to write what would look like a Victorian Rom-com, I knew exactly whom to trust with my vision. Shaela with Blue Water Books is a genius, and I hope my book lives up to its cover.

Jolene Perry, this book is very different from when I first sent it to you. Thanks for pointing me in the right direction and helping me turn this very messy manuscript into something legible and meaningful.

Julianne Donaldson, I'm pretty sure being an editor on this book was more work than you had thought it would be. Thanks for being there with me during the final week of edits and cleaning up my ridiculous sentences. I always felt a sense of comfort and camaraderie knowing we would be getting this book ready for press together.

To Covenant Communications, so much of the success of this book is because you took a chance on me and have promoted my books. I look forward to a long relationship together for many more years.

A huge thanks to my scream team! Your reviews and excitement have been critical for this book's success.

And to my family: This one was a hard one. We made it through, and in the end we have come together stronger for it. I love you all.

ABOUT THE AUTHOR

Esther Hatch never dreamed of writing books, she enjoyed reading them too much. Then one day her sisters-in-law made her try it. After a two year trial period, she is now hooked.

Sign up for Esther's newsletter at estherhatch.com/subscribe

Follow on Instagram and Facebook as Author Esther Hatch

Made in the USA
Middletown, DE
14 July 2021